crawling at night

nani power

crawling at night

```
FIC
POWER
N
```

Atlantic Monthly Press / New York

Published simultaneously in Canada
Printed in the United States of America

FIRST EDITION

Library of Congress Cataloging-in-Publication Data
Power, Nani.
    Crawling at night / Nani Power.
      p. cm.
    ISBN 0-87113-784-4
    1. Japanese Americans—Fiction.   2. Cookery, Japanese—Fiction.   3. New York
(N.Y.)—Fiction.   4. Restaurants—Fiction.   5. Waitresses—Fiction.   6. Cooks—
Fiction.   I. Title.
PS3566.O83577 C7 2001
813'.6—dc21   00-050821

Design by Laura Hammond Hough

Atlantic Monthly Press
841 Broadway
New York, NY 10003
01 02 03 04   10 9 8 7 6 5 4 3 2 1

for Russell, Ivan and Sunny

I would like to thank the following people:

My parents, Ann and John McCarty, and Mark Power, for unwavering love and support. Sylvia and Murray Kronick for consistent enthusiasm and kindness shown toward my writing. Also, Russell, Ivan and Sunny Power-Kronick for patience and sacrifices made on my behalf.

My agent, Wendy Sherman, who has been a godsend. Likewise, a huge thanks to Elisabeth Schmitz and Morgan Entrekin for intelligent, thoughtful editing.

To Liam Callanan for his fine writing class at Georgetown University, as well as Richard Peabody for truly generous encouragement.

Lastly, I'd like to thank Kenji, Akio, and Onosan at Cafe Japone for introducing me to the world of sushi. Thanks for all the *uni*, all the *toro* through the years. Thanks, Akio, for the sashimi knife.

Yobai (*crawling at night*) is an antiquated expression born of the Japanese farmer's tradition of accommodating large groups of overnight visitors on futons across the floor. If a gentleman visitor wished to attempt to share the futon of a fellow lady traveler, he would cover his face with cloth in a gesture of anonymity, proceed to crawl to her futon and invite himself. If rejected, he could return to his futon unknown, at least in theory.

chapter one

Menu:

Fatty Tuna

Rice

Sake

More Sake

Carrots, 1 case
Lettuce, 2 case
Scallion, 2 box
Pork, side meat, 10 lbs.
Fish—Tuna, 2
Sardine, 1
Yellowtail, 1
Clown Anemone, 3
Crab, 4 box
Octopus, 1
Flounder, 3
Rice, 1 sack
Sake, medium grade, 3 box

Lists are life.

For example:
Katsuyuki Ito writes forty-two years in shorthand.

Always the same, few numbers change (perhaps one less tuna, a few more flounder, rice OK that day).

Folds an envelope from the Con Ed phone bill squarely across his soft middle. Tracks down a pen in the cash register (*bing!*). It bleeds ink. He wipes it with a tissue and itemizes. Jots his needs for tomorrow in the restaurant, in summation. A list of dead things wrenched from the ocean floor, arriving daily in their iced beds.

His needs.

Mr. Ito being a master of the chiseled shape, *shokunin*.

To you and me: *some sushi chef.*

The list is a scratchy thing, to see it. Symbols.

He stops writing, uses the metallic end piece as a makeshift toothpick and stares out the window to the street, people in their business clothes shuffling by in the jaundiced afternoon light.

Cold outside. Still.

Gorrud owsigh. Stirru.

He says this out loud, in English. To practice the sounds, like an actor.

Another need, to have something to say to customers. To *chat.*

To the junior marketing exec in the crinkled gray suit with fake orange nails that jut oddly curved and glossed from her hands, who mumbles *hello, hello, the usual, please,* meaning two California rolls and a glass of iced white zinfandel, he'll say *Gorrud owsigh stirru,* she'll smile and say *tell me about it,* to the trio of men from the office down the street, who blast in carrying a pocket of wind from outside, reeking of spices and metal, each sporting thick gold bands on their hairy knuckles, slamming the glass top of the sushi bar in happy-houred raucousness *how ya doing, Ito! Ito!*

Gorrud owsigh. Stirru.

Damn straight! Cold as a bitch. Laughter served up like a brisk, cold wave.

Loneliness is another matter. He doesn't expect miracles.

Speaking, it's the staccato chunks of a toddler. *Hello, good-bye, yes, thank you, please, oh, good.* But in there, deep down, where nobody goes but him, his head bobs with Basho haiku and *The Tale of Genji*, with all the *moon-viewing*, all the *willow-leaves*, all the *autumn dusks* snagged with the tidbits of his trade. How he judges tuna for its fat content with a flashlight in the dawn fish market alongside the haiku image *on a barren branch*. All thoughts whirling like flimsy scales flashing in a sink's wetness, yet they get sieved along the way. Somewhere there's a set of orange cones, an embargo. He pauses, his face reddens. His thoughts jettison to his tongue as babble, and he is treated as such, he is talked to as if he is a green employee, a big babyman, and the shame and awkwardness of this feeling, despite being an old pro, colors his days.

He thinks:

> *Aimimu to*
> *Omou kokoro wa*
> *Matsura naru*
> *Kagami no kami ya*
> *Sora ni miruramu*

(To meet again/Is my desire/The mirror god/At Matsura/Can see it in the sky) as his mouth says, *please, enjoy,* passing the tiny plate of sliced squid to the waiting hands of a customer.

So, writing the list, the man is toast. Can't get anyone to understand. He stands on a shelf, dusty. Feeling the familiar gnaw of shame, a left-out-on-the-edge feeling, as he scratches the damn list, recalling *The Tale of Genji*, the words of Murasaki Shikibu, *They all moved onto the bridge and started their drunken racket again.*

I am always on the bridge, thinks Ito, *I am always on the outskirts, the drunken racket somewhere down the road.*

Waiting for the evening and the shuffle of hungry stomachs. Lost in some modern form of court life. The nightly adornment of victuals. Anticipating the *drunken racket* of the evening, the spoiling of all he carefully prepares.

1 box carrots
2 case lettuce
2 box scallion

In the beginning, Ito walked in the back door—

Back in *Nihon* when he was eighteen in blue cotton pants and hair cut shaggy. A haze of pimples across the cheeks gave him a rosy tinge of permanent embarrassment. *Katsu-chan!* or *hey, new boy!* they called out to him in the harsh, smoky grunts of work.

Sweep, Katsuchan! He was handed a broom by the head chef. Everyone scurried by as if on wheels. Young Ito swept, all stiff with ineptitude and shyness. Great piles of rice, dirty slivers of vegetables, dust, dried pieces of meat, fish scales, bones, paper, each day a different blend. In his boredom he devised stories from this detritus. One day, he sweeps the silvery fins of tuna from the morning, and, with the endless *swish-swish* of his broom, he thinks:

A tuna found its way to Tokyo. It was large and silvery. It lay on the cold wooden slats with hundreds of other cold, white torsos of fish, gutted, their white skin curling and hardened at their eviscerated cores like pale shells. It was sold at 5 A.M. to a chef for all his money. He nods his head, standing on the wooden platform where the auctioneer babbles. The tuna had lived for thirteen months as a fierce sea vessel and now lay headless, flashlights beaming on a gash in the tail. The pinkest fish, *toro,* is chosen by the chef, he knows in a glance from the hue of the rosy flesh whether it died on a net or was caught by a hook. He knows also the exact percentage of fat in every segment of its flesh. He hooks it with his fish claw and swings it into his cart, bumpily wheels it to his truck, shields his hands and lights a cigarette, then rides the squat truck through the black streets of the freshly washed city. When he gets back, he'll get the new boys to unload the fish from the back, grayed and matted with fish blood.

The trucks pour in from the countryside as the light loses the cold blueness of dawn. Fires burn in the corner, leaking cedar smells from ripped-up fish boxes. An old farmer drives a green truck with an open bed. He also was up at 3 A.M. and was surprised by his old wife of forty years, who woke him naked, with her bony elbow. They made love slowly as light crept into the room and the nutty smell of the morning's rice seeped into the air. He moved inside his old wife who had borne him three sons and thought not of love but of fried fish, rice, pickles and tea. It felt soft and slack inside his wife but he was old and slack, too, and it had been perhaps two years since he had been inside her and they were both grateful that everything worked and that she had gotten through some of her sadness, the sadness she felt like a blanket over her most days, a strange thing, but her eyes seemed warm and happy to him now, she had come to him naked, of such familiarity, in the moment before dawn as the fires of the night trickled out, as the trash trucks barreled by outside, and as he moved slowly in the semidark, he could hear the *clank-clank-clank* of their bumpers on the uneven road.

They picked ten bushels of carrots yesterday, maybe this is why she is happy, ten bushels of gleaming orange rods out of the dark earth, each one perfect and straight, no bends or gnarls like last year, and undoubtedly the seaweed mix had helped, the days of stewing it and mixing, the early mornings of carrying it in buckets to the rows, his old back creaking, feeling skin on bones, no fat, had paid off, he had ten bushels of carrots this morning to bring on the dusty road, his wife held him in her quivery arms and smiled, he would smoke a pack of Winstons in the truck on the way to the market, he would listen to his radio and sing some old songs, he would eat a tiny grilled mackerel on rice and later a *bento* bought from a bicycling boy, and feel indescribable serenity when his life simply presented itself as it should be. The chef, after

getting the tuna, stops by the vegetable market and gets some of
those carrots (*very sweet, tender,* the seller pleaded),

Pork, side meat, 10 lbs.

and at the same time a butcher slices pork inside a grimy shop with
cloth hanging down, across the street from young Ito's restaurant
(where Ito has a full view as he sweeps) with big men in the back
playing cards and eating fried pork on rice and talking of southside
whores who do wondrous things, the smell of pork everywhere,
everyone understands the soft gumminess of a meaty pork bone as
opposed to a spindly fish bone, they all have dulled soft edges lined
with fat, not unlike the pork, discussing, with occasional laughing
bursts, the subtle differences of the whores of last night, who was
younger, smaller, who had starry nipples, but that younger pork
worker, just married last fall (Ito sees him, looking out the window
in his pork apron), is plagued as he gnaws the pork, hearing the
talk, he knows the whores in question with Western names, Candy,
Dawn, Melinda, has seen them at the bar they frequent, has had
sake poured in tiny cupfuls down his throat, has come home to his
doll-like wife, in her robe, her jewel body, so quiet, has thrust himself inside her in the quickest way, and is scared of his recent actions in the pig locker, where the scraped, sour carcasses of the pigs
lay in darkness, where odd mashed pieces of pork fat catch the
bottom of his shoes with sticky obtrusion, a place where he has
groped a fellow pork worker (the small fellow by the grinder, with
the dark red mouth), felt his bare bottom, gripped his penis, placed
it in his mouth, its hardness ramming down his throat, gagging him,
pleasing him to no end, the dead smell of pig fat and flesh, the brack-
ish flood of semen, and the confusing pain he feels, liking his wife,
their home, their kitchen with its small warm ricemaker, a pleasant
iron kettle given as a gift, a futon with its red cover, her tiny ivory

feet, the aesthetics of it all, the pleasantness, like reading a book in a sunny corner, like bundled cats huddled in a chair, like good soup on a frosty day, ephemeral, destroyable.

The skin around the pork worker's eyes is stained as if from tea.

(Ito thinks this all in his fertile mind as he sweeps. He sees him still looking out the window. He knows his name, Ken, because of the small *kanji* script on his work jacket. Young Ito has more sweeping to do.)

> *Fish—Tuna 2*
> *Sardine 1*
> *Yellowtail 1*
> *Clown Anemone 3*
> *Crab 4 box*
> *Octopus 1*
> *Flounder 3*

Young Ito's mind wavers to *that old carrot farmer,* returning from the day with his carrot money, the truck needs gas so he fills it up, he buys one pound of *O-toro,* the highest-grade fatty tuna, pale pink, wrapped in paper, slid next to a hunk of ice. No worms. A fishmonger, a reputable one, is trained to place the fish slice against the light, and through the flecked flesh, the tiny grain like wood, they can see the dark patch of worminess, they sever it out with the point of their steel knife, and it recedes and falls away, but the bad ones don't do this, the worm stays hidden, you eat it and it lies in your warm stomach cavity and grows, eating your predigested matter, growing larger, wedging itself into wet intestines, consuming them, creating fissures and pain, until one day you feel indescribable pain, hunker over and fall down dead, an empty hollowed torso.

Consider *O-toro* again and realize that the *O* is honorific, used for holy men and emperors, used here to signify the high level of excellence in the shimmering chunks, the velvety fat that washes across the mouth.

In the U.S., the same tuna, the bluefin, is caught for cat food. Fishermen off the coast of Maine are surprised to find that their poles have bent and almost snapped and they wrench in, with all their strength, a silver elephant-sized fish up on the wet and dazzling boat floor, a cool, serene monster, with arching fins and tiny teeth like a cat's ridged in its fawning mouth. Its eyes are round hunks of steel and carbon, layers of translucency between the metals, some ancient glimmer of subterranean instinct, a fleeting awareness of the moment.

In disgust, they ease it back. Too heavy and cumbersome to lumber to the fish market, where tired men in overalls and stiff rubber gloves smoke in the world of dirty ice in cardboard boxes, vast seas of frozen blocks, thick leaden walls of walk-in refrigerators, where boxes of shrimp and squid lie, men who plod around heaving huge fish by their tails and scratch out illegible receipts on their messy desks, dusty, with scattered papers flying. Outside the dawn is stiff and cyanic, trucks pull in and leave. Fires burn in rusted barrels and the men gather around them, warming their fingers which pop out of fingerless gloves. The cat food market is down, they would say, and the hefty tuna would be worth maybe twenty dollars for all the muscle it took to haul.

Across the oceans, in cooler waters, across the Pacific, this tuna is a mine of value, a retirement, a Mercedes. An ounce of tuna is equal to gold.

The old carrot farmer has just finished listening to "Holiday" by Madonna, staticky, in his truck as he pulls into his small house. Evening is setting in. He pulls the *O-toro* out, his satchels, his body as tired as death, as old as winter, a face like a stiffened work glove. His old wife greets him with a soft hello, steam hangs around her face as she stirs a pot of fish cakes and miso. Her neck is long and brown, like a turtle's. He kisses it, coming up from behind, unexpectedly. An unprecedented boldness. She burns her hand, he shuffles in embarrassment. The O-*toro* falls to the floor, she asks what is that, he explains. Her delight, not having had this treat in many years. Her hand on his cheek for a moment. Night sets in. (Young Ito's chef turns off the lights in the restaurant. He tells young Ito to go home. It has been two years now and tomorrow Ito learns to make rice, the beginning of his ascent to *shokunin*.)

It is evening, yes, and Ken, the pork seller, and his wife, a ceramic kitten of a girl, watch a famous soap opera about a Tokyo housewife who becomes the man of the family and her husband becomes the wife. It is fraught with ridicule at his situation. Her cool hand lies in his. She made a delightful dinner of fried tofu and salmon croquettes, boiled daikon root. He is full and relaxed, lounging in a T-shirt and boxer shorts. His penis grows slightly hard, memories of today in the cool meat locker flit through his head, the other man's eager whine, his navy blue underwear, his peony smell. His wife smiles at him. During the advertisement, she snuggles up to him. He closes his eyes. He is confused.

rice, 1 sack

And now, Ito rubs his face a few times, scattering his tangled daydreams, and makes a sighing sound. He has long left the days of sweeping. He rises, stretches, yawns, shuffles to the coffee machine, pours a fresh cup, the first from a new pot he made, having recently switched from tea to coffee, in the U.S.A. for a few months and subtle changes take place. It is the quiet hour of the restaurant, the lull between lunch and dinner, a hiatus, an ordering time, a time to lie on the back banquette (the leather is smooth, dark red and cool, his warm hands folded under his face), as he does daily, at table 42, and catch a brief nap, then read a Tokyo newspaper brought in, slice white radishes paper thin, make miso soup (whisking ocher clumps of paste atop a sieve in a steaming bath of fish broth), cook an employee meal (tonight the simple and typical *Kare* rice, a thick glutinous curry sauce with lumps of potato, carrots and pork over rice, sweet and heavy, the food of college cafeterias and elementary school children).

He prepares to make rice. The very word *gohan* can substitute for *meal*. It is the substance, the base of all. It lays in a giant metal tub. The top makes a templelike low gong as he removes the lid. If he turned to the clock, he would find it is four-thirty, the exact same moment of this gong every evening, the next minutes all following the same pattern and sounds, the crisp, shoveling sound of measuring the rice, the rocky sound of its landing in a large metal bowl. The cunning way it moves as one large form yet is composed of so many little pieces, the pale whiteness of it all, a tinge of gray, he turns on the water and they disperse and clump, tiny babies, whirling in a cloud.

The front door's little bell jingles and Ito knows it is a waitress, perhaps Delia or probably Mariane, his favorite, slightly older than the others, a little clumsy, eyes averted, a plainly sensuous face, choppy brown hair, crude makeup, slim body. Through the *noren* curtain, from the kitchen, he sees her whisk by, to the bathroom.

The chemistry of his body steps up a bit.

His thick, browned arms, sensual for a man his age, accented by a rolled-up short-sleeved shirt, are elbow level in the watery mound of rice, disappearing in a sea of opaqueness. Mariane walks in, skitters in, licking lips rather quickly, stopping in front of him by a little shelf sanctioned for the waitstaff, with several dirty ashtrays on a rubber matting. She lights a Virginia Slim, puffs a few times.

Sake, medium grade, 3 box

Hey there, Mr. Ito, she says.

She appears to be repeatedly stabbing with her nail for a trace of tobacco on her tongue, as smoke trickles out.

No, no. Please. *Itosan, Itosan,* he says grinning.

Itosan, then.

Good evening to you, Mariane. Good day?

Uh, fair. About the same. Crappy.

Crappy. Bad?

Bad. Sucky—

He notices her hands shake.

Same old, same old. Nothing unusual.

She cracks a smile and it has an imperfection to it, frail Dresden china with a crack, a flash of watery blue eyes and folding lips amongst some wreckage, some travesty of beauty going on. A confusing image.

She wears some old leggings and a large man's shirt, draping around her like a falling parachute, a jumble of silver bracelets on her left hand, red lipstick, big hoop earrings and ballet shoes. A certain lankiness to her legs gives her a coltish appeal. A certain crumpling around her mouth dashes any coltishness to the floor.

She reaches for her special cup amidst all the waitstaff's. Hers is brown and says *Damn I'm Good* in large white letters.

Oh, coffee. Got to *love* coffee.

She goes out to the front of the restaurant, the front and the back, two different worlds, the border where the illusion begins, *the back of the house* is where things dropped get scooped up and replated, whisked to *the front of the house,* the parlor, a mirror of the menu. The gateway to the outside world. Her body is visible in slat views through the *noren* by Ito, his following eyes, his eyes peeking under lids.

And then, in the casual way a shoplifter places an item in a bag, humming even, Mariane places her coffee cup under the cool, plastic sake machine, hidden from Ito's view by the bar, pushes the little rectangular button and hungrily awaits the lukewarm urinish stream, soundlessly filling her cup. Safely hidden from the kitchen by said *noren,* traditional dark blue with a calligraphic slashing of the word *sakana* (fish), Mariane places the cup to her lips and drinks freely, in the lusty way a runner chugs water. Her daily ritual. Her reward.

Ito turns to pour the wet rice into the large chrome ricemaker, and for a brief second catches a different angle of Mariane and a section of her throat. As his hands take on a clamlike shape, he deftly and methodically scoops the transparent grains and at the same time sieves an image flashing in his brain, beyond the chimera of language and culture he crisscrosses daily, the basic knowledge imparted in the tiny muscles in her throat as she drinks from her cup, and how those muscles move like an animal under cloth. He rips a briny segment of seaweed to add to the cloudy rice water and he knows, *he knows,* with clear instinct, that coffee is hot, very hot, too hot to drink quickly without burning, and that what poured down her throat at this moment, and—quick inventory of other days—pours down her throat *every* day, is sake.

He pauses for a moment. Mariane breezes in again, tying an apron around her middle. She scoots by him, but the space is narrow.

Excuse me, big guy.

No problem, Mariane.

Her hips leave a trail of sensation on his. He stands still, absentmindedly flicking the ricemaker on, his eyes blinking slowly.

During the rush of the evening, he watches her, she skims and dives, carrying the wooden blocks of sushi to the waiting customers. She flirts a bit, even with him, squeezes his shoulder and

Ito carries his knowledge like a heavy gift, one he can't wait to open. At the end of the evening, he finds a scrap of paper and writes, the pointy English from his brief school days, stiff and foreign. When Mariane begins to leave for the night, after counting tips, Ito stands up quickly and catches her at the door, he crumples the note in her hand. She says, *what's this?* but he says, *shh, read later, later.* She smiles a questioning smile and pulls her leather coat around her thin face, preparing for the cold blast of winter outside. In the heat of a cab, she reads.

Please come Tomm. 192 20 street. Aparto. 2. Dinner.
Itosan. I wait.

chapter two

Heaven:

For this *gal,* on a night off, there is the ritual: four ice cubes in a striped glass (left by someone once), a healthy pour of Smirnoff to the level of the ice, cranberry juice to the top, half a lime, sixteen steps *precisely* to the bath wearing a petunia-shaded robe, hair in a knot, touching each slippery side of the tiles, *two touches each,* heaven is a bath and a drink and precision and good luck.

Anything off kilter, and things could foul up. Go wrong. One becomes skilled at these forms of insurance. Mariane does.

In ritual lies calm, and enough said, Mariane lolls in the cloudy bubbles and sips the icy slurry.

Deciding, indeed, in that warm cab of last night, hurrying through the blurred lights of the city, to go to the old sushi guy's house, Itowhatever, on her night off, for the hell of it.

For the different thing to do, for the possible freeness of it all, the drinks, dinner, money in her pocket untouched. For the *attention.*

Because, let's face it: She's not getting any younger and hasn't been asked out on a date in maybe ten years, maybe twenty years, maybe never? Who even asked women on dates anymore, with the overwhelming *pressure* of that type of advance, it's just so much easier to run into people, *hang out for a while, see what develops,* mention in a casual way, *Hey, I'll catch you at Sam's. Maybe I'll see you around?*

★ ★ ★

Oh, she's pretty in some kind of eye-squinting, off-center way, or more specifically, she had been years back, for a brief while, when several drinks flushed cheeks attractively and smeared mascara took the clean edge off beauty, young skin peeking through like a hazy, pearlish light, back when she wore small, unfaded jeans, smoking *ciggy-butts,* and wore halter tops crisscrossed against her pointy shoulder blades, slopping around in flipflops, her toes a chipped red, even singing in a band once in a while. Glossy, black hair (creosote locks, now), swimming-pool blue eyes rimmed in dark, a small doughy mouth (now flattened, with lines surrounding starlike) that men liked to trace with their fingers, their tongues, all put together in a tiny package, a rack-up-the-pool-balls snappiness, an energy as shiny, as mechanical as a yo-yo slapping against your palm.

Shedding the clothes became her great moment, the quick rush of weakness from the men as her breasts popped out of her bra, two firm, pink birthday balloons, skin so soft and pale a sheen danced from it (observe: flattened disks half exposed in the bath's bubbles), the running river course of curves, nonstop from shoulder to tummy, perfect shading (now, bloated), strong smooth legs (spindly, varicose on left side), a sumptuous, velveteen landscape (correction: a dry desert, ill, poisoned).

Because, baby, a drink takes the edge off.

Most of the cool people drink.

I'm not one of those A.A. freaks, I just like people. I like to live it up.

She thinks, *I don't look half bad. For my age. Plenty others look older.*

No *dates,* but there were men—there being a vast distinction in her mind between a *date* and a *man*—a whole slew of names spoken with her tinny voice between the hours of 10 P.M. (when the kitchen closes and she goes out) and 5 A.M., names she didn't recognize the next day (Artie, Chris W., Dodgie, Timmy Myers, Tre), men who left traces of various drugstore colognes on her pillow or scraggly dark hairs (the bartender at Hacienda del Rey in the blue vest, Greggie over at Clyde's, Sammy T., who tends at J.C.'s Lounge or just that guy, *that guy who gave me a Camel Light, the nice one talking*), men whose presence she assumed by the crowded cigarette butts, the ones missing the red lipstick stains, bent shapes in her metal plaid sandbag ashtray, along with the sore edges of her body.

Like, there was this Roger guy.

Yeah, like he started hanging around in the light hours a few months ago, snoring loudly in bursts until three or so. Then he got up and called in some Chinese food, standing there in big, paisley boxers at the phone.

Best way chase a hangover's with some salty-as-hell Chinese, you know what I'm saying? Hey. Mariane. You know what I'm talking about? Hunh?

She watched him from the bed, a big hairy mass with a gray beard which later caught sesame noodles like seaweed caught in a net.

Is that so? Hunh. Never thought of that, Roger. Guess you learn something new every day.

He put the phone down and crawled on his elbows over to her in the bed.

Hell, I could get used to this, grabbing her waist as she got up to dress.

Hey, Mariane protested, I've got to get ready for work.

She sat in his lap, staring at his polyfoam plate beading with oyster sauce.

Oh, *screw* that.

Roger hung around for a week or so, frying eggs for her when she came home, sprawling out in front of the TV during the days, working the bar in the evenings, until Mariane brought home a quiet man named Howard, a sixty-year-old bartender at Morris's Hitchstop, and had him answer the phone when Roger called and when she saw Roger again, a few days later in a bar across town, his eyes flicked her way, and she heard his large, artificial laughter. Howard, though, only crashed for a night, curled up like a child on a chair, and left early while she slept.

Thing is, she had liked Roger when he tended bar. She likes all male bartenders when they stand up straight, drying glasses. Their shoulders always square and uplifted, emanating control. Owning the room, walking slowly back and forth, interrupting at the perfect time, picking up punch lines, segueing to swift yet succinct comments, a wink thrown in. She likes their black vests, crisp, pale shirts as they stand above her, paying attention and replacing her drink when she's halfway through the other one, often *on the house,* and if need be, they will interfere when they sense trouble, when someone seems rude or disrespectful. He may cater to drunks, assist in their disease, but there will be order and decorum. To Mariane, he's a deity, a supreme being, someone she'd like to lay, *The Man.*

> *Mornings are important to me.*
> *I need my downtime, my Good Morning America.*
> *No man needs to see me in the morning before I put my face on.*

She wonders what would happen if she didn't drink one day, one whole day.

Once, she tried it, back in October, almost a year ago. She woke up early, and took a shower. She left the TV off. She felt like a normal person and had fried eggs for breakfast, something she always did without. She put on makeup, and curled her hair with a curling iron. She opened the crank windows and dull air from the city poured in, but it had an element of freshness to it, an edged coldness, and it represented to her a Fresh Start, that it was just a bad direction she had taken that could be reversed. She had stepped forward into a regrettable path of sloth and she could change, and maybe her life would be productive, she would be one of them, the regulars, she would go to restaurants, and have vacations, even a family, she would sleep at night and exist in the day, eat salads and cottage cheese for lunch with cling pears, use panty liners, wear perfume, use hair mousse appropriately, date men with jobs and incomes and suits, men who had neat closets, with orderly drawers, men with black toiletry bags and shiny shoes, with patterned yellow ties and gleaming short hair, who would spend two months salary on a crisp solitaire they would present in a glass of Dom Pérignon in a swank restaurant, a bistro, where the waiter knew them, and knew they liked dressing on the side and would recommend the special sea bass with wilted greens and they would *kiss kiss kiss.*

R.G. (*Regular Guy*): God. Do you like it? Do you? I just—

Mariane: Oh, oh, it's just, incredible, look how it sparkles. OH MY GOD! I love you.

R.G.: I just want you to know, how much you mean, to me, Mariane—what I'm trying to say is, marry me, Mariane. Make me the happiest man in the world!

Mariane: Yes! Ever since we met at the firm's Christmas party I knew!

R.G: You knew? So did I! It was fated or something. Oh, Mariane, we have to do it soon, I can't stand another day without—Mariane?! God, you don't look so hot. Are, are you OK? Gee, you're shaking like a leaf! You're—

Shaking, the water spills out of her glass. Desire to puke. And then she got sick, it started slowly, her hand shaking imperceptibly, until she trembled all over, and sweat broke out. And she felt pretty near shitty, and things subtly changed then, see, that's when her drinkies became more than fun, they became necessity and process, process most of all.

Mornings:
Empty bottles lined up on the kitchen floor like bowling pins. *Mornings are important to me.* Lying in bed, the soaps on in the background, filling the apartment with their silky voices of urgency. *In the morning, I make a new start.* The TV on all day and night, even while gone or sleeping. Most of the night, the busy sound of static, the bugle of a closing station. Geraldo at nine. Jenny Jones at three, Oprah at four, time to take a shower for work at five. *I have a schedule, a plan of action.*

The dread of 5 A.M. *A nasty hour for anyone.* If walking home or in a taxi, she avoids the glow of any watch, in order to avoid the sickening feeling this hour gives her, the hour her drinking would stop, the inevitability of sleep looming, climbing the precipice of drunkenness back to sobriety *Is there any way I could just get another Capecodder? Please?* Carefully, like the tidiest of nurses, dealing with her body and its complaints from the nightly abuse, *hush you gotta be quiet in the elevator because the super'll wake,* sleep is the first cure she clumsily reaches for, *Honey, you and me, you and me, you and me,* falling softly in her rumpled bed *pass me a smoke, will you,* her head whirling and rushing, a howling sound in her ears every night *excuse me, whoa, let me through,* sometimes, sometimes she crawls like an infant to the bathroom and pukes in the eggy-smelling bowl, where she thinks of fresh, cool grass *I have a plan, a way I'm working towards* or clear, alpine streams from calenders and patchworks of her youth *you like me, don't you?* some part unremembered and put in a corner to retrieve, someone she's supposed to remember, to get back, then the vomit wells up quickly *I'm sorry, baby, oh, shit, sorry, baby,* sour and burning, smelling like spaghetti sauce and gin, she sinks to the old white tile floor, her face a heavy chunk of dough conforming to and retaining the pattern of the grout, lying there for who knows how long, waking later to the crackle of a stream of urine, resounding in the bowl by her head on the white tile, arching from a young, hungover boy with his eyes closed, groaning softly.

In the mornings, there is something I need to remember, someone. I have a plan of action.

I am working towards some direction.

chapter three

(If you take the train across the Manhattan Bridge into the lower East Side, at a certain point the train dips down and skims right past the apartment buildings, torturously close, giving all the passengers a quick feeling of flying, especially in the blue twilight hour, like some night-borne vampire or bird creature.)

So if you could *fly above the city*

(In that moment as the train's level creates that illusion, there is this certain joy in the car, a look the passengers assume as they feel this shared fantasy. They glide by the windows. They see a milk carton on the counter in someone's kitchen.)

If you could *soar*

(Remember when you get that first flying dream, usually around age four, you are swinging on a swing and you take off, and you're light and airbound and you don't fall, you're not even scared?)

If you could really fly, above the blinking grids of pinlights, some constant, some fading, gliding smoothly above the tarry gravel of rooftops or fancier ones with potted trees and iron terraces, and dip even below these levels and fly by the windows and see the people up close, stirring food in pans, combing hair in mirrors, eyes peering hurriedly through slatted blinds, twisting in crumpled beds. Faces bouncing with TV's moonstone light on old couches or contorted in soundless conversation or arguments. Some rooms simply black, empty and contained like a pocket. Others, softly lit, with lovers shuffling in a dance to unheard music or removing each other's clothes, slowly or quickly, depending on their time and passion.

You'd fly by these and then you'd see, behind one frosted pane, Mariane in her cloudy bath, her drink raised to her mouth, and ten streets away, at another window, Ito, a bent form, vacuuming his couch.

There was this Beyers of Manhattan Furniture Rental Company Catalog, on page four, that Ito had earmarked—MODERN MANHATTAN CONTEMPO (after page two, DESERT SHADES, and page three, RELAXING COUNTRY JAMBOREE)—and picked for his apartment, with its *Italian leather coordinates hand-fashioned by craftsmen in Milan,* and its *sleek urban hues of slate and charcoal;* it was, in fact, this very couch that he vacuums at this moment. Often, he napped on the couch and drifted off to the buttery smell of the leather, *hand-selected by our expert design team.* He had chosen the couch for its durability, its clean masculine lines. The model, draped across the cushions, with blond, feathered hair, may have been a deciding factor, on some level. The couch, then, became a focal point, an advertisement of his good taste and sophistication, yet, really, it often provided a warm repose for his tired body as he watched TV after work.

Right now, he vacuums that couch, dumps ashtrays, circling a wet paper towel in the glass to clean the ash patina. Removes the piles of Japanese and American pornography lying on the coffee table and hides them in his closet, along with his collection of pornographic videos, featuring sinuous golden-limbed Swedish women, and replaces them with a diary written by Murasaki (*"He's far too old for such goings on!" we all whispered among ourselves, but he took not the slightest notice; he took our fans instead and made a number of smutty jokes, the master of the household Tadanobu brought some sake to where the nobles were sitting and, despite the fact that it was a mere formal gesture, gave a very attractive rendition of "Minoyama." Leaning against a pillar two spans to the east, Major Captain of the Right Sanesuke began to check the hems and sleeves of our robes. It was most odd. Under the impression that he was befuddled with drink, we made light of him, and, assuming that he would never recognize them, some of the women even started flirting with him, only to find that he was far from being a flamboyant character; he quite put us to shame."*)

He composes a still life on the coffee table: the diary, a fancy lighter, a *TV Guide,* a book of haiku. (*He rehearses a conversation in his mind:* This? This book? Oh, it's some very fine haiku. Read? Oh, oh, certainly. You like poetry, Mariane? Oh!)

He took a steaming-hot bath. Not in quiet contemplation like Mariane, but in rigorous scrubbing with a sturdy scouring brush of vegetable fibers, the same type his mother used on him in his childhood, roughly scraping his skin in the raw cold air of Sapporo where he grew up, reaching in all the corners, her concentration apparent as she made her coarse *eh . . . eh . . . eh* sounds as she worked. Ito stood up to reach his legs and found it hard to reach down past his stomach, finding himself absentmindedly making the same sounds as his mother, wrapping himself in a thin blue and white *yukata,* like the type found in the country spas of Japan, lounging on the couch enjoying a cigarette and a sufficiently icy beer, contemplating Mariane and the evening.

As an older man of a fatherly age, and her boss, her leader, he felt, in true *Japanese company manner,* an obligation to the good of the whole, the family of the work, in the traditional sense, and Ito was Tradition (in a paternal, if you will, way) and therefore felt obliged to assuage the damage and betrayal she might be choosing to inflict upon herself and the company, the family. As a boss he is responsible to her as a parent to a child, to assist in times of trouble, to procure habitat, or help with bills, or offer advice, it was not the owner who now had this ultimate responsibility, it was him, as high sushi chef, *shokunin,* he must speak, not let the company deteriorate, not allow mutiny amongst the ranks.

He will get to the point.

You were drinking sake. Please stop.

What?

Sake drinking at work not good. Must stop.

But, he is opportunistic. He feels excited in a dark, hungry way, a heart-beating way, and not in the soft, plodding caring of a boss that he imagined. He has other ideas. A veil of images follows in *kanji* in his mind, a segment still pure and untouched by English, vivid in archaic impression, of contorted limbs, senses flaying, the smells of cane and ricepaper, wet bamboo in the morning, red cotton quilts and futons, black pubic hair as straight as cat's fur, paper-white skin, napes of necks, the nutty smell of rice, the burst of images of tiny red mouths, black sooty hair, his own Japanese women with hard, brown nipples, hips brushing against his, piny-smelling arms, women who speak his language, green tea foamed by a whisk, bitter lacquered woman, collaged against the others here with pale, pink buttocks, girls with blue eyes, *he reaches in his pants, his penis semihard,* blue eyes like frosty waves, green eyes like fern fronds, big, drooping peachy breasts, Ito would like to know, to compare, it's simple really:

What are the women here really like; what's Mariane like?

Back in Japan, Ito had a wife named Tomoko, rather homely, round-shouldered with a tiny mouth like a raccoon and sharp, dark eyes, who died of stomach cancer. She told him he smelled of fish and after they had one child, a boy, refused him in the night, sleeping with the child pulled to her side. Ito began to frequent the hostess bars late at night and favored one whore, a certain Xiu-Xiu, a

Chinese girl, tiny and slender with a tattoo on her stomach of a dragon that Ito gripped while she rode his hips naked. There were hints of that girl in Mariane.

His wife stopped talking to him, a little bit more every year, though Ito loved her. He loved a home, a warm spot, he loved her presence in that home. He loved the hot noodle soup she made, slurping it with her in the evening, bone-weary from cutting fish all day, from standing on his swollen feet. He loved the small form of his son, Daisuke, on the futon across the room, mouth open, and at times in the night, he would reach over to touch her shoulder and she would shrug him off, the next night Ito stopping at Flower Farm, as they called it, Xiu-Xiu, in tiny platforms and a crochet dress, always linked her arm in his, smelling a bit too sweet, like gum, and got right down to business, brought him to the back room, wiggled her clothes off, folded them on a stool and kept the platforms on. Wore a little thong and often just pushed the crotch aside for entry. It was afterwards he liked best, which he paid extra for, when she took the platforms off, walked barefoot on his back, smoked cigarettes, giggled at his bad jokes, massaged his back for hours, told about her grandparents in the country, how they farmed pigs on the coast (first generation), how they think she does secretary work, her boyfriend last year who she misses, a salaryman, Toyota, to be exact (but he decided he wasn't able to handle her profession or her family), her kitten, her collection of purses, anything at all, drinking beer, going to all-night sushi bars, bad off-color jokes between Ito, her, and the other sushi chefs, an old tradition, her tinkling laughter, red lips, ordering ten orders of sea urchin sushi and not touching it, and eventually, when he went there to the Flower Farm, she was gone. Just like that. They said she met a monkey-faced man with a perm, Japanese mafia. Took off with him to Tokyo. She was gone.

Three months ago, Ito sat in an airplane gushing through dark clouds, his slumped head shot through with gray flecks, beside him a young boy in sweats jiggling to a headphone. He heaved two pale blue suitcases, *Young Voyagers,* above his seat.

In a small satchel by his feet, he kept a Hokkaido paper, a few rice balls he made at early dawn, a roll of money and a letter of introduction from a certain Yoshi Takahara, owner of Sugi Sushi Bar, a letter of apologies and promises, descriptions of an employment role, and long paragraphs, in a completely protocolic way, of his numerous gracious thanks. Plus directions. And an address.

Careening over the pale brown island of Japan, perhaps his last view ever, a flight attendant offered him a plate of broiled fish, which he politely declined. She spoke in Japanese, and for this he was grateful, for at this point, his English was sparse. He reached for his rice balls, rolled in crinkled foil, still warm, the insides wet and red.

For a while he slept, strange dreams flitting through his head like odd birds, sounds and smells he barely discerned, yet seemed familiar. Animals crashing through wet forests, Ito's bare feet making soft crunching sounds as he ran behind, his breath choppy. Finally, he grabbed the stunned animal and they fell on the wet leaves, the mossy smells mingling with the dark, spicy odor of the deer. It uttered a high-pitched honk as he bit into its neck, hot, wet blood rushing in his mouth. The mingling of fur and pink flesh.

Ito awoke. The airplane was dark, except for the tiny pinlights rimming the edge of the luggage rack. They jounced through the black sky, a mix of people with mixed routes and sleepy breath.

Ito has an erection and wishes to sleep. He hears the tinny sound of the music from earphones. He gets up and goes to the bathroom, swaying slightly. In the plastic interior, he masturbates briefly, ejaculating on the seat, and reaches for the tissues but then stops and doesn't clean it, in his own way he feels he has invaded some space in a small desperate way, some intimacy taken without its having been offered.

★ ★ ★

It is raining when he lands at JFK. He stands still at the lobby, not knowing where to turn, but Yoshi runs up, skittering like a crab. He fetches Ito's bags and shakes his hand, he bows, he smiles, laughs nervously; Ito is formal and quiet. Yoshi chatters in the cab about brands of ginger, fish, rice delivery, Ito's apartment. After a while, he notices he is jabbering to a sleeping man. When they arrive at the apartment house, he shakes Ito's shoulder gently, as if he is a small child.

When Yoshi leaves, Ito watches American T.V.

So much space, so many people, when you are one, he thinks.

In this country, one wears loneliness like a coat.

So now it's 4:59 P.M. Sunday, Ito gets up from the couch, a bit spent from thinking of *too many women,* his penis crumpled and damp, tosses a tissue in the trash, wipes himself off with a damp towel in the bathroom, splashes on some cologne, puts on a colorful Hawaiian shirt and jeans he thinks make him appear more young, and as he hums, he walks to the kitchen, checking on the rice cooking, steam piping out, the sake warming, a hunk of *hamachi,* in a brine of salt, salmon skin crisping in the oven to be wrapped in rolls, and at this exact moment, across town in her twelfth-floor apartment building on Fourteenth Street, The Imperial, Mariane's head falls back on the tile of her bath, her hair damp and plastered to her forehead, dreaming of babies, the voice of her mother, smells she had forgotten, and then just a soft, cotton sleep holds her drunken cerebrum, while water drops sporadically from the faucet.

If she had a clock, she would have realized, upon awakening, that hours had slipped by and Ito had waited, but she wouldn't have known how he had waited and sighed, waited and breathed fog on the window viewing the lobby's entrance again and again. She wouldn't have known how he sat on the couch, smoking cigarettes and sipping sake the first hour she was late (getting up to view the aforementioned window ten times), then changing to beer, drunk from the bottle, then spending a torturous half hour attempting to locate her number (speaking to the operator, *I'm sorry, sir, I cannot understand, Mary Parker? Molly?* Finally hanging up in frustration), or how he tossed the fish in the trash, or how he ate roast beef straight from its deli paper wrapping, hunkered over the coffee table, big folded slices of beef.

And how, drunk and clumsy, slightly sad, he had pulled off his Hawaiian shirt and his jeans and stood silently for a bit, wearing only his white Jockey underwear.

Nor would she have known that he fell asleep with the Swedish porn video at 2 A.M., his mouth gaping and snoring, the VCR finally stopping to a blue screen.

chapter four

Who's on top?

Yoshi, the owner of Sugibar, is a man who appears as if always running, tripping forward, even in the boxy confines of his little bar. Always in the same T-shirt and pants, tight and black as a wetsuit, he is sinewy and childlike, and when not playing *pachinko* or reading Japanese adult comics (*manga*), he is slurping noodles quickly in the few moments he allows. Behind Ito's back, Yoshi refers to him as the old man or lately, the bumbling old man, the slow old man, the crawling crab:

Today, he says, let's pay fifteen dollars a pound more for tuna, fifteen dollars.
He says this to his young sushi chef, Koji, who listens as he slaps rice behind the glass sushi counter, then slaps his hands.
Aaaah, shit. Americans don't know the difference between *O-toro* and *Chuu-toro*. Goddamn *O-toro*. What a waste. What a fucking waste.
Old follow old ways, *ne?* says Koji. New is more hard for them, *slap, slap* go his hands.

Old man needs a woman, you know? When he comes here, his wife died before, when my cousin call me from Tokyo, he says, this guy can come cheap, top *shokunin,* because he needs change, dead wife. But—

Slap, slap, wife dies he can still work there, no? Why leave? It's a heartbreak kind of thing.

Ah. *Slap, slap.* Bad memories, *ne?* It's a tragic kind of death? Childhood sweethearts?

Kind of like this, I think. Kind of too sad for him, but, oh, I don't know—

Slap, slap, old people get used to each other, you know.

I don't know, maybe not going to work out, maybe too old-fashioned. Everything always, he say, *fresh, fresh, top quality.* Expensive Japanese ginger, instead of Chinese. Chinese, you know, *cheaper,* but no problem. People don't know differences—

The door jingles and Ito walks in fast, with a paper bag,

Konnichiwa, konnichiwa, Yoshisan, Kojichan. Oh! I get flounder. Flounder?

More, other too old.

Aaaah, you can cook. Pickle or something. Shit. Stew it or, or fry. We don't need waste all the time, every time.

I'll call Sunshine Seafood and order. I need more money.

Ito has stopped at the counter, talks almost to himself.

Come, aaah, *come on.*

Yoshi gets up, scowling, and Ito looks down, recognizing that *aaah* sound, when Yoshi is irritated or uneasy.

Yoshi leads Ito down the back stairs to his little crammed office, amidst smells of vinegar (a waitress dropped a glass jar of rice vinegar on the stairs two months ago) and furnace oil, pushing open the little door and pulling a string light which illuminates a pile of papers and boxes filling the corners, boxes of ramen noodles and flour; several out-of-date calendars line the walls, bent magazines and *manga* comics, crushed cigarette packs. Yoshi reaches under the desk and pulls out a dried-seaweed tin, square and bright orange. He clicks it open and Ito sees a sea of green bills.

Everything so expensive, don't you think, Itosan?

Most quality.

Ha, quality. Listen now, here, he says as he pulls out a small roll, this is thousand, only thousand. Only this. No more. Get simple stuff, crabcake, red tuna, smoked salmon, you know, stuff that lasts, not too special. No *O-toro,* no prawn.

Yes.

Come on, this is business here, different. American way.

Oh. I see.

Tomorrow, tomorrow we go to Fantasy Island, huh? You, me and Koji, *ne?* Beautiful girls dancing, *ne?* Have dinner?

Maybe, let me tell you later—

No, no, you come.

Yes, I think about—

Tomorrow, after work, we go. Come on, old man. Yoshi puts his arm around him, thinking, *It is hard to adjust for old grandfather.*

I think about. I think.

There is a certain way the Japanese tend to treat the word *no,* it is basically an unacceptable usage, you can say *maybe* or *let me think about it,* or *I wouldn't want to trouble you,* which all could, from an older generation mean *no,* and from a younger generation could really mean *maybe,* or you might hear *I can't take up your time, it is a waste for you,* or *I would be an inconvenience, surely,* all in avoidance of the blastingly harsh finality of *no (iie),* because it could embarrass, or sadden unduly or even madden people, so it is avoided politely, skirted around, and in this hidden dance, all is well understood.

Yoshi recognizes this, but will insist later, as they walk up the stairs from the office, his hand on Ito's back, the vinegar smell becoming entwined with the implicit *no* floating in the air. *There is a master shokunin from Hokkaido, from the south of Sapporo, I heard,* his cousin had said, *he wants a new start and is willing to go work for cheap, for starting price, he can even come next week,* and it happened Yoshi was at the tail end of a string of unfortunate, badly trained sushi chefs, with dull knifes that hacked at the fish or produced mounds of sickly sweet rice, and he jumped on the situation, and before Ito came, he pranced about Sugibar, chattering about the new chef, *from Sapporo! forty-five years' practice!* And it was only at the airport, seeing the old man stumbling down the stairs, his moppy head down, the creases in his face hardened from the long flight, that Yoshi saw the burden in his life, this old man's happiness, which could be defined as keeping him fed, in many ways, like a large infant. He fed him special food, padded his check with extra from time to time, arranged and payed for his apartment, drove him around town in his Jeep to the Empire State Building, Ellis Island, the Statue of Liberty, but now, seeing the man in his linty sweater and dark, tired eyes, Yoshi sought to find for him the arms of a woman, someone to kiss him and keep his bed warm, to hold him, to occupy him as if loneliness is a virus that one can prevent, Yoshi saw it glaring in the eyes of Ito and it made him feel edgy and sad—

Itosan, Itosan, you haven't had an American *girl*—

What?

You need to try one. You need to sleep with one, to try, *ne*?

Oh, heh, heh, I see.

And it was in silence they finished walking up the stairs, each filled with the image of American women: Yoshi, flicking the lights, held, for a second in his mind, the hard breasts of the dancers at Fantasy Island and their brassy legs, while Ito scanned his Rolodex of memories for an instant, and he paused on a film clip: Scarlett O'Hara, in a green velvet dress, smiling, under the porch of a southern manse, and not coincidentally there was something of Mariane there in her green eyes and the hair, as if Mariane were the face of old American dreams.

★ ★ ★

When Yoshi first opened the restaurant five years ago, he had been on the edge of his thirties with smoother skin; he wore Giorgio Armani suits and went to Tokyo often. He wore tight silk T-shirts on his wiry body and grew his hair long, in a braid, and his wife, Theresa, a small girl with red hair from Queens whom he'd met in a bar in Soho, was pregnant with his first child, and Yoshi started spending longer hours at Sugi, because Theresa went to bed early. Yoshi would count the register and pour raisin-flavored plum wine for the waitresses who sat at the glossy sushi bar counting tips, loud Japanese pop blasting, a cigarette always hanging from the maroon slash of his mouth, he'd make jokes about sushi and sex, combining the two, he'd call *akagai,* the red clam, a woman's vagina, and *giant clam,* long, wrinkled and phallic, a penis, and he'd say to the waitresses, *akagai genki? Is your red clam OK?* and they'd all giggle and smirk in that silly, offhand way they do in restaurants or hotels, everyone's language and time short, most people tired from supporting families or habits, and they make quick little fourth-grade jokes for some kind of proto-bonding, *my giant clam always good,* he'd say, which is true, last year he flew to Tokyo and had small pellets placed under the skin *to make better for woman, before use metal balls but this is no good, now use soft plastic, so it moves, now woman happy in five minutes, five minutes!* and everyone laughed, this was before Mariane, before Ito, this was the time of Angela, Maggie and Todd, three NYU students, and Angela seemed to be his favorite, she had lovely pooling eyes, a crisp buzz cut and wore a small T-shirt with the glittered words *Superstar,* with rounded grapefruit breasts, she majored in Women's Studies with a philosophy minor, very fond of Camille Paglia (though he could care less— *Polly who?*)—he said, *Mountain Potato gives big power,* wink, wink, and they all cackled as he dished out tiny square plates of diced tuna with grated Mountain Potato, unctuous and snotlike, and poured more plum wine all around, cigarettes lit by everyone, but then

Todd sat up, he had to run, *I'm catching some friends uptown,* and he got his coat and then Maggie swallowed her plum wine fast, *wait, I'll catch a cab with you, Toddie,* and she puts the dishes in the back sink, and calls out, *hey, Ange, you want to come?* but Angela says, *nah, I'll finish my plum wine and hang with ol' Yosh here,* and they rush to the door, the cold air hurtles in for a brief moment and then they are alone, he tops off her plum wine and skitters over to the sushi bar, *how about sushi? you want sushi?*

OK, sure. A little bit.

Uni? Eel?

Umm.

You like Unigasm?

Hee, hee. Yes, I would.

They have a tradition amongst the staff at Sugi; The *Unigasm*—Uni (sea urchin roe)—is so revered that during the consumption of it no one can talk to the consumer lest it mar the enjoyment of the cat-tongue texture, the creamy mustardy roe.

So they have a few more plum wines, some cigarettes, he makes sushi and feeds her a few pieces and she just accepts that, aware that it implies a notch of intimacy crossed, then he, at one point while discussing her parents' visit in a few weeks, reaches over and massages her neck and she says *ooh, that feels good,* and he reaches down and kisses her neck softly and she says *ummm,* and Yoshi feels some wildly overpowering lightness of breath, and Angela is intrigued by this experience, she turns and their lips meet, and Yoshi is kissing a waitress for the first time, a singular thrill, then she is fast and poised, her quick tongue darts around with its cold pierced little stud and he cups her breasts, and Angela pushes him away and stands up, slowly pulling up her T-shirt and her round, pale breasts bounce down and then Yoshi zooms forward, his warm mouth sucks them, and leaning forward, they lose balance for a few seconds and he guides her down to the floor by her waist, her eyes are staring straight into his as he tongues her teeth, her throat, the harsh industrial-gray carpet under his back, he wiggles her jeans off as she touches his surgically altered penis through his black serge trousers, she feels the soft give of the pellets, he shimmies out of the pants, and in a flash Angie straddles him, he guides himself in and she arches, feels the pellets, they rock and careen, he grabs the floor with his toes, holding her ass, and she says *whoa, Yosh, whoa,* her knees are burned against the chemical pile of the carpet, then even before the end of the song, she is crumpled on his chest, his cedary smell leaking, his face quiet and pink, he says, *You need ride?* and she says, *Yeah, that'd be cool,* her jeans like a discarded skin on the floor, she sees her roughened pink cheeks in the wall mirrors, rubs her sore knees, he acts subdued, but his life takes a subtle swinging shift in direction, he has crossed an invisible line now, he has had *sex with a waitress* and he becomes a boss who does those things with ease, a few more times with Angela (until she started getting involved with Claude), another named Julie, whom he took to a hotel a few times, Marguerite late at night in his car, and the list goes on, so when she, Mariane, came for a job, her tangled face and weary eyes, his sporting side appreciated her hungry-looking mouth and he thought, *This is what I do now, this is my thing, I am a man who enjoys the company of women.*

One night he moved in on Mariane, and it wasn't a pretty sight.

A Saturday night, when they were friendly and laughing, too much sake, and all others had left, she trusted this man, he approached her, his hands outstretched, her back falling on some bottles, knocking a few down as he kissed her hard and she tried to push away, and had no strength anymore.

Yoshi could taste and smell the old sourness of her alcoholism and pushed on, she was mouthing *No,* directly, a very American *no,* but it rather excited him, he pushed her back and felt it was a game, she actually fell to the floor and he was laughing, Yoshi was, and he thought he heard her giggle, he thought that her *no,* meant something else, like *challenge,* and he was filled not with the urge to rape but a feeling of symbolic conquering, and she seemed game for it, she was squirming and angry, biting even, and he breathed hard, and grew stronger, he pulled up her skirt and saw her green polka-dotted underwear, wiggled his hand in and she was moist, *he was right!* she had wiggled her butt to the back wall, he reached for his zipper and sprung out, he pushed himself in her, thinking *she will like the pellets,* thinking *this is a fine, rough game,* and as he pumped he stopped suddenly, for underneath him she was crying, he looked down and her face was red and wet and she was only whispering *no, please* and he felt a paralyzing shame, he got up and said nothing as she lay there sniffling, as she got up and walked to the door, crying still, and went outside, and Yoshi stood behind the bar, he zipped up his pants and stood in confusion, staring at the door.

And he was not a bad man. He went to the bar, and back to the sink. He smelled of her body and his excitement, it had unleashed a certain grenade of hormones in him as he pushed her down and his thoughts (as he drank more plum wine) dashed around like shiny pool balls, clacking against each other, thoughts of *she started it, did I hurt her?* colliding thoughts of fear and danger and guilt, fear of being found out, but worst of all, the fear of feeling pleasure at another's discomfort. A new sensation.

And Mariane just went home that night, no bars, no meeting friends, leftovers of winter's dirt lay in the streets after the ravages of snow and sleet, she punctured the frozen sheet of dirt with her small galoshes and walked home, no taxi, still crying, stopping at the liquor store on the corner, which smelled strong and spicy as she walked in. She saw a young Indian man behind the counter, his hair tied in a red cloth, eyes like pieces of dark felt with orangy whites, behind him a small girl in a ruffled dress sat on a stool, eating ice cream, a radio from somewhere a woman singing in lilting Urdu, and to this man, Aparjeet Rungibab, life at this moment appeared as such:

When we meet, your eyes are bold/but you are not for me/you are another's/the spring is coming/I wish to hold you/I tell my parents I cannot live/Love is a sad thing.

Aparjeet has all fourteen of Mamila Sahb's tapes stacked on the side wall by his small tape player, tapes of the lovely woman from Kerela who sings of Love's misfortunes, who lives in New Delhi and finds one thousand flowers at her apartment's entrance daily from admirers, sometimes even whole bouquets of roses and other times just simple wild blossoms, or even scribbled desperate notes, or blurred pictures of men, one day Aparjeet had been sixteen, smoking a cinnamon *bidi* on the corner with his friends after a Saturday lunch with his parents and grandparents, when a glossy car drove by and inside he saw for a millisecond the silhouette of Mamila *Mamila Mamila Mamila,* voices chanted behind her car, he saw her glittering, red mouth *lips like dazzling rubies!* her kohled eye like a black bead, and the herds of people following her on dusty feet or ringing bicycle, that black of an eye fixed on Aparjeet for a fleeting second, as the *bidi* reached his mouth, she winked slowly, he heard his friend exclaim, *Mamila darling,* as Aparjeet for one long second lay in the cupped vision of her eye.

Mariane watches through the dull, scratched Plexiglas as Aparjeet scuffles in his mud colored slippers up to the front, *Can I help you, miss?*

Uh, yes, I would like, uh.

Aparjeet focuses on the face of the woman, puffed, pink and wet as a wad of gum, her makeup smudged and shiny, and he wonders if she has been crying, or if the weather has wrecked her

face, but he has learned to wonder and not involve and at the same
time the little girl gets up and pulls on his shirt with her tiny hand,
Papa, Papa, and he says, *wait a minute, Puhna—*

Yeah, I'll take some vodka, uh—

Ma'am. Are you—

His eyes have a deep shine as if oiled and she smiles an embarrassed smile, pushes some hair to the side of her wet face,

Are you, can I be of assistance for you?

Oh. Oh. I'm, I'm just tired, but. Thanks.

Yes, I am tired as well—*Papa!*—please, Puhna—

OK, well, so, a small vodka and a liter, too. Cheapest.

Yes, yes, (poor woman is a drunk perhaps) *Papa, I want Mommy
now, can I call her?*

Yes, Puhna, in a minute, That will be ten fifty-eight, *Puhna!*

There is a crash as the girl knocks over the stool, and she pays
the money in exact change on the heavy rubber mat that says *Win-
ston Lights,* she turns and the door chimes, an automatic lock clicks
in place, the warble of Mamila Sahb is shut off, Aparjeet Rungibab
decides to count the drawer as it is late, he gives Puhna a Snickers
bar and drops a slipper as he sits on the stool to count, a song ends
and there is a millisecond of static, and he looks up and sees the
huddled form of the woman leave the street, and he thinks *unfortunate,* and turns to the money.

Mariane walks home slowly, clutching the bag, sipping the
small flask of vodka when no one is around, keeping her mind on
each thing in her path, a newsstand, streetlights, restaurants, passing a tree she knows well, a small elm near her apartment, now
covered in tiny pale green buds, when this winter in the pale snow
she had rested against the barren tree and swallowed consecutively
coffee, wine and aspirin. Big ragged chunks had fallen and spiraled
down so slowly, and smaller ones caught in little eddies in the gray
air, settling on the top of the big city bus pulled up by the stop-

light, like a shroud. An old lady had walked by, scarf-clad head star-ing at the ground, unaware of the festive polka dots of lacy snow on her back and shoulders, they covered the lady's 7–Eleven bag, her shoes, her body and Mariane had said *hello,* and the lady looked up and saw her bag with the wine poking out and ignored her, kept her head bowed over, flecked with snow.

Past the elm, on the corner is Mariane's building and she goes in, remembering the lady, remembering Yoshi and the evening and she cries in the elevator (coldly gray, with graffiti she has seen a million times—a heart with T.M. scratched into the brass of the control knob panel), fumbling with the keys in the long hall of roasted meats and babbling TV muffles, finally falling on her bed in her coat, sobbing, rising to chug from the vodka; she vows:

When I get you back in my life, Daisy, said with the Smirnoff high in the air, at the same time noting the wavy fluctuations of her ceiling light through her tears and the liquid of the vodka bottle, *I'm going to make a good life, I'd like to have a house with wind chimes on a porch,* she hears simultaneously the faraway bell of the chapel on the other street, chiming softly, *and vases of flowers and cats, and I'd like to learn to weave, and you'll have your own room, in a little town upstate, I'll be on the PTC, we'll have a porch, like I said, to drink coffee with friends and watch you grow and braid your hair. When I get you back, when I fully activate my plan. My baby, Daisy.*

She fell asleep this way, dreaming. The bottle tipped and left a pooling circle of gray.

chapter five

Menu:

Bourbon and Water

Froot Loops

Mead

Vodka Tonic

Lists compose us.

The next day Ito writes his list again and he is thinking of Mariane and why she didn't show, *O-toro, 5 piece, Prawn, 20 piece,* flitting between each scribble with anger, wonder, confusion as Yoshi drives around and around the block, his nightly routine, an inching red Jeep, searching for a parking spot, refusing year after year to rent a space (*Four hundred fifty! Expensive*). Thinking, as he drapes the wheel, in the agitated way he has nightly for three weeks since the incident with Mariane, trying to decide what to do—(woven with his bursts of parking space inquiry) although in his polite, cool transactions with Mariane in the last few days some decision had been made, it was not enough for him—(*Is it a space? Is that woman pulling out? Is she? Goddamn!*)—he could not abide by the gnawing feeling that he had misunderstood, that he had not seduced but forced, that Mariane was secretly joining forces with the other waitresses (or policeman or *lawyers*), this nagging cloud of paranoia, quilted with frequent sniffs of cocaine a friend had given him at lunch, got him in a frenzied, shaking state (*Leaving? Mister. Mister! Are you leaving? Goddamn! Fuck, fuck, he's leaving*) and he was getting slightly sweaty, lurching in the stick shift (*OK, OK, this space, here, here*) as he turned, reversed for a small space just short of the hydrant allowance, parking in little bursts, finally closing at a deciduous angle, but *Goddamn,*

Mariane, you Mariane, he thinks, *what I am going to do about this Mariane?*

It's about now that Mariane wakes up (as Yoshi walks into the restaurant to Ito at the window), her head confused, as if sections of thought have been shut off and covered in cloth, (*I'm every woman, I'm every woman,* sings the *Oprah* theme song, as she rushes out on stage in her medium-weight phase and the audience breaks into applause). Mariane first feels the edge of the bath against her chin, then the coldness of the water, then hears the familiar warmth of Oprah's voice introducing her guests (*Today we got a great show, let's give it up for*) and she knows it's four, she rises up and her body is waterlogged and shriveled, the glass of melted ice falls into the bath, and then she remembers her intention with a jolt, *please come, aparto 20,* she rises up and grabs a towel, she finds a beer in the fridge, cracks it and sucks down the cold bubbles, and plans her reaction. She will be silent and wait for him to make the first move, as she did with Yoshi.

She redraws a bath. Again, *sixteen steps, touch the walls four times.* Petunia robe. Beer in hand. Work preparations.

If you are wondering where, out of the endless flux of genetic mishmash, comes a Mariane like we have here, the story started so long ago, trekking back across the span of wine-swilling, beer-swilling, mead-swilling eons of barbarians, humping at all hours, breeding, birthing ancestors, each driven in their own ways, fighting wars, making love, drinking, working, sweating, crossing oceans, betraying, following plans and honor and mistakes as faithfully as dogs seek smells, tossing sperm and spittle and flesh across the generations and out of the spasm of centuries we alight upon the girl known as Poppy Howell, real name of Catherine but nicknamed for her bright red hair, only child of the respectable and properly drab Wasps Billings (Bill) and Margaret Taylor, tasteful arbiters of Virginian aristocracy, Margaret coming from a long line of pale banking sorts, brittle as onion skins, and Billings a rather handsome doctor, outdoorsy in a purplish way, a thoracic surgeon, a Yalie, a tweedy type, tall and stooping when approaching door entrances, a soft, scaly handshake, and accompanying laugh, ha, ha, ha, nicely deep, terribly fond of Poppy and all her antics and proud Miss Poppy (*Pops. Pippsy. Popcorn.*) was attending The University (It is Ivy League, after all . . .) and so delighted that Poppy plans to study English lit and be a teacher, and, best yet, join a sorority house, then the big *M* with a proper sort, a sailing sort, a bourbony sort, a 100-percent-cotton sort, it's all a perfect plan, except for the slight tendency that Margaret has to put away too many bourbon and waters late in the evenings and has always, but God, everyone drinks back then, Good Lord, and Billings is no slouch in that department. Poppy has fit the mold quite succinctly in many ways, except for her faddish tendency to wear beat clothes, black turtlenecks and ballet shoes and Margaret would say, *well, dear, it's a bit too funereal for my tastes* and send her packages from Lord & Taylor with cashmere twin sets in peach and buttercup and Poppy refused to wear them, in her coy baby rebellious way, and she would haunt the poetry readings on campus with fellow beatnik wanna-bes and that is where she met McClellan Hackett, scruffy, black-haired son of Phillip W. and Mary Hackett, of Oyster Bay, Long Island, Macky Hackett, famous on campus for his bravado poet snorts of irreverence, they take to each other like hounds in a pack, lost in the bush, it is simply a few beers, a few wild kisses, a few car rides in the night, before Macky and Poppy are a mated, glued item, a streak of whining lust in the safe, Jeffersonian brick of the campus, flinging their pillowy traditions aside like spurned cafeteria rice puddings, they hang out, get wild, jargon-clad ideas about *living free,* and Phillip and Mary Hackett, Billings and Margaret become discarded paper doll figurines with sketched in O's for mouths.

In fact, when these two leave campus and find a trashy apartment in Richmond, drop out of school and decide to find a real life in 1960, on the verge of a new happening, a new way of existence and Poppy has no idea of the fleeting superiority of lust and its quick-slap disappearing act, it is one year later that she has kicked out Macky for 1) drinking 2) drinking, she is alone with the water faucet dripping, pregnant, she is not a teacher in some fine university after all, she is not picking curtains from a large, awkward book of fabric samples in a gleaming wood-floored cottage in Long Island, or eating warmed Triscuits and cheddar from a wax package on a crisp, Deer Isle lawn, she is instead, as promised by her mead-swilling ancestors, an alcoholic who doesn't know it, pregnant with a worse case, living on a check sent by Billings and Margaret and nothing left to do but pick up the leftover Poppy charm, the fire hair, the brown smoky eyes, and place them in front of men in bars, who would respond with warm arms, drinks, nicotine kisses.

Then Poppy had a baby in November that year, a tiny fuzz-haired thing. She looked at the girl and named her, named that little bundle of red skin and squinty eyes Mariane Louisa, after her grandmother, and then, she called that baby Mariane, after Marianne Faithfull, but dropped an *n* for no good reason.

Margaret (Maggie) had Bill drive her in the Lincoln, they had discussed it for weeks and she wore wool slacks and a turtleneck, her antiquing outfit (she had owned an antique shop for a bit, even), they packed a little cooler with bourbon and ice, they brought Timmy and Tina, their two drooling Labs that turned around and around in the backseat, mashing dog drool into the leather seats covered with old towels, and a frosted plastic water bottle, empty, stood on guard in the back for impromptu pee relief (she crouched on the side of the road, over the bottle), while Billings nervously perused the traffic, because she couldn't dare enter the bathrooms, the smell, the people crowding around, the noise, and Billings had grown used to protecting this fragility, a human tarp he became.

They edge the Lincoln around in the crumbling district where Poppy lives, searching for a space, fearful of the indefinite lines of poverty clutter around, fearful of Poppy, of the child, what if it is imperfect (what if it isn't *OK,* says Margaret), and Billings says it'll be fine, soon they are at the door and Poppy is there, overweight to their horror, but they tell her she looks darling in that black smock, the baby is tiny and Margaret holds her and feels love for the little thing, but they leave later and she drinks up the bottle in the car (we'll need to stop for ice) and Timmy throws up in the back, she is worn as they approach home, they are silent, they fall into their twin beds, pictures of Poppy lining them, glossy in her neat skirts and shining teeth, they don't really say it to each other, but it is how it will be: They will not go there again, to that place, they will not let that picture replace the one on the walls. Instead, they send checks with warm notes and Poppy slowly fades away. *Popcorn, Poppums, Popsy.*

That baby grows, becomes an adult at age five, making breakfast, coffee, cleaning, sewing, washing the laundry, bringing mother sliced bananas, peanut butter, Froot Loops in bed, child's food, her mother laying her head on Mariane's shoulder to say, *what do I do, Mariane?* talking about some man. Mariane was the mother, her mother the child. Technically, *parentification.*

A person can do that for a childhood and then when they're older they just don't want to go further.

They stop.

So, here we are, she is walking up the stairs to Sugi, it is a coldish evening, five o'clock, losing the blue tones and becoming dark gracefully, she is on time, her cheeks are flushed, her lips look full and shiny, she walks in, hears the familiar drone of the Japanese CD, sees Yoshi nod his head in greeting, Ito lifts his hand as he chops clams, subtly subdued, yes, but normal, yet his eyes are down, *I've fucked up,* she thinks, and begins repair mode as usual, a slight

bit more helpful, more smiling, sweeping up the broken pieces, offering Ito coffee, bringing Yoshi his dinner, serving the customers
with extra smiles, washing the counters in her free time, ignoring
the sake machine (her hand is shaking slightly), then finally counting her tips slowly, shift drink in hand, not sitting with the staff,
stooped alone against the end of the bar.

Yoshi comes to her.

Mariane, sit, sit, he says in an artificial light tone, sit. He leads
her to a table where the staff usually sit for dinner.

Drink?

Oh, uh, I already. She lifts her vodka and tonic.

OK, Mariane. Listen, aaaah, I notice.

Notice?

You, you seem so *tired,* maybe need little *vacation,* he pushes
a little envelope across the table, you know, I like to help out, maybe
take a few days off, relax—he is edging towards her, holding her
hand.

You're firing me?

No, I—

Firing me now?

A break, just—there seem problems—

Problems, you goddamn you. Goddamn you to hell.

Shh, no, Mariane—

Her face is a wet mess. All the staff stops and stares in her direction, the sumo wrestlers on TV the only movement.

I hate this place. I hate you.

Yoshi stops talking, folding his arms across his chest.

And Mariane leans into his face as he pulls back.

You are evil. You are.

But she couldn't say *rape,* although the word lies on her
tongue, she couldn't say what she wanted, and at the same moment Yoshi felt the word *drunk* but he also couldn't say it, and Ito

watches from the sushi bar, where he pours little bucketfuls of water against the display case, creating a wall of transparency, and finally he bursts out a long torrent of Japanese words without expression directed at Yoshi, but Yoshi only shakes his head.

After a while, Yoshi says, Please go. Please.

And Mariane turns to the door, then turns back and grabs the envelope, her coat and flees to the street, the cold air stinging her wet face, the lights making trails in her eyes, then as she goes down the stairs she looks up and sees Yoshi looking at her, their eyes meet.

Drunk.

Rapist.

chapter six

Menu:

Margaritas with Salt

Fish Cake

Nostalgia

Saudade

Natsukashii

Nostalgia and the hotel lobby: (or perhaps untranslatable but more apt and vivid, the Brazilian term *saudade,* implying longing, want, remembrance and need, in one package. Or the Japanese term *natsukashii,* implying the same with a sweeter infantile edge.)

First, there's the softness, the quiet. The velvety welcome of immaculately dressed attendants, escorts to the brink of what used to be, an old-world form of elegance. A superior life. A certain level of ease.

And for this reason, though certainly not in any conscious sense, when particularly down-and-out, needing more than comfort, needing in fact a cradle of plush security, Mariane would go to such a space, the Barclay, perhaps, with its subtle suede walls and glimmering brass accents or even the Plaza, full guns-on crystal and expensive glitter.

She finds one four blocks away, a swanky place with a brassy, fern-filled lobby, big plush couches, the rich smell of leather, walks in and hears the gentle tinkling of a piano ebbing from a corner and follows the mirrored partition. In the pocket of her leather coat, she fingers the envelope of twenties and tens, and feels a familiar pang, *the last of money for a while, the last of that place.*

Walking into the bar, a gleaming piano, clusters of small couch worlds with spool-like tables, and bowls of dusty smoked almonds,

a long, cold, glacial bar, she hears the singer's words, low and crooning, singing *The Girl from Ipanema,* Mariane's favorite song, one her
mother played for her as a child over and over, the bossa nova horns,
the sound of swishing palms and crooning sadness. Mariane sits at
the bar, singing along, next to a man in a bright blue shirt, a polo
shirt it could be called, and sings, and hums a bit, finds her eyes
watering and orders a margarita, six dollars but who cares about rent,
the future, in a world of immediacy one can rationalize, always. Now
tears are just part of Mariane's face, she's given up wiping them, she
knows she looks like hell, owl eyes with the mascara, but she's beginning to maybe feel, what's the use, anyway, she's been fired two
times this year, and *although she has a plan, an idea,* it may be starting
to seem less important, yet most mornings she wakes up and thinks,
I've saved four hundred twenty dollars now (in a shoebox in her
closet), I will get five hundred more, and then I'll pack a simple duffel
bag, a green nylon one that she likes (the man at the bar has turned
to her, offering a tissue, she blows her nose and thanks him), and
pack that bag with only the necessities:

> *A few shirts*
> *Underwear*
> *One dress, for the plane*
> *Liquid refreshments*
> *Jeans*
> *Bras*
> *A picture of her mother, a cross she found on the street, a turquoise*
>   *ring a man gave her*
> *The money*
> *Diapers, formula, bottles, pacifiers, a few onesies*

It is a good list, she thinks, the margarita patting her veins
and head like a comforting hand, loosening her movements, a good
list, but flawed, old, out-of-date, yet Mariane is oblivious to this,

it is too painful a fact to realize, and Mariane can afford to skirt issues, because that has become the important thing, the problem being:

She doesn't really own a dress "for the plane." (This is some antiquated notion she has adopted, that of the rarefied new world she will be assuming, where one favors old-fashioned habits, like dressing elegantly for travel. Did her mother, Poppy, instill that in her? Did Poppy talk nostalgically of the days when her mother, Maggie, dressed in trim suit with gloves and hat for excursions?) In fact, what Mariane owns is ripped or too old or ruined for the word *elegance* to be applied.

Her mother has been dead the last few years.

The money isn't there. She's scraped bits of it through the weeks, and the envelope is empty and crumpled.

The cross is lost, as is the ring. Or she gave it to someone.

And the baby in question doesn't need diapers or formula or bottles, the baby Mariane longs for and dreams of, but has mostly forgotten, is thirteen, attentive, a pom-pom girl, unaware of her mother, unaware that Mariane is troubled and seeking her out, thinking her mother died years back in childbirth ("It was a terrible pain for me, Daisy, as your mother lay bleeding and I could do nothing. Not a damn thing."), not knowing, even a tad, that her mother had been court-authorized to treatment in Raleigh, a shrieking baby in a pink terry stretch suit taken from Mariane, a young girl of seventeen, sobbing, tears everywhere, Mariane driven in a station wagon down the interstate between Charlotte and Raleigh, North Carolina, the clutching feeling always that she lost something somewhere, left her purse in a rest room feeling, a pit of discontent, knowing she'll drink every chance she gets, walking out of the treatment center, the pale smell of salt and cleaners, the chumminess of it all, slowly now the baby stayed a baby, an icon, a symbol, a dream, a pocket of her youth, a goal, a plan, but, the thing is, children grow up and move on and this one had.

All that was left of the list, at this point, was: *Liquid refreshments.*

(The blue polo man lights her cigarette, and points with a tan, stubby hand to her drink, dregs left with an irregular line of salt, and she nods and a fresh tinkling one is set down by the crisp, white-shirted bartender.)

More words of sambas and beaches from the singer, Mariane is swaying now, half drunk, and the man is also, his fourth Johnnie Walker Red on ice, a man traveling from Dallas for *business,* always a bland and scary generalization, a man with a gold bracelet of some Venetian link pattern, probably bought by his wife at a mall jewelry store, for their tenth anniversary, and he says (you like that song, huh? it's so much better in Portuguese, I went to Rio, I mean, *Hio,* as they say, and went to the *real* Girl from Ipanema bar where the guy saw that girl *every day,* and I learned the real, you know, way it goes, um, something like, something like, oh, uh, *Fuck it,* it's hard to translate, um, but something about this beach and that girl and blah blah blah), Mariane barely listens to his words rambling on, snippets of jumbled Portuguese and travel, Mariane singing in English only, sipping tequila, forgetting about Ito, Sugibar, the list, her life, just the glossy here and now, all of it pretty and immediate (the end, he says, is cool, because he talks about like why he's so sad and stuff and life is short, etc.) you know it's Portuguese, see, well, it's similar, it's, it's similar to Spanish, but in the English version, they like, change it, so dumb, to *all this* bogus romance stuff, you know, like I think he meant some other kind of thing, I mean, ha! what about poetics, people!).

This man in question apparently had ordered a seafood salad, which Mariane notices in a glance, a large, showy display that gets ceremoniously presented in front of him, a virtual condominium of a dish, with architectural "crab" and "lobster" piles drizzled with herbaceous ranch-dressing pools, and a lemon wearing a cheese-cloth cap for squeezing,

Holy Christ, he says, turning to her to laugh, this isn't even fucking real, it's that crab with a capital *K,* you know, fake shit, it's crabcake, for fourteen ninety-five, you'd hope for more, right?

It looks fresh, at least, she says. It's got some good cherry to-matoes there.

It looks like a piece of *plastic!*

I like the lemon.

The lemon is cool.

He stabs a piece of artfully reddened "lobster."

It's, umm, actually not bad. Here.

Mariane eats a chunk. *Stage one* crossed in a series leading to-ward seduction—the sharing of food from the same utensil, imply-ing mother love and lack of fear in sharing germs. Both acknowledge this on lower-conscious levels.

She likes it. Tasted for its actual existence—a new species, a seafood biscuit, a casserole of proteins with sea flavors—it is tasty.

(In Japan, it is *surimi,* fish pounded and flavored to imply a different food, not in an imitative way, but in a complimentary way, a poetic salute, fish cakes fashioned to resemble bamboo and other shapes, with the word *Modoki* on the cover. *Remembered experience.* A poetic salute to the remembered experience of bamboo, in a fishy form.)

It is a few more margaritas and Johnnie Walker Reds later. The seafood platter is almost scraped gone, both Mariane and the man eat it lustily. They eat the lettuce garnish, they suck the lemon. They sing along to other lounge-y songs the singer croons, like *Hotel California,* and then due to Mariane's hoots and *encore!*s the old piano player agrees to sing *The Girl from Ipanema* again (I mean, these Brazilians have this term, *saudade,* it's hard to explain, but it's the whole feeling of that song, you know, this fella told me over a Caipirinha, this nifty lime drink, strong as hell, about that *saudade,* we don't even have a word for it, it's like longing, and homesickness and sadness and, *shit.*)

Mariane is up at her chair swaying softly, sipping the margarita to the icy end (Hey, my man, another roundaroo here, please), and Blue Polo Guy gets up and dances awkwardly, a little too hip-thrusting, until she puts her arms up and they slow-dance, the bar is fairly empty, except for White Crisp Shirt Bartender, similarly White Tuxedo Blouse Young Waitress, who mans the few couch ensemble clusters, and then rushes to the back to puff on cigarettes, a couple at a couch, Older Trim Man of Arabic Origins and His Mistress, Himself in an Expensive Suit, and a Threesome of Women, Giving Themselves a Treat Night. Blue Polo Guy sways as does she clumsily to the music, turned on in a nanosecond, aware of his erection awakening in his khakis, grabbing Mariane's ass as delicately as possible, really just caressing it gently, Mariane singing hotly in his ear, liking his arms, the hard penis she feels on her thigh, trying not to take that any further in her mind, especially loving his hand occasionally holding the small of her back, moving together completely, the song ends, the singer takes a break, Blue Polo pays the tab, suggests they share some drinks in his suite, a drink or two, he says, the casualness he employs as light as the cocktail napkins crumpled and damp under their drinks, Mariane, speed-thinking, remembers she has a condom in her purse, her light reply in the elevator, *sure,* he leans over, cups her chin, and their tongues slip over each other, *really* cupping her ass this time, the plastic card to enter the room, its odd click when allowing entry, a seamless blue bed, his things on a table, coins, tickets, a brochure about hospital HMO plans, a warm can of Coke, a certain look in his eyes, like children get, a reckless glee, she sits on his lap, she unzips his pants, he's in his underwear, Tommy Hilfigers with a nautical stripe, his penis prongs out, smooth as wallpaper, she sits on it, doesn't feel a lot because of drinkies, an unfortunate problem, he shakes her up and down, lots of sounds around them, turns her over on the bed, sinks himself into her quickly, and she sees his face from an odd angle, faraway, a golfing expression, a man-in-a-dentist-chair look, vague with some slight grimace of pleasure, but layers of denial too, and almost a need to get it over with, as if this is a chore but needed, back and forth he lurches, then lets out a huge, thunderous belching sound, he rams it up her a final time, she feels hot spurts, feels his sweat, his last small breaths, he tears out fast, pats her head, lies back, a faint junglish reek in the air of trampled plants, resinous, and then he is out like death (unlike men in love, who are fragile at this point, *soft and crushed* around the edges).

Mariane lies back for a while, she smokes a cigarette and wipes herself, knowing it will leak for a while, feeling sore, but still giddy and good, she gets up and pulls on her sticky clothes, goes out the door, her last sight of him, his greasy, limp penis, khaki pants crumpled around his hips, his mouth open, arms outstretched, Christ-like. She turns on the TV for him, for company. An infomercial.

She wants to sleep, it is about two, the city is black and sharp. A warm cab rolls her through the streets. She is starting to feel sober, and with it, shame. She fumbles for keys at her apartment, the door swings open and she glances at the simple lobby, the small crystal chandelier, a few tired Easter decorations, a bluish, aqua couch.

A small Japanese man sitting on that couch, staring at her with his black pitchy eyes.

A familiar face.
Ito.

chapter seven

Attendants brought over various boxes and containers from His Excellency's quarters and lined them up along the balustrades, but the light from the firebrands in the garden was insufficient so Minor Captain of Fourth Rank Masamichi, among others, was ordered to hold up torches so that everyone could see. The gifts were in any case due to be taken over to the Table Room in the Palace, but they were all being rushed over this evening because from tomorrow the palace was to enter a period of abstinence.

Ito thinks, *When, when, was my dear Murasaki born? I was taught of her death—at the traditionally dangerous age of thirty-seven, for a courtesan—but of her birth? In her last days her eyesight failed, she wrote, "I have lost what attachment I retained for the trials and pains that life has to offer. . . ."*

—Fresh? I mean, I've tried the crab before, but this is pretty unusual.

Nani? Oh, please repeat, sorry, *ne?* Hearing not so good.

An American man sits at the sushi bar, a *yuppie* he could be described as, slicked-back hair the color of hard rain, carbon eyes, a linear mouth. Ito is busy rolling *maki*, broiling eel, scooping translucent balls of roe with a spoon,

—I was wondering what that, that raw shrimp was like, I mean I love the cooked one but raw, is it, kinda, you *know*, slimy?

It's good. Very good.
Good, hunh?
Delicious, very fresh.

He is deeply disappointed that Mariane didn't show to dinner at his house, even slightly angry, wondering if she has a boyfriend and glancing at her as he slaps the rice and cuts the pale fish, watching her turn or smile, he is noticing a guardedness in her manner, and Yoshi is running around, in a bad mood, jittery, turning up the music, smoking cigarettes, and Ito is watching carefully, like a child who observes his parents silently, picking out tiny details of discord,
—When I was in Tokyo, for business, you know.
Ito brings his head back to the man, draws his eyes away from Mariane.
Oh. You in Japan?
Yeah, Tokyo, Kyoto.

Mariane is perhaps thirty-seven. The dangerous age.
A woman of the Heian period, as was Murasaki, especially if a courtesan, was kept from the world, from the work of the world and its commerce. They consumed and feted, but did not see the roots of whence it came.

—Yeah, I liked Kyoto a lot, the geishas were something. I love that sukiyaki, too.
Oh, yes, *good,* he says as he hands him a rectangular wooden block with two transparent peach-colored lozenges of shrimp,
Whoa, that looks cool, oh I was in Hokkaido, too. In Sapporo, saw this ice festival, totally amazing. You know it?
Uh, yes. I know.

Ito's first memories pass in front of him like strange phantoms:
(Early morning mist rising above my bedroom window. Mother feeding me soft clumps of miso-flavored rice in my waiting mouth,

not watching her face, but the steaming window as the film so condensed, awaiting a long drop to fall and land on the tatami mat. Drop, drop, cool plop of wetness. Chopsticks loom again in my focus, presenting golden mouthful, I obediently open my mouth, like a small baby bird. A sickly child, one would say, most of the childhood period, lying in a shadow-flecked bedroom, coughing, chest burning, or just weak, slightly sweaty, touching my penis frequently, hairless and warm, reading *The Tale of Genji* or *The Pillow Book,* so lost in that world of courts and samurais, building villages on my bed, and destroying them, the evil wrath of cruel ancestors, a small wooden box was delivered by the doctor once a month and inside, kept on the second shelf of the kitchen space, were the powders, elixirs and ointments necessary for health, delivered and picked up once a month, only charging for what was used. Most of the time, emptying box, cleaning it out, using it to play with and it became the palace of the emperors, but Mother always needed it back, to give back to the needle-faced doctor, Ryogo San.

So much of the day under a quilt, silent, watching the shadows on the wall, the sound of trees outside, imagining evil ghosts or *Oni-baba,* a she-devil, coming to suck out my brains like tasty *udon* noodles.

Seven, or eight, living in Kusharo, off the coast of Hokkaido, cold and windy. Father bringing me to Snow Festival, because he has entered a piece in the snow sculpture contest, a large, clear, nude woman. With fruit in one hand and a bird in the other, and she has round eyes and father calls her Maiden in English, perhaps my first *gaijin* word, maiden, maiden, I say over and over. The judges are confused by the sculpture, Father says, used to the endless ice pagodas, Buddhas and animals the others offer. A judge deems it "artistic" and Father receives Honorable Mention and we celebrate at a small, smelly *Okonomi-yaki* restaurant nearby, where father gleefully sprinkles powdered green seaweed on the oily pancakes, speaking of his "Maiden."

I told you, he said, I didn't work hard for nothing.

His face is as crinkled as hands after a long, hot bath. He fishes squid in the gelid water of Kusharo, and his face and limbs had been beaten by the wind like wind chimes in a maelstrom, after fishing he would spend long hours in the cold shed, with a single lantern, heating and chipping blocks of ice for the great festival, ending in puddles in the morning, but he wasn't distressed. When he made a good one, he would wheel it out for Mother, my mother couldn't walk, a strange influenza attack as a child left her forever immobilized in a wooden wheelchair, and they would stay out there, talking as he chopped the ice.

Trying to hug Mother but she would say no, it hurts her legs too much, she would pat my hand instead. Her legs were in need of constant attention. She would spend hours in the hot bath, soaking them, and then it's my job to massage them, or help her with the exercises, because Father was on the boat, I also became in charge of fixing her meals, first Father would make the rice early, a giant vat, and the miso soup before he left, and when I awoke, I would build a fire and broil fish for us and then I keep the fires going all day, I was taught to write and read by both parents, not attending school, because of Mother. I see the kids walking together to go to school. I hear their songs, and I study them, watching the way they tie their books with string and I try this at home, and my mother gets mad. I read, I read *The Tale of Genji* and everything I can take from the library. I write haiku in journal after journal, I tell Mother and Father I want to be a poet and they laugh, it was a dinner on a weekend because Father was talking, not tired and it was day outside, he is telling us about a fisher's mate who wrote a haiku and I blurt out that I want to be a poet when I grow up and they laugh, light, unserious laughter, oh, that's good, no, no, Katsu, no. This is not possible. You can be sushi chef, because I have connections in town, you can start apprenticeship in a few years—)

—And ate this wonderful stew. Do you know this?

Stew?

Yeah, this stew in Hokkaido. You know it?

The yuppie stares at him, smiling. Ito rubs the edge of his headband.

Oh, *oh, oh.* Yes. Hokkaido food good. Very good. Uh, sorry. Last call please. Something else?

Five of ten and the kitchen is closing and now Ito must break down the sushi, wrap each piece carefully as he has about fourteen thousand times at this point in his life, fourteen thousand times he has scrubbed the clear glass of a sushi bar, the only difference here at Sugi is that he must grapple with his English at the same time as his preparation and at the same time as his constant whirling thoughts in Japanese, he is trying to please this customer, but is really distracted and now he sees Yoshi counting tips and Mariane standing by herself at the edge of the counter, like a wary animal, sidelong glances at Yoshi, and he had noticed she was deferential to him all evening but removed, distant, and he wonders if he should ask her for a drink somewhere, to talk (and *then maybe*) just to talk, and share his concerns, the yuppie is jabbering about Korea now, and Ito is completely lost, he smiles, laughs lightly, he smiles again, the guy is standing, thanking him, speaking all sorts of mangled Japanese in a well-meaning way, and he passes Ito a folded twenty, and Ito says, *no, no,* and the guy says, *please,* and then he leaves, the last customer to leave, and they turn up the music, and then he sees drinks being poured, the shift drink, and Mariane kind of huddled in a corner, and then he sees Yoshi talk softly to her, they move to a table together, they speak quietly, but Ito manages to hear Yoshi say *vacation* and *seem so tired* and Ito stitches this to the stricken look on Mariane's face and quickly realizes she is being fired, he pours water on the sushi bar to clean and says, loudly, in Japanese:

Yoshisan, no! Don't do this, she is excellent—

Aaaah, old man, please—

This is mistake—
What, mistake, shh—
She OK—
This is my business, not yours.

And Ito falls silent. He finishes cleaning, he watches Mariane crying, her anger, he sees her leave. Ito is quiet and doesn't mention it to Yoshi again, and when he leaves, he checks Yoshi's black leather phone book by the front, and gets her address.

And hurtling through the dark cold streets of the large city, he fingers the twenty to pay the taxi driver, feels the carefully folded corners, thinks about the yuppie man, and feels a little sad, and distant again, after all, in his bumbling approach the man was only trying to connect on some level, scanning his mind for the obvious cultural pinpoints, Japan, sushi, and pushing those buttons and actually seeing Ito's distraction and rote answers, and still keeping on, wondering who is this old man, butting his head with his postcard-polished questions against the austere facade of Ito's armor, but it would take years to melt it down, to get a real answer, and would the yuppie really want to know, driving home in his BMW convertible across the George Washington Bridge, on the upper level, smoking a cigarette, half his brain on the song on the radio (Lenny Kravitz) and a bit on Ito, for a millisecond, *hunh, what's it like for that guy?* he wonders, *where's he live?,* and it's not the formal temples of Kyoto that pop in his head or the cramped, concrete high-rises of Tokyo, but a girl the yuppie met in Roppongi one drunken night, a tall Japanese girl whose name he could never remember, a slim thing with a miniskirt and silvery eyelids, whose hands fluttered against his neck as they danced, it was she who he longed to connect with through Ito—this phantom girl—he imagines her on a tiny futon somewhere, he wonders if she has kids now, a husband, he sees her naked in a flash of a once popular fantasy, her delicate body on all fours in her platformed boots, then he flicks this away (too arousing), switches on the car in front, on his girlfriend Beverly, on kayaking (*go by the store and talk to Raymond about that silver one*), Beverly again, Beverly, he zooms off the ramp, into the streets of Fort Lee, he can hear the coarse bark of his doorman, already, *Evening to you, Mr.*—

Getting deep into the core of Ito would be unpleasant, if it ever happened. It would be like going into the back of a four-star restaurant after a sumptuous feast to see the real workings behind the magic, and have them slice open a live chicken in front of you, just as the door swings open, a squawking chicken, and placing its hot little liver in your clean, pink hands. Not that he really wanted to, anyway. A polite, futile attempt.

So his silver car disappears into the seamless door of the garage, coincidentally as Ito reaches Mariane's apartment.

The sound of slamming car doors.

The beginning of the night.

chapter eight

Bunny.

You, bunny.

Ito sits on the uncomfortable couch in the lobby, talking to the plastic Easter bunny on the wall.

The bunny, he feels, has a malevolent curve to his eyes. They are not friendly eyes. He is beginning to gather some ideas that this bunny is indeed some incorrect, evil spirit, some mischievous deity in hiding.

Bunny, you stupid bunny.

It seems his eye moved. Did it move? Ito turns his large head around, looking to see if a super or tenant is in the shadows. There is no one.

The bunny glares, carrying his confectionery basket of bright eggs.

Goddamn bunny. Ito lunges up and grabs the bunny off the wall, it feels light and ineffectual, but somehow perhaps it is cursed and ruining Mariane's life, he snatches it down and glances around, trying to decide what to do with it, he runs to the incinerator, but then freezes, worrying the superintendent might find it and blame Mariane, and have her kicked out of the building, so he runs to the door and folds up the stiff bunny, saying, damn you, bunny, damn you, feeling victorious, not foolish at all, almost knightly in his purification ritual, he flings open the door, then sticks his wallet in the crack to hold it open, and proceeds to run to the close-by trash can on the street, but fear grips him, what if Mariane comes along now? How do I explain this? So he skitters over, pushing the bunny deep in the papers and wrappings, and runs back, grabbing his wallet, the door closing, he darts to the couch and sits abruptly on the pale green couch, out of breath, wiping his hands on the pillows, the stress of this rescue has made him tired, and on the edge of sleep, his thoughts hurtling in another dimension of evil animals, bunnies, hedgehogs, impure *Kami* of the Shinto religion, and then the cold blast of air wakes him, he sees her smudged face and feels pity and attraction, and pity and strength, and of all this waterfall of images he can only mouth:

Mariane. Mariane. Please.

Shit, oh, shit. She stops and looks at him, What'll *you* want? Come to rag me out, too? Is the whole damn world now, ready to pounce on me? Kick my ass?

No, no. Just, maybe talking little bit.

He walks over. He wears a mustard-toned leather coat. Pleather, really. She stares at a button.

Talk? What are we going to talk about? Did Yoshi send you?

No. I just come. I see tonight.

See what? That jerk throw me out? Or are you mad or something—

She drops back onto the aqua couch, without looking back, like a skydiver.

I didn't mean to, like stand you up and all, I fell asleep. I'm sorry, but—

You like Mongolian beef?

Huh?

Chinese food.

Mariane stares at the door, a little depressed Ito wasn't sent by Yoshi to beg her to work again, her body is just weary and it's late, must be threeish, still black outside, still too early for her to hit the sack, she looks at him, he is poised and silent, and his eyes, though murky, seem kind.

I am hungry, I guess. I guess I could use some food.

Out in the frigid air, Ito raises his maple syrup–colored hand, waves a taxi down. He runs to her side, shuffles, really, and holds her elbow delicately, as if it is a tiny knob of some sort, then opens her door with an old courtliness Mariane has seen in movies before, but not in real life, not real men, he squishes in the back of the taxi and says *Chinatown,* looking in the taxi's rearview mirror he takes out a tiny comb and arranges his hair in heavy bangs, like a dark fringe, directs the driver to a plain, empty street in the middle of the Chinese section, he whisks around again, cool air rushing with the door, he holds her arm.

Forget about tonight, bad memories. *Badu mem-oleez.*

She is accustomed to his accent, translates quickly in her mind.

He thinks of her fragility in aching terms, like a disease he knows the cure to, thinking of her as the passing of seasons, the artist Murasaki, the moon shining above, so gossamer, sliced cleanly in half as if with a razor, the horrible seizure of his language, the comfort of his thoughts, *Now I see, This lovely maiden flower, In bloom, I know for certain, That the dew discriminates,* then he says:

Good Chinese show.

Stopping before a dark, somber building, the door buzzed open at his grunt of *Mr. Ito,* a narrow corridor, a stained green carpet and from somewhere in waves the sound of a high-pitched woman singing, waves of sesame oil, fried garlic hang in the air, he pushes on a heavy door at the end of a hall, opening to a bright blood-colored room, with black plastic chairs surrounding a stage, a sea of Asian faces staring at a woman on stage, dressed in a satiny tight gown of sun-colored polyester, her hair permed and pulled back in a clasp. Behind her sits a group of old Chinese men wearing faded tuxedos, playing exotic instruments, keyboards conjuring dreamlike tones.

Here, here, sit.

Boy, where the hell are we? This is something, Itosan.

You like? You like?

A waiter brings in an instant a bottle of Chivas, with a paper label on it that says "Ito," scribbled in that particular style of English by an Asian hand, the letters formed subtly with pointy triangles.

Ito screams over the music, his face close to her. Semen drips from her.

You like Chivas? When he says it, it sounds like *shivers*.

She nods and he pours a water glass full, neat. After a bit, a team of waiters fills their table with a sea of covered metal dishes, Ito pulls off the shiny tops to reveal steaming mounds of beef, seared with garlic and scallions and hot fresh chilis, bone white rice, soups swimming with tofu and shreds of pork, hunks of crab in peppers. Ito spears beef with his chopsticks, and an eddy of thought spins in Mariane's mind, little details have all merged and she becomes aware that Ito is comfortable around women, that he is aware of their tastes and needs, his politesse displays a deference to them, an old-fashioned courtliness she finds warming and trustworthy, and faintly sexy, implying knowledge of women, of their needs, of their bodies. As if he is *taking control*.

Eat, Mariane, come on.

OK, OK.

Like a starved animal, her body sore and drippy, she plunges in, between mouthfuls of juicy meat, Chinese broccoli, stir-fried watercress, tofu sticks, feeling empty and desperate for food, slurping crab and hot soup, the Chivas speeding the action forward as if on film, and Ito stops, wraps a morsel of food with his chopstick into a tiny bundle and tenderly places it in Mariane's mouth, watching her carefully, like a mother watches a baby.

She looks at him with side glances, feels an ephemeral change in her feelings, a gratefulness, she feels full, happy, a slight attraction starts, or better yet a curiosity, the very beginning of attraction. She wonders how he would feel to kiss, how it would feel to have his tongue fill her mouth like the food, to remove worn pockets of emptiness. Then, she is aware of her appearance this night, aware that women at the various tables seem glossy, coiffed, curled. Their lips are bright shades of shiny grease, glittering nails, even their dresses shine in waves of satin, like Asian Barbies, and Mariane starts to feel drab, matte, as if powdered from head to toe with silt. Her nails are broken and dirty and she hides them under the table. She drinks sharp bites of Chivas, catching glimpses of his round, oily face, his mushroom nose with its flaring nostrils (like a baby bull). She guesses he is sixty. His hair is gray in strands.

Both of them are mesmerized by the singer and her tiny, shrill voice, which sings a piece of an operatic movement, her motions are mechanical and sudden, exaggerated. Lots of *shh* sounds, and as she sings she becomes faster, harsher, stares in their direction. She holds the last piercing notes at the end, her tiny white neck bulging with a vein, and the people, the people rise in exclamations, rising from their seats, yelling in Chinese, *Hao!Hao!* clapping, a thunderous sound like beating rugs outside on a line.

Only Ito remains seated, smiling with his shiny face. His mind whirls with confused chunks of action and sounds, smells and reasons, small feet the color of zinc, cinnabar toenails on his back, the crunching of fragile bones, his soft damp skin, the latissimus dorsi clothed underneath the thin, glutenous butter-colored fat, a field below of dendritic neurons sending the warm impulse of pleasure, alpha waves as cool as green soybean fields, cool transparent streams and below the viscera, the plunging, throbbing course of hematic rivers, her feet above his pulsing heart, his heart as lavender as a tulip bud, beating in tempo, succinctly content, not so much physical, *If one could explain,* his mind grapples, like a song, inexplicable, like a poem, like Murasaki, of course, *Hidden in the darkness, Of a spring night, It has no color, An aged heart, Intent on the fragrance.*

Mariane is stunned, horrified to see the woman, the beautiful singer, dart from the stage in their direction, people milling to the bathrooms, getting drinks, powdering noses, intermission perhaps, and, like a whisper in yellow, a flickering Bic lighter flame, she comes up to Ito, standing above, him looking up at her, her eyes angry and sad, Ito's eyes only sad, Mariane watches and the woman says No! No! to him No! Like a mewing kitten, No! and she pushes his shoulder, and he says nothing, she pushes, No! No! so she turns to Mariane with wet, beanlike eyes and looks deeply at her, for a long minute.

Then, she walks away.

It is quiet after that, Ito smokes and Mariane is still. She lights up a cigarette, blows a wave of smoke in his direction.

So, what the hell was that all about?

Oh, oh.

It would be impossible in English, or Japanese, to describe the heavy perforated feeling he has across his chest, the intense pain, but why bother, years of Japanese, an inadequate language for exacting personal, subtle hues of intimacy, has left him fairly mute, combined with an Eastern male tradition of smothered expressions, and this icing of an unfamiliar language, its cadences and words, wholly unsatisfactory to explain this battered-chest pain. Feelings heavy as rocks lie behind his fragmented words. Ito is trapped in a textual plain, a desert of insufficiency—

A woman friend.

Duh. Obviously, a little more, right, a lot more. Damn, that was some drama.

Yes. yes.

But you like her, right?

Yes. I like her.

So, why doesn't she, well, what's this *no, no* business? Did you do something bad?

Bad? No.

Is she your girlfriend?

Before.

Before?

She drinks the glass of Chivas, he refills it, and then his glass.

Before, in Japan, she was. My girlfriend.

You're kidding? So, what's she doing here? Did you come together?

No.

So—

We are not together for a long time.

It was a coincidence?

No.

I'm lost.

I took a job here. For her. To follow her.

Why?

To follow her.

But—

For the reason of love.

And she?

Does not. Return this love. It is simple.

Of course, no one takes a job across the seas, a lower position than before, less money, a single apartment, stripped trees outside brandishing worn windblown plastic bags in their limbs, dirty snow, a language they can't get around, herds of people unlike themselves, the cloak of loneliness, unless they seek love in some form of its dementia, a new start or a righting of wrongs, sometimes when a person has felt love for a fleeting time, despite the uprooting, the difficulties, they will seek its source again, for the comfort, simply the quiet comfort of mutual space. To know that person lives in the same city, breathing the same air.

That of all the soft yellow lights that shine at night throughout the dusky night, one is hers, one light is hers. And even if it isn't the same person, really, one can convince oneself it is. One can see, say, the same mouth of a beloved on someone else and feel the hurtle of love again, the aimless, silly loss of equilibrium, simply because of a mouth, and it can even be planted on the most unlikely sort, but it is their mouth and a badge of nostalgia. So sometimes, a person can seem like a beloved and be so similar as to be frightening, and then there are problems.

There are problems when what is called *ardor* spills over in the gray area called *stalking*.

Back when it was his second week at Sugi's, Mariane had not started there yet, and Ito was tired of strippers with Yoshi, tired of Fantasy Island with its fake palm trees and beach posters, weary of the charms of odd dancers, Darla or Susy who were Yoshi's favorites, ample women with the husky, flower-tinged smell of sweat encased in nylon frilly underwear. Darla had frizzy blond hair that blurred the hard bones of her cheekbones. Susy was redheaded with fake breasts that jutted like cantaloupes from a bony bird chest, and both had the flat, lightless orange skin from years of sunbed tanning, and they poured themselves around the Japanese threesome, sitting on their laps, tinkling laughter at their jokes, sounding like someone had dropped a bag of small bells.

Already, he was weary and confused by the Americans and their thievish ways with his skills, using too much soy sauce, trying so hard with their bumbling hands to manipulate chopsticks, pounding the sushi into the little sauce bowl and ruining its articulation, leaving a pool of soy sauce–soaked rice kernels, the obscene amount of soy sauce they cloaked on the pure, fresh flavor of the fish, the big show of rubbing the chopsticks together (if Ito did this as a child, his father took away his dinner, with a scowl, *you think this is a cheap noodle shop?*), the constant yammering *where are you from, how long did it take you to learn* and not understanding them so much of the time, canceling orders by mistake, not knowing if they want more, what was it she just said? One can only say *Nani? What, I am sorry, hearing not so good,* his rote answer when his mind whirled, he practically knows *The Tale of Genji* by heart, he could speak of Murasaki for hours, he could quote maybe six hundred haiku and poems and out of his mouth in the mumbled language, he stammered, *yes, OK, good-bye,* so the waitresses and clients treat him like a big child, like a lovable panda bear, blond made-up American women said, *Oh, isn't he cute, I just love him!* and their husbands would say, *Now watch yourself, Ito, that's my girl,* with some sort of bravado and they'd all chuckle, *what do you have that's cooked, you know, not raw?* And Ito's heart would sink, hand shaping rice into slim bar, one-two-three, *wow, he's fast! Look at him go* as if he is some type of trained performer, a circus animal, when in Japan, his hand shaping rice in that very pose is likened to the En-lightenment Pose of the Buddha, grabbing each time the exact same amount of rice to the kernel, mating it gracefully with artfully hewn fish like a subtle dance, where in Japan he could say, to Mr. Kawasaki, *belly of tuna very fresh today,* and Mr. Kawasaki would nod seriously and graciously accept this fine tip, and later mumble, with almost religious awe, *oishii, oishii,* whereas at Sugi's, the people ask, Califor-nia Rolls in mouth, *do you guys have karaoke?*

So, on a Saturday night, one week before the hiring of Mariane, Ito is cagey with Yoshi when he offers the strippers, the nightclub with his companion, Koji. He thinks *no,* but waffles politely.

Come on, old man, let's go drink, says Yoshi, the huge wheel of keys in his hand, clicking all the lights of the restaurant in sections.

Oh, Kenjisan. I am bad company. Boring.

Tired, he anticipates an icy beer on his leather couch, quietly reading the *manga* comics Koji lent him, eating some roast beef, wearing his cotton blue robe. He looks forward to the Playboy channel at one o'clock when *Candy and Her Friends* comes on. He is growing to be familiar with his new single, quiet existence.

What, what? Come on.

Oh, bad headache, bad.

I give you pills.

No, no, I'm OK. No problem.

So they dropped the old man at his apartment, teasing him about too much masturbation. As he left the car, he felt the same crushing emptiness, his apartment looked dark and tall, like a giant box, and he remembers the feeling, in an instant, of the muffled sound of his apartment as he enters the door, after the clicking sound of the key, the dull roar of his refrigerator, and then the electric click of the control, and the spunky out-of-sync rush of canned laughter from the TV, he feels a rushing jolt of horror and then he decides to go with them after all, he runs foolishly to the curb, and bangs on the door of the van.

Yoshi laughs, unrolling his window, *what, what, old man?*

Com-ing, coming, huh!

OK, catch your breath. Going first to Chinatown, eat something.

OK, OK.

He gets in and the city careens around him, lights dashing like colored beads running across a smooth table and Koji says, there is a good club here, and they park and they walk in a door that pushes into the heaving smell of garlic and sesame and fried pork, the waiters in those red tuxedos and napkins on their wrists, and they find a table and order quickly because the kitchen is closing, Ito smooths down the tablecloth as the clinking metal plates are placed, the smells pouring out with the steam rising, then a Chinese man stops singing to applause, a man in elaborate embroidered costume with pink-shadowed eyes singing Beijing opera, his headpiece shaking with prongs, and then the stage darkens and they introduce Madame Ling, the stage darkens further, and then in a column of red light the singer comes out, Ito is busy wrestling with a crab leg as her voice warbles with delicate Mandarin sh-sh sounds, his sucking rewards him with a tender hunk of crabmeat, just as he turns his eyes to the stage, and he stops as he sees her in the gleaming column of yellow fabric, his chopsticks drop to the floor with a loud clatter, his eyes widen, he says,

Nandesuka? Nani? (What is this?)

What happen, you eat *fugu*? Now poisoned? (Referring to the popular yet deadly treat of *fugu* fish, available in Japan only in special *fugu* restaurants and prepared by licensed specialists who are trained to cut away the poisonous liver which contains a deadly nerve poison, and yet, to leave a trace amount for its scintillating effects, fugu is a great delicacy it is said, combining the subtly of its wonderful flavor and the slightly narcotic effect of the soupçon of poison, yet the arduous preparation is so difficult, many Japanese die each year, heralded by the clattering of their chopsticks which fall from their paralyzed hands. Clients at *fugu* restaurants have been known to blanch in horror, only to discover that a reddened waiter has dropped chopsticks while clearing a table.)

Pulling a *Bando, ne, Itosan*? Yoshi chuckled, your lips numb now? (He referred to the great and famous Kabuki actor *Mitsugoro Bando*, who died from ingesting *fugu*, no doubt due to his macho insistence on eating the guts of the fish, although his friends protested, although the chef demurred, Bando insisted, and instantly died.)

Maybe *Bando* sees a ghost, said Koji.

Ito looked confused, he looked around stricken, he grabbed for his scotch and sucked it down as the woman sang, he felt odd and nervous, and in his mind there was one thought:

Xiu-Xiu? Xiu-Xiu? How can she be here?

—*It was weird, this guy, you know, I go on a few dates with him and he like goes crazy, he's like a freak or something. What? Oh, I think it is I-T-O. Yeah, EE-to. Mine? It's, uh, Miss Ling, Miss Ling Yu. Yeah, like "you." But he call me Xiu-Xiu all the time, which is not my name, at all, he follow me home, he leave things in my car, flowers and perfume, he always sometimes standing outside my apartment, in the garden, say, Come back, Xiu-Xiu! I make mistake, he say, like a crazy or something. He's like a loser or something. This is high-class club, very important, and he just ruining things coming here, just keep him away, like far away, I don't want to see his face, oh yeah, my address is 231 Ludlow Street, yes. Thank you.*

After that night, for a month after work, Ito leaves quickly, saying breathlessly to Yoshi,

Yoshi, you go club? *Ne?* You go club?

No, Old Man, go to strip place tonight, come on. You come on.

No, no. I go to club.

Forget that club, come on.

I need to go to club, Yoshi.

Why club all the time, hunh? Club, every time.

On the first night, after initially seeing the singer, Ito was deeply shaken, he drank and drank the Chivas, while Yoshi and Koji went on laughing about *Fugu* fish and then about the singer and then their cars, he drank the Chivas while she sang and each sip brought her features closer to Xiu-Xiu, the alcohol smoothed her face into a mask of his old love, and his brain became slaggardly and jumbled and he wondered how she could be here, he became sloppy and spilled his food, he became sentimental and as she finished her set, he said out loud *Xiu-Xui,* and Yoshi said, what are you talking about, Old Man? and they laughed, Ito put his head in his arms as the bar closed up, as the waiters rolled out their carts to clean, Yoshi and Koji picked up the drunken man and carried him out, as he sobbed and Yoshi said to Koji, I feel bad for Old Man, I feel bad, and they stopped laughing. They put him carefully in the back of the car and Yoshi dropped off Koji and whipped around in his red Jeep, across the bridge to his high-rise, and had the doorman, Jerry, help him with Ito, help him in the elevator, *this old cousin of mine, drinking too much,* he said to Jerry, and they both looked at Ito's wide oily face in the elevator going up to the fifty-fifth floor, they watched his large nostrils flare, and they didn't speak, Yoshi's hand against the brass panel, Jerry's against the raised velvet of the interior, both eyes on Ito. *What'd he do? Mix 'em up? That'll get you every time,* says Jerry. *You got to go by the color method, you know? All browns together, or all whites, but don't mix, never bourbon and vodka, say. Try it and see.* But Yoshi doesn't answer, because they are at the apartment, they drag him in and heave him on the couch, on Yoshi's big soft Italian leather couch, color of light river mud, and Yoshi thanks Jerry, slips him a twenty, offers him a beer, but Jerry says, *Oh, no, thanks, Mr. Yoshi,* and then he is gone, and Yoshi covers Ito in his coat, and joins Stella on the futon in their red and black bedroom, she mumbles and he just answers *Ito, Ito is here,* and then they are asleep.

In the morning, Ito stares for a good long while at the large expanse of window that is in Yoshi's apartment, and doesn't know where he is, his head pounds and then he hears the laughter and voice of Yoshi's six-year-old daughter, and Stella, his wife, comes to him with a mug of coffee, and he says, *I am sorry,* and she says, *Oh, come on, Mr. Ito. We all tie one on once in a while,* and it is only when he is on the train going back to the city that he remembers Xiu-Xiu, it seems like a dream. It is the beginning of his times spent at the club, where he begins to go nightly, beginning that very night, ordering Mongolian beef, crab, his own bottle of Chivas, waiting for the girl to come out, impatiently tapping his lighter against the table, eyes darting to the side curtains. Then he asked a waiter, after her number, if he could *meet the lovely young woman,* and the waiter said please write down request on this paper and perhaps include *gift,* so this gave him a great boost of confidence, because he understood that it must be her as she is a prostitute. Looking at her sing he thinks, she is the same, same tiny face, hair a bit different texture, but the eyes are uncanny, luminous and gleaming with long edges, and Ito knew only Xiu-Xiu could have those cat eyes, and after the set she did come over, perfumed, smelling of sink water and crushed rose petals and cheap hairspray, smiling at him and thanking him *for his most generous gift, how delightful* (two crisp one- hundred-dollar bills) and he said, *you are very beautiful,* and she replied *you are too kind,* and he replies, *have we met before? No, no, I don't think so,* there is that split second of panicked appraisal in her eyes that he catches, to him meaning recognition, to her a fleeting question of safety, but she regains her calm and says, *no, I don't think so, I would have remembered a gentleman of such elegance,* and he thinks, ah! Xiu-Xiu! and says calmly, *well, I would very much like to know you,* and she says, *good, is tonight convenient to make an acquaintance?*

Instantly, Ito feels his penis fill his pants, he shifts his weight under the table and says, *of course, yes, yes,* and thinks of his apartment with porno strewn everywhere, says *how about a little later on?* and she says, *OK, how about midnight, then? OK, OK,* he answers quickly and she says write your address here, and with the jolting ecstasy running through his veins feeling druggy and elated, he produces a card for her (made for him by Yoshi) which says:

Katsuyuki Ito—Top Sushi Shokunin
Sugi Bar
Manhattan's Top Sushi Bar
223 W 16th Street
New York, New York
(212) 663-0034
We have the freshest fish in Manhattan!

And he scribbles below, 192 20 street. Aparto. 2.

He then sped to his apartment in a taxi, showered (using Irish Spring, he is the type who scrubs most arduously, soaping viciously in every corner, especially pulling back the dark, purplish foreskin of his penis and washing the red, beady tip, then, since he was hard, and to feel control in the evening, he masturbated rapidly against the tiles with a dollop of shampoo), then afterwards, he smoked a cigarette in the hall as not to contaminate the apartment, piled the porno in his closet, scrubbed the floor with a towel, leaning and pushing it across the floor, then preselected some CDs for his turntable, all Japanese lounge singers, and then hid his *manga* comics in the closet also. He made sure the sake was reheating in a double boiler on the stove and he placed a few bowls of wasabi peas out on the tables for snacks. Then he waited.

He waited for Xiu-Xiu to return.

chapter nine

That woman in the yellow dress runs out the back door, pulling out her cell phone, little huffs of Cantonese spoken furiously: *Fuck, it's him again. Motherfucker! I will, I will. They don't give a shit, restraining order. Oh, goddamn. I'm going home. Later.*

She clicks down the street in her heels, her hair shining in the streetlight, gleaming in harsh streaks of white, from her lips to her phosphorescent eye shadow. After a minute, she finds a taxi, it bumps her viciously along the winter-ravaged streets. You have to walk five flights up to her small studio, so she carries her heels and once inside the small delicate apartment, swathed in shades of peach and pearl, this woman peels her clothes and gets underneath the covers of her bed, a large flouncy thing with many layers. Then she puts a tape in her cassette player, drinks a Champale, smokes a tiny cigar. Presses *record:*

This is the true account of my life, Miss Ling Yu. I am twenty-two years old. I am unmarried.

Nobody owns me. This is the most important rule, more than *be kind* or *honor your family.*

I am not kind, nor do I have a family. I am an orphan, the only daughter of a waiter who worked in a dim sum restaurant on lower Broadway, under a dirty tunnel where many people go to buy rolls of satin material (*she pauses for a deep puff on that little cigar, a sweet slim*) or buy those cat statues with their paws outstretched, that mean: *Come in, coming in, buy, please!*

When this waiter died, my father, it's cold day and I'm waiting for him to come home. He's late and I'm wondering why, then two men, his bosses, come by the apartment and give me a bag. Inside was:

> *A wallet with my picture and two condoms*
> *Watch, the strap broken*
> *A jade amulet on a thin chain, a money good-luck symbol*

They told me I was to be calm, that my father's heart had exploded when working and he fell on the noodles he was making. Here is his paycheck, plus fifty dollars to get rid of the bad luck from his death. Then, the skinny one, the son, took me to the back room, while the other man, his father, watched at the door, rubbing his self on the outside through his shiny cheap suit. I could've said no, at this point, I suppose. Looking back, I realize that.

But I already know them this way. Father had sold me to them many times, and others. The old man had never done it, he preferred to watch.

These were the others:

> *The tiny one who made dumplings, who smelled bad from*
>   *under his arms*
> *The waiter with the big tummy and the long skinny item,*
>   *who moved in circles, who had many tattoos*
> *Beanpole, a soup-maker, with long yellow teeth*
> *The youngest, baby, who had just begun to grow hair around his*
>   *soft, silken item*
> *The goat, with sharp bristles, who pinched me hard and sucked*
>   *my earlobes*

After they left, I did the Coke trick Father said got rid of babies. Brown foam flooded from me, mixed with his cloudy juices. I wiped it up and made Oodles of Noodles. I adjusted to the quiet apartment. I had to call my teacher at school for help with the funeral. We went to McDonald's and she paid. She told me the proper thing to do, and she knew a church that could pay. I had a fish sandwich. I don't remember what she had, though she had really dark lipstick. A wine color. She was from Taipei.

That was when I was fifteen. For the next few years I go work for Mr. Chen, who owned Red Dream Palace on Mott Street. Like my father, I pushed the cart full of dim sum, for fat American ladies wearing hard, shiny gold collars around their tanned, wrinkled necks and mainland families exploding with children and grandmas in cheap flip-flops. I preferred to push the dried squid cart or the chicken feet one, so I could sail past the white people, just say "chicken feet" and watch their face wrinkle up and be relieved when I go by.

I let the Chinese men know little secrets. I wear jade bracelets, perfume and high-strapped heels. I send them the message with my eyes when I hand them little hot plates of taro pancakes. I lean down quickly while their wife wipes the baby's face and they see my French bra in my shirt, upside down. Or I touch their arm. They come back the next day, wet sweat on their foreheads, smell like metal leaking through the layer of Aqua Velva they splashed on, last minute.

This is what I see behind the counter at Red Dream Palace:

A little gold statue, the food god, for good luck
Tiny bottles of Grand Marnier
Rubber bands
Lotto machine
Bowl of lotus nuts, left over from New Year's

I look at this a lot. Sometimes, Mr. Chen wants me to stand behind counter and look into mirrored back, while he punches register and plays with my ass through my skirt. I am told, with his garlic grunts in my face, to wear satin underwear. He pays me ten extra for this. He prefers pale pink. One day, he calls me to his office. He tells me to lift my skirt. He tells me he knows I am too smart to work there and should attend secretarial school, talks about his cousin who makes thirty thousand a year as an administrative assistant, but he has lifted my skirt and is pulling down my underwear. Luckily, as he exposes his small, wood-colored item, his wife walks in. She drops a bowl of broccoli and meat. *(Another big inhale, a sip of Champale.)*

His wife told me, *little whores can get out.* So I did. Some people say they need help in south Chinatown, at a big restaurant there. I have made my apartment so nice since I've been on my own. I have lamps like flowers, with frosted pink petals. And my favorite, a light that has a waterfall over it, and it plays music, famous song, "Lover in the Garden." I sing it all the time, and some men have said my voice is even more beautiful than my other face.

Like everything in life, it turns out the restaurant is a big joke. He was a stupid, greasy man who didn't do the proper celebrations for business. He was too cheap. He invited bad thoughts. And of course, it has no business. Mai Yan says there is nightclub opening in the old bank, Chinese style. You must sing, but you can, Ling Yu. You must be really friendly to men, also, but that is no problem, I say.

I am always friendly to men.

I think of them as a different race.

It will be good money.

I go there and I meet Mrs. Chang. She has big legs and a big ass and likes money. Her face is flat and powdery and she has long dog teeth.

You need to sell your ass here, she says, *no wastrels.*

When I sing for her, she smiles, big chunks of rice in her mouth as she eats her lunch, shoveling it from a round bowl on her lap. *If you screw as well as you sing, I make good money, she say.* Ugly woman.

He had come in for a while, maybe a few months. He would watch me sing, then put some money in the crystal bowl by the stage. He had dinner sometimes. I guessed he wasn't Chinese, but I thought maybe Korean. No other girls been with him. One day he sent me a *gift* and asked for me to join him at the table. I did.

His apartment was small and not fancy. I did not like the smell: oceany, salty. Like sand. And hair. He was a sushi chef from Sapporo, some place in Japan where it is cold and they like ice.

First, we went to dinner at a sushi bar downtown. I never had sushi. The place was all wood, dull, and not expensive decoration or fancy. Nothing shining. I wore my favorite yellow satin sheath, with underneath, my French look, white merry widow and hook-on stockings in white also. Later, he told me never wear this again. Only small cotton underwear, like a child.

I said, so plain this place. Not fancy. He smiles and say, this wood is mahogany and teak. Hidden money, he say. I don't understand. Sushi comes on wood, too. They cannot afford plates, I say. This is Japanese style, he says. Discreet.

For dinner, we have:

Octopus, sliced, in a sweet brown cold sauce
Paper-thin flounder, fanned, in a lemony sauce
Liver of whale, with scallions
Sea urchin sashimi
Mountain Potato grated with chunks of fatty tuna

He slurps the Mountain Potato, white and cloudy like men's essence.

Gives big power, he says winking.

I tell him I like the tuna. He tells me it is the most like a woman's *manko*. His Japanese word, but I know the meaning. He says the more fat tuna, the better. There are sixteen different types, each a paler pink as the fat increases. I like *toro,* the fattest, most expensive, pale like inside of a conch shell. It's silver and glimmers in the light, like Maybelline shell pink eye shadow.

I am wondering right now, what will he be like? I have only been with Chinese guys. The raw fish, the warm sake and the spicy wasabi make me feel curious. The sushi is good, amazing. I feel like I live in the sea, that I taste the waves.

Buzzed on the sake, I return with him to the smelly apartment. I take off my clothes. He looks at me for a long time while I stand there, naked, not smiling, not frowning. His eyes travel every inch, carefully, like he's shopping for a car. He draws me a boiling hot bath, and he lifts me in his arms like tiny baby.

Turns out, he's got clothes all set up for me on the bed, bell-bottoms, little halter top, even tiny butterfly clips. He dries me off, powders me, spends a good hour buffing my feet and painting them red.

So, I say, when I'm all dressed up, *You want me to take this off now?*

No, no.

Then, mouth?

No, no.

Then?

He takes off his clothes. He's not even hard.

Play with me this game, he says.

I like games.

Walk on my back with your feet. Massage my neck. I call you Xiu-Xiu.

Xiu-Xiu?

Yes.
Like a fantasy?
Like this.

Who is this Xiu-Xiu, anyway?

It's an hour later. I walked on his back. I massaged his neck. He pulled me to him, I sat on him. He cried her name a few times. He had a thick item. I covered it in a green condom. It felt fine. I did not climax. He did.

It was like this: UNgaUnga, nuh, nuh, nuh, nuh, Xiu, XIU, XIU, ooohuh.

This is exactly the sound he made. I have another tape I keep of each man's sounds at that time. I write it down. I think I'm getting some kind of love theory here, about them. The silent ones, the loud ones and what they say, at that time.

I am kind of like a scientist. That's how I view it. I have a theory:

Quiet guys are often the most passionate.

The guys who are least smart say the most stuff.

When I retire, which I plan in five years, I want to do several things.

One: design own line of perfume. I like to make a special blend, that reminds of a good childhood and love in the future. Not for making money. To make people feel happy. I'm thinking of peaches, jasmine tea, the smell of bacon, lemons. This one will be called *Sweet Childhood of Happy Times*. I made a little sample I keep in my bedroom, for when I sleep. I dream of beaches, mothers, soft children faces. I dream of people cooking food for parties, a house where you live, a swing from a tree. Picnics. I dream of my father, back to me, money no problem. We both have time. He watches TV, plays with my children. I cook him *gyoza* dumplings, and we eat smiling.

Another blend I call *The Core of You.* I collect from every man a drop of their essence (from the condoms), I mix with violets, almond oil, one piece of Tiger Balm to preserve. This is like a memory smell for me. I use it when I bathe, to remember my life, to make amends, to plan the future.

The second thing I do when I retire is write my memory, and that is why I keep the sound of all the men, because this is when they lose themselves and some truth come out. It is something important.

Common things to say are: I love you, oh, that's good (seventeen guys said exactly this). One guy said: Fuck you, mother (in Cantonese), as his eyes squeezed shut, as he plunged that last surge in me.

So, who is this Xiu-Xiu?
Old girlfriend.
You love her, hunh?
Yes.

I stayed the night. I was lounging in one of his bathrobes, after a shower. Luckily, I had brought makeup in my bag and painted my lips the color of shells with a touch of gold in the center. I had made myself some tea, although I prefer oolong, green tea tastes bitter to me. I opened a window and fresh spring morning air, flower air, filled the room. It made me think of Father, and how he loved picnics. Sometimes, the only time he relaxed was in spring. He'd make noodles for us, special *dan-dan,* with spicy sesame sauce and he'd bring Cokes and we'd sit in the park.

Father had a special velvet blanket for picnics. Father who never stopped working, who died in a vat of noodles, who came home and scraped his arms with a spatula to take off the layer of flour. And on the picnics, he was quiet. I asked the questions.

Do I have a mother? I asked, often.

No.

But I must, somewhere.

No mother.

I knew to stop when he had that dark look in his eyes. When he spat in the grass, big globs of brown tobacco goo. Little mud-colored wet flowers on the road. He sighed. I hated when he sighed, felt sad and bad and worthless. I stopped asking.

He would never tell me anything. I used my brain hard and thought of all details he might've shared. I know he is my father. He said once my mother died. I know I've never known her.

Maybe if I had a mother, now would be different. She could've kept me from the men. She would've saved the money. She would tell me, stay away from that Japanese man. I who know nothing, no woman to tell me things, stayed in his apartment because he said so. That was always my job, do what a man says.

After that first night at Ito's, he leaves the next morning without a sound, leaves when the sky is silent and blue. I watch his dark body in the cool light sit at the edge of the bed for a while and I wondered what he was thinking and what he wanted me there for. The door quietly closed and I saw his note by my pillow:

> *I buy fish. Please—tea for you (arrow pointing) anything you wish.*
>
> *Ito.*
>
> *happiness for me if you coming tonight 7:00*

and underneath the note were two crisp fifty-dollar bills, covered by the note almost, in a discreet way.

Today was planned to be a beauty day.

I had appointments at Mary's Beauty Salon for a waxing, massage, manicure, pedicure and facial, that I did every week. Mary was an old Chinese woman, an ex-whore who saved her money and opened the small pink place in Chinatown. Most of the best workers went there, she was cheap and efficient and knew our business. I decided I would go, but first, I wanted to prowl around.

First, I checked out the bathroom.

I hear the crackle of the key in the door. It is him.

Xiu-Xiu! Up, up. I have a surprise. Good luck at the fish market.

I stood up.

He looked at me for a long moment.

Very lovely, you. Look!

In the kitchen, he has spread open newspapers to reveal a silvery fish, with gray eyes.

First Bonito of the spring. This is special fish. You will stay and eat, please? His eyes were dark as wood, and shine wetly.

I will stay, if proper accommodations.

By saying this, I meant *money*. I must always think of job.

Of course. Course.

He washes the fish, and lays it on the counter. I sit up on counter. He frowns and points me off with knife.

No. Get chair.

· Then he hums as he runs the silver blade on his sharpening stone, one way, making a gritty sound. It is different from the Chinese way.

I grow up in restaurant, I tell him. He looks up and stares at me. I tell him my father makes noodles. I tell him more than I expect, how he sold me.

Where's mother?

I tell him I don't know. Everyone has mother, he says. Mother forms soul, father forms character. I say, maybe I have no soul.

His mouth click, clicks. He hums.

Behold the Green Leaves!
A Thrush singing in the hills—
The first Bonito.

★   ★   ★

Bonito in Japanese, *Katsuo,* my name *Katsuyuki,* he says, so Mother call me Katsuchan, little Bonito.

Little fish?

Yes. Me, little fish.

After the fish was sliced, he heated a large black pan. Smoke trailed from it in a few minutes and he placed the fish down and it sizzled. After a few minutes, he flipped it over.

Raw inside. *Tataki.* Now cold is better.

He put the fish in the refrigerator. (*Then she sits up and snuffs out the little cigar. The sound of a siren blasts from outside her window.*)

I watch him wash his hands in his metal sink. He dried them carefully and turned to me. He undid my robe and rubbed my chest, carefully, like a massage. I have small breasts, with deep brown nipples. Rather large nipples. Some men call them mushrooms. I mention this.

Ha. *Shiitake!* he says. I remember his large pink tongue. Kind of repulsive. He eats and circles each nipple. I feel dreamy, melting. After a while, he stops, nothing more.

I have special things. You will like.

I smile. He is a nice man. He made me want him, slowly, like an artist. I am used to fast men, holding the mattress edge.

Time to eat.

He takes the fish and slices it into neat rectangles. An edge of cooked gray fish surrounds an oval of deep pink. He grates ginger over it, and scallion. It lies in a pale blue bowl he brings up from somewhere, and then he dribbles a sauce over it.

Big fish! Bonito in spring.

He places it in my mouth and the tenderness scares my mouth, as if I am eating the flesh of babies. It gives with gentleness, and the ginger and scallion add bite to the creamy flavor.

You like, Xiu-Xiu? You like?

If you like this, this Xiu-Xiu so much, how come you don't be with her? You're a nice guy, make money.

Come on, come on, now.

Come on where?

Come on, no more joke with me, more Bonito in my mouth.

After the Bonito with Ito, I say, *well.* I stretch. *Gotta go.*

Go? No, I give more money. One hundred dollar, stay until evening, I get.

Nah, I have to do hair. And I have appointment tonight.

No, two hundred.

You see, I have—

No. He grabbed my throat, pushing me against the refrigerator, he said, no, Xiu-Xiu—he was rough and scary.

I'm not, *ow,* playing that stupid game, I said—

No. no.

—*Xiu-Xiu* or whoever the bitch is—

Now, he was looking sad, he says, *Please.*

Get off of me, I'm yelling.

And he goes, *Please, pretty Xiu-Xiu,* and all this crap.

I kick him in the nuts, knocking over the sake bottle on the counter, I duck under him.

Stop! he's screaming, and I'm running to get my purse.

No, this is mistake, I'm sorry! he says.

Get away from me. You're weird.

Xiu-Xiu! He lunged for me.

I race to the door, it was bolted, he came up behind me, put his hands on my breasts, he goes *always,* he whispered, *always Xiu-Xiu, think of you, I'm—*

And I'm trying to say, I'm not this Xiu-Xiu!

So sorry, baby. Always, then, lots of Japanese words come from his mouth, just when I'm getting free, opening the door, running down the hall.

Stumbling out, I remember him falling on his knees.

Sorry, he yelled. So sorry, my Xiu-Xiu.

On the way down, I twist my ankle, I swore right there, never again.

I didn't know it was only the beginning. (*Her kitten has jumped on her bed—You little thing! Where were you!* she teases him.)

Most times he just came to the bar, buying Chivas and sending me money wrapped up in notes, *sorry* or *I love you*. I ignored them, but kept the money. For a few weeks, this is all he did, but then one night he followed me to a party in midtown at a bar, I was dressed in a red velvet pantsuit and it was a private party for the son of Mr. Chen, the owner of the bar. It was for his son, a bachelor party. He had paid me and a friend, Deborah, one thousand dollars to treat him well all evening, to smile and flirt, to pour his champagne, to feed him shrimp and lobster and to go home with him and sleep with him. We were not to let him sleep. We were to exhaust him thoroughly. As I went to get more lobster from the steam table, Ito was there. He said, *Miss Xiu-Xiu, I am so sad.* And I whispered, get out or I call police. He said, *Oh, make me sad in heart.* I went back to the party. He stayed all night on a bar stool, staring at me.

After a while, he would be outside my apartment. On those days, just to get rid of him, I brought him in and he would take me, very quickly and fast, and I would say please go, and he would beg, but then leave. This was a mistake. He started coming every night, and then I call the police. They call him and call his boss. He stop for a while, but he send things, bags of white underwear or tiny shoes. Then, I don't see him for a long time, until he comes to the club with the girl. I thought I was rid of him. I think about having him killed. Such a nuisance in my life.

Everyone is *sad in heart*. Who the hell tell you otherwise. That is kind of life.

★　★　★

There was this one boy I liked, Ton.

He hung out in the club my father worked, sweeping floors. This is when I was thirteen, and fourteen. I had to wait long hours for Father working and I would sit on the floor or lay on his jacket. Father brought me bowls of rice with hacked, roast duck and stringy pieces of water spinach and I would noisily suck this down, not having eaten since morning time, usually a few pink iced donuts from the Chinese coffee shop where Father and I drank coffee in the morning, so by the time the duck came, it was two o'clock and I was drooling with the smells from the restaurant. So this Ton would start sweeping in the far corner, slowly getting closer, his hair was like a shimmering black curtain over his face, he wore a two-tone western shirt usually, and suede shoes in blue. Later, I learned why.

You like Elvis? he said, the first time he ever talked. He said this so quietly I wasn't sure he had really spoken.

I guess. I like other music better. Madonna.

Oh. Oh. He's King, Elvis.

He sat down shaking with excitement.

You go to Graceland, you change. You see, you see, he was laughing. The lady in the back was his mother, the one who folded dumplings as if they were flowers she just picked up and dropped from her hands, she was so fast. I heard some people call him "Dumb Ton," saying he was slow, dull-witted. But when I squinted my eyes and looked close, he seemed OK.

He had a little pink boom box and he threw the broom down and clicked on a tape of Elvis.

Then he did a little hip-swinging dance for me, which looked like he was just one skinny rubber band with his thin boy body, no muscles or anything. He was kind of grossing me out, you know that sickly feeling when someone thinks they are hot and you feel exactly the opposite and it's getting worse and worse? That was happening.

OK. OK. I get it, I said. You play cards?

He swung down. Just twenty-one. And poker, five-card draw. Real good.

I pulled out a deck I carried everywhere and proceeded to beat him bad.

After that, he took his long yellowish fingers, covered his eyes and sobbed. Hard, honking noises. I just sat there. I had never seen anyone cry. It's the truth. Father never cried. I cried as a baby, but Father would slap me so hard if I did that my eyes were permanently dry. I watched wet rivers coming from under the hands, and I heard the scuffling of Ton's skinny mother running, in her reed slippers, yelling *Ton! Ton!* She ran over and grabbed him up, kissing his head, his face.

What happen, my baby? You evil girl! What you do to my Ton?

He just sat there, sniffling. She looked down at the scattered cards.

Did you beat him at cards? Fool! He can't handle, can't handle. She cradled him and rocked him in her arms, the skin wiggling.

The next day, he stayed by the edges, sweeping. I called him over.

You can play with my hair, if you want.

He put the broom down, and walked on his knees to me.

You know Elvis had a brother, a twin? He died a long time ago. You know he ate fried peanut butter sandwiches?

His fingers were gently waving through my hair like bird wings.

How come you know so much about Elvis, Ton? He'd found an old elastic and he was braiding my hair.

You a retard or something, Ton?

Before he could answer, Father came out with that look. His arms were pale and dusty from rice flour.

Jing-li upstairs. I brushed off my skirt and said good-bye to Ton. Jing-li meant *manager* and I knew what that meant—Zhang Xinxin, in the red office. The small fat man with pockmarks who smelled of almonds. The one who liked my tongue to be a slithery snake up his body.

It meant more money in Father's tin box in the ceiling and maybe a new VCR.

I wondered if Ton was jealous, or if he even knew. He was a virgin, I was sure.

Couple of days later, Ton is braiding my hair again.

You know what Elvis really liked? His boom box played "Jailhouse Rock."

No, what? His eyes lit up.

He liked to be naked with women. He liked to touch them, and they touched him.

H-He did? You sure?

Oh, sure. Everybody knows this. You want to try?

We went to the broom closet. I took off my dress with blue flowers. I only had red silk underwear on, no bra, because sometimes Mr. Chang liked me on Fridays. I peeled off his clothes, and he was grunting slowly. His item was flat against his stomach, it was so hard.

What did Elvis do? He was breathing hard.

Well, he liked to do this. I put his hands on my breasts and moved them in soft circles. I felt so soft, so creamy between my legs I thought I might faint. I had never felt the pleasure myself. All the old men swoon in my arms, and I remained cold as butter.

Yeah, yeah, Elvis like. He like. He was panting, getting carried away.

And, this, he like this, too, Ton.

No, call me Elvis, I'm Elvis now.

Elvis, do this, now, Elvis. His hand sunk into me. I was so wet and I guided his hand inside, and then in two seconds as he grunted like a pig, I had slipped onto his item and he sat back on the mop bucket and I used my legs on the ground and rubbed against him, and he shivered and moaned and yelled, and I covered his mouth. I worked faster, and felt tension rise and screeched softly and my insides came falling out and shuddered down my legs. His eyes were bulging as he came, his mouth held hard and pulled back to his gums.

We lay back, a sweaty pile, gasping for breath.

After that, I needed Ton, and he needed me. He killed the sadness I felt from the Mr. Changs and gave me pleasure. All I had to do was call him *Elvis* and he was back, in the broom closet, unzipping fast. He kissed me softly. I think this was some sort of love. I am sure.

Ton taught me the words to all the Elvis songs. My favorite was that one "Suspicious Minds," which Ton could sing perfectly, his voice dark and strong, just like Elvis's. I wasn't sure why people thought Ton was retarded. He learned so fast. In the broom closet every day, Ton learned more and more. He knew my body like a song he had memorized. He knew to stroke the back of my neck, to blow wind there, to kiss me not too softly or hard. He knew to wait a bit before he grasped me hard and plunged himself deeply inside. He would kiss my hair and call me *little bird* in Vietnamese. He brought me metal tins of curried frog legs and rice, fresh spring rolls with rice wrappers, shadows of shrimp and cilantro underneath. But sometimes his words made no sense. Sometimes, he made odd sounds and shushed me away or swept all day and didn't answer my words.

His eyes were black, innocent buttons. I could read nothing from them. When Father would call me for my work, he would stare. His lip would tremble. I didn't know how he knew. I never told him.

One day I came back. Guan-xo and Mr. Lee had both had fun with me in the red banquet room. They had tied me up. Father said just pretend, this meant lots of money and a special bonus. He said soon, we would be able to buy a little apartment in Queens, and he would start his noodle business. Only a little bit longer, but I would have to work hard. He said, don't worry, you will never have to do this again, he will buy me jewels and pretty clothes. He already was looking for a match for me from Taiwan, he said. They wouldn't know about my past. I might have to work a few parties sometimes. I cried. I did it once, twelve different men inside me for hours.

Please no, I said.

Remember Queens, he said.

When I come back from the men, Ton looks at me. You smell like dog, he says. I don't love you, not even a little bit. I lead him to the closet. He falls softly against my shoulder, like a baby's head. The door flies open and his mother gasps, finding us naked, wrapped up together on the dirty floor.

She beats me with her heavy broom. Ton tries to pull her off. Everyone comes around to see the commotion. She drags him away by the ear.

Ton is gone after that.

A fat Korean woman does the floors then, and she doesn't even speak to me.

After Ton disappear, about a month later, Father died. You know what happened. Those men came and gave me fifty dollars. I spent days looking for the tin of money, his savings for Queens. At least, I could move there. Finally, I found it, lodged in the wall. I jimmied it open with a metal nail file. It fell to the ground and it was empty. The inside was rusty and there were candy wrappers.

I wonder then, Is this a dirty world? A bad world?

I told myself, I'll save my money. Then I'll find Ton. I'll fix up a pretty place for him. I'll take him to Graceland.

After Ton, I became a kept woman for a guy named Sam Johnson. He's a businessman who lived on 43rd and Sixth. He says he designs bras. I tell him, then make me a bunch of them, of pure silk. He says, I don't make them, I design them.

Says, a bunch of guys get around in a room, and point to drawings that look like textbooks and they talk of weight distribution, fabric density and stuff. Really boring stuff. I could teach them a thing or two, like to make bras in green. Men really like green bras, or purple. Lace is the most popular, though some insist on the eighteen-hour bra. Some, like Ito, only want white cotton, like a training bra. Brazilian women wear these paste-on things, which I tried once and it really threw my job, because they wouldn't come off and then left ugly, gluey spots for weeks.

What Sam Johnson really liked was for me to be a wife, and I liked that, for a change, though it's not my thing. I ironed shirts, washed dishes, even though he only came once a week: Every Friday from six to nine. He would walk in, I would remove his jacket. Then, he sat in a chair in the living room and I would massage his feet. He would be quiet. Then, I'd fix him a perfect Manhattan, and serve it with some potato chips. He'd listen to Mozart. I wore a gown of fuchsia or a robe. Then maybe we'd do it, but very traditional and boring, him on top, over in a few minutes. He'd linger, watch TV. But there was something odd going on that took me weeks to notice. First, I thought he was clumsy. He'd bump into my shin or hip as he went by, but slowly I realized it was intentional. He wouldn't say anything, just—*whack!*—as he'd walk by, a smack to my arm, or leg, then face, getting harder. If I said, what was that, he'd do it harder, and not speak. After a while, he was just beating me, and then a little sex, beating me. I was black and blue and then I had a whole week of nothing. He was paying me good money, all rent and costs, plus a thousand a week.

(*More Champale, relights another cigar.*)

But Sam Johnson didn't seem mean. He just needed to get this out. Something bad must've happened to him.

I think about Ton a lot. Yeah, I loved a retard. But he was kind to me, you know? It had been a couple of years. I was a woman now. I hid my bruises with Dermablend. I walked through the streets and felt proud and independent. I could've been with a lot of guys and been in all types of bad situations. Men could be cruel to women like me. They considered me a plaything, and sometimes, they like to hurt things they play with, torture them, toss them around. Sam Johnson was kind, to compare.

One day, I walk to Chinatown to find a roast duck for Sam. He likes that crisp, dark skin. I ached thinking of what he'd do tonight. I'd lost weight. I was trying to be OK, but I was fading. *Sad in heart.*

The place was called 66 Mott Street. I found the spot. A lady told me it was the best in town, home-smoked and their own spice blend. I walked in and the place smelled like caramel and warm, people coming and going, round tables with groups of mainland families, a small place. But I was surprised and my heart was squeezed dry for a moment.

It was Ton. Standing there in a brown smeared apron, chopping duck. When he saw me, he dropped his cleaver, and I could hear, though my sight was filled with his sweet face, a woman's voice in Chinese,

Oh, careful! Stupid! be careful!

Ton wasn't a boy anymore. And Ton wasn't dumb.

Ton had grown sleek and handsome. He had sideburns and he squeezed my hand hard as we drove fiercely through the streets of Chinatown. He threw down his bike in the stinky hall of an herbalist's shop, pulling me back to a small apartment.

He didn't say anything. Neither did I.

The apartment was neat, and quietly arranged. A big altar with oranges was the first thing I noticed. Then the smell, sweet, powdery.

Mother's not home until late. She works.

Ton, I said as he kissed me.

I was crying, I felt like years of sorrow were pouring from my eyes as he kissed the lids, kissed the drops pouring from them.

Where did you go, Ton?

I was always here.

Here?

I worked for East Winds, and then, duck shop. I carry this.

He pulled out a small ribbon I gave him once.

Mother said you are a whore. This is true? You give yourself to men for money, is it true?

You work for money?

Yes.

I work for money, too.

But.

I don't know anything else.

Softness. Ton is the softest of men, the strongest and the softest. It is the sweetest of contrasts to taste a kind man, to feel powder-soft skin above a hard muscle. And the eyes of this one. They give up themselves to me. I can open up my body to this one, and look him in the eye at every moment. The sounds he utters, the words are lost in the room. My sounds cover his. (*Stops for a bit, smoking. Hears honking outside, a shout. The kitten's tiny teeth bite her hand.*)

Men of the Star in Sky restaurant, 123 Lafayette.

1) Mr. Choi:

Oh, oh, oh, oh, ph—ph—oooo, ph—oooo.
Yeah, yeah, yeaaaaah,unh.
I like it, I, I .

2) Sam Tuong Li:

Mmhhh.
Waaagh.
Haaaaaaooo.

Preserved and spoken by Ying Lu, April, Year of the Dragon, 4:43 A.M.

chapter ten

Menu:

Twinkies

Sake

Wasabi Fried Peas

Bonito

Mariane and Ito sit for a while, as the place closes. Chinese waiters move rapidly, closing folded chairs with hard snaps and crumpling white tablecloths into piles of cloth. An older one comes over.

If anything is required?

No, no. Thank you.

Mariane offers a wrinkled twenty from her pocket and Ito pushes her hand away with a hiss. He lays three perfectly smooth bills on the table and sits up, helping her to her feet, his head bent low, his breath tarry and hot,

Come. Come on. I make tea.

Tea?

My home. Come on. Then, we talk.

They leave. By then, the waiters had the big vacuum cleaners out, chrome machines pushed against the deep red carpets, and as they walk on the dirty streets, seeking a cab, not speaking, oddly holding hands like a couple together for many, many years, the sky is lightening around the edges of the horizon, although is it still dark, still dark and crisp as charcoal.

In the elevator, the chrome walls are too shiny and their faces look greenish and blemished, the speakers pipe out "Yesterday" and Mariane sings along, under her breath, Ito smiles, his cheeks oily pink balls,

You sing nice, maybe karaoke.
I used to, in a band.
Really?
They have come to his door where he fumbles with keys. The carpet is the color of dried blood, meat smells from neighbors' dinners hang in the halls, Ito removes his shoes, motions her to sit down, runs into the kitchen as she stands.

Movements for Mariane are long and prethought, steady, cautious from years of being unwelcome in places, years of being dizzy or unsteady, from injuries (a fractured ankle, tibula, nose, cut lip) of the body and the soul (*the baby*), from not knowing if she'll be yelled at or hit, lightly, she touches the lamp, exploringly, moves to the big, black leather couch, it oozes air luxuriously. Japanese *Manga* comics are strewn on the table, skimming through them she realizes they are for adults, scenes of gory violence or sex, naked women with big Western eyes, round globe breasts, Ito comes over,

<u>Three quarters of a bottle of Chivas, two large bottles of sake (accompanied by dried wasabi peas).</u>

He places a tray on the coffee table, he pours, offers the snacks, she drinks, the process begins again, the inebriation, they begin to feel it,
It's you who fired me, isn't it? Your idea.
He pauses.
It was not his idea, but he considers a lie. Considers what it will bring him. The moments pass, she looks at him, her hard eyes sad, open, she waits.
No. I tried to stop.
Ito doesn't lie, after all.
I saw you drink sake. I saw from the kitchen.
Is that why? You told?

No, Yoshi finds out. Smells your cup. It's not only this. Big problem. He says you steal.

What? *What?*

Fifty dollars.

That bastard!

But you don't.

I never did, what happened, is *totally* different. *Fucker.* Last week, when you are off, Yoshi—

Last Wednesday?

Last Wednesday, Yoshi counts my tips, Carlie is gone already, Janet, Miyako, finished and he, he gives me a vodka tonic. And, *yuck,* makes a move, he puts his gross little mouth on mine and wiggles his hands on me, and I said, get off, and then, he doesn't speak to me for a while and then, then, that jerk fires me, like that,

(Since we all bob around in the liquidy creek of our own *versions of occurrence,* bending, shifting each word or incident, blurring the sense of incorrectness to suit our sense of ourselves, her version of how it happened:

She is rather out of it, dancing around, everyone had left, she's waiting for her tips, Yoshi offers her a vodka tonic, of course she accepts, he leans over her to make the drink, tells her she smells good, he kisses her, they fall against bottles, some almost fall, Yoshi palms her breast, she says Yoshi! he says, come on, I like you, she says, well, I like you, too, but, he says, you are beautiful, unbuttons her blouse, sees a lacy pink bra, pulls down one cup, her breast he tongues, she lies quietly, then she comes to, pulls away, buttoning, he says oh, Mariane, please, comes towards her, she slaps his face hard, a cracking sound. Note: She leaves out the really painful part, the penetration, the look on his face, the forgetting she was there. Then, Yoshi holds his face, looks at her, walks away. She leaves.)

This is no good.

I should sue the guy.

It is no good.

Fucking sexual harassment.
But you drink.
Hunh?
You steal sake. I saw.
Well, yeah. Yeah. Just a few drinkies don't hurt.

He drinks more sake, refills her glass,

<u>Three quarters of a bottle of Chivas, four large bottles of sake
(accompanied by dried wasabi peas, some roast beef on a plate).</u>

Feeling luxuriant, like velvet, her legs touch his slightly as he
sits down next to her this time, on that airy couch, a little more
soft and informal, he smiles more, she says,
I want to hear about this girl, that Chinese girl, aren't you
married and all, anyway?
And he says, I was. But she die, but I love her, too, but it is
different, Xiu-Xiu I met in Hokkaido.
Where?
Island off Japan, I meet her in special bar, for company, you
know, how about where men go for company of pretty ladies.
I get your drift, sort of.
I meet Xiu-Xiu here and find her very perfect.
A whore?
No, no, she is different than this.
A whore.
Oh. Everybody whore. Waitress is whore—
Not *spreading my legs*.
She giving a lot to me, her heart.
She loved you?
Maybe not, she's giving her heart, though.
She left you?
She disappear, with man of mafia.

Mafia? Don Corleone?

Japanese *Yakuza,* very bad. Dragon tattoos. Very violent.

How do you find her?

I find her. I invite job, I leave son. And then, I find her. Like miracle.

You have a son?

His arm is around her neck, she rests her head on his shoulder, his house smells like paper, like a box of different papers, like newspaper and tissues, all with their slight cedary essences.

You have a son?

Yes.

<u>Three quarters of a bottle of Chivas, six large bottles of sake (accompanied by dried wasabi peas, some roast beef on a plate).</u>

You, Mariane, who are you, where you from?

Just places, nothing special, here, there, hell and back. She laughs.

Tell me.

Well. Here's the thing. You got a son?

Yes. Do you?

No. I have a baby.

A baby?

Yup, the most perfect baby in the world. The *prettiest* thing you ever saw, like a little angel or something, but, but, they took her away from me, and, and, I'm going to get her back, I am, I'm going to if it's the damn last thing I do.

How old? Take away?

Let's see, oh, maybe six months, eight months, or maybe a year now, or hell, I guess, I guess, maybe even two, shit, can it be that long? Goddamn it might be, I, no, about eight months.

Who's the father?

It's all fucked up, just a guy I met on the road. Name of Carl.

Kind of a weirdo. Old guy. I like those old-guy types. And before that, I grew up in Richmond, Virginia, in a small apartment, just me and Mother, she was a secretary and no dad, never knew him, and she had to work a lot, but she had her social life, too, don't we all. So, I stayed downstairs with Tom and Fran sometimes when she worked, made her feel I was safe or something, they had cats, lots of them I remember, black ones, fluffy white ones, every sort, Tom was nice enough, had a limp, was kind of a sweetie, he knit- ted sweaters for everyone, and Fran was OK, taught me to cook some stuff, I remember, and on weekends he was a security guard for an all-girl school in town, drove his truck around the grounds, and brought me along, and he always had these, these whiskey sours, little premixed bottles in a big Igloo cooler in the back, so I think back to those cute little orange bottles, drinking them up, he'd give me one or two. And all his shit back there, pieces of wood, metal bars, tire jacks, a toolbox I sat on, sitting on hard-ass stuff, drinking sweet, magical juice, sweet, sweet, stuff—

Teenager, he says.

Yeah. One time, I was waiting for Mom, she's late, her Gremlin broke, won't come until late, which means Jack's in town or Robert, her lawyer friend, so I have to stay over there, and I'd had about six of those things to drink and Tom said Fran was out shopping, I said how, by the way, did you hurt that leg, Tom? And he goes, you wanna hear about that?

So I says, sure, and then he goes, Come on over here then. Now, that was odd, he was patting his lap, but OK, I get up and he says, well, I was stationed in Florida with the Navy, back in '62, in Tampa. You know it? And he says, as I recall, well, it's nice down there, but you cut the grass all the damn time, I'm riding a riding mower, you know what a riding mower is? Of course I says, sure, and then he slides his big, meaty hand under my blouse, really nonchalant, which shocked the hell out of me since he's *gay,* you know? And he goes, Yeah, well it started raining and something got caught under there, grinding up, and I got off to check her out, his hands cupping my boobs, without acting like he knew it, he says, grass so slippery, my foot slid underneath, quick as a whistle. Like a slide. Foot opened up like a book from the blade. By now, he was in my underwear, a large, callused hand in my privates, saying *my shoe went one way, my foot the other and my tendon another,* and he goes, you could say I've known a bottle or two of Tylenol Three in my day. Whiskey sours help.

Like that night with Yoshi, you know? You don't know if it's you that did it or them. You don't know if you gave them the, the *wrong idea* or something. Then, what happens then is, he lays me down on the shag carpet. Someone's dog barked outside in the yard. I looked outside and saw a cloudless day, trails of airplanes, an old basketball hoop. I'm just waiting. I could hear children, from the pool outside, laughing. Under his clothes, he was waxy white, with black hairs on his thighs. His penis was like his hurt foot, gnarled-looking, purplish, stumpy. I only saw it for a second. He rubbed it against my leg, fast, humping like an old dog. Afterwards, he sat up and said, I don't think it's a good idea to tell Fran about this. I mean, he wouldn't get it, you know? That's what he said.

Did you tell mother? Police?

I told my mother, he was creepy and I couldn't go back there, but she said, he's *queer,* honey, and therefore harmless and everything I said or tried to sounded off and suspicious, and *weird, so I gave up, and how did I know I didn't cause it? How did I know?* because she didn't believe me. That's when I took off. I packed a bag and left, and went south along 95, hitchhiking, that's when I meet Carl.

And nothing happens to this man?

No. I'm not really sure it happened. Maybe I started it.

Carl is your baby's father.

Carl is my husband.

Oh, you are married.

Yeah, he's old, too. It was weird, see, he's sitting drinking coffee in a diner in North Carolina, have you been down there? Barbecue lodges and stuff, furniture stores, you know, they make most of the stuff you see around in the new shops down there.

Couches, things?

All that shit, got factories down there, he was sitting drinking in a, in a diner, the poor old dude, do you know about diners?

Is restaurant, cheap ones?

Yeah, yeah. You got them in Japan?

Like this.

So, this old guy's talking to the waitress about his wife's cancer, can you believe, just babbling on, how it's eating her alive, I'm sitting there thinking, I've been on the road one whole night, *I'll take more sake there, please, ah, that's good,* so, I, I got a ride from a nice husband-and-wife team, who told me they had fourteen grandchildren, one with cerebral palsy, they dropped me in Raleigh early in the morning, gave me twenty bucks, said "call your mama," and dropped me off at Dottie's Diner here, at six A.M., I ordered a bowl of chili, and coconut pie, and I ate each bite as slow as possible, added all the saltines in, crushed them up, just to buy time, when you are sixteen, seventeen, what the hell can you do, the business of life is moving on, I see people going to work, grabbing coffee on the run, sun is starting to shine, I'm wearing the, the same clothes—

Where is mother? Mother gone?

I told you. I split. Left. Didn't want to hang out out with that weirdo anymore, besides I was ready to cut out, I wanted to be on my own, I was sick of our smelly house and her lying in bed all day and waiting on her, and why did I have to stay with those weird neighbors anyway, I was *sixteen,* for Christ's sake.

So you find husband?

It wasn't like *that,* I didn't find him, I just, I overheard him talking all sad and felt for him, I started talking to him, to *Carl* talking about his wife, how bad things are, how he's just got to get a break sometime, poor old dude, balding, broken glasses patched up with tape in the middle, old jeans and a shirt that got stains. Like maybe his wife was some kind of Susie Homemaker before and now she's all hard up and things are falling apart.

And Ito says,

This is unfortunate situation.

Ito fades away, thinking back to the fall years ago. A *nabemono* of a certain fall, a seasonal Japanese food cooked in a ceramic pot, a fall tradition as the weather cools, the pale brown coolness of the pot hauled from the top shelf in his kitchen, dusted off, he puts it on the kitchen table, writes a list on a scrap of paper, puts on his shoes at the door, he bundles Daisuke, his young son, in his felt coat, his little frog boots by the door, Saga, the cat, runs to the door as Ito attempts to open it, but he pushes her away, the pleasant chill of the air, pulling Daisuke in the wagon, stopping two blocks away at the cloth banners of the fish stall, Kanekosan, the owner, procuring a fillet of salmon, some squid, some octopus, a nice fall *nabemono* of seafood, he pays the bill, swings by the tofu shop, a large block of firm tofu, vegetables, chrysanthemum leaves, bean sprouts, spinach, seaweed chunks for the broth, all in the wagon, Daisuke holding the bag, coming in the door (Saga darts for it again), starting the fire, Daisuke sits on the table, stirs the broth, a warm smell in the air, rice cooking, and adding the fish, turning opaque and hard and cooked, noodles swirling in the hot soup, the spinach leaves dissolving into green compliance, steam of indescribable sweetness filling the air, and bringing her to the table, wrapped in her quilt, light as a broom, Tomoko, her stomach nearly gone from surgeries.

But it is fall, and she grew sick in May, and she wishes for *nabemono,* as her father made it, as Ito always has, Daisuke and Ito carry her, keeping the ends of the quilt from dangling down, she sits up straight, her eyes eager round beans, a small bowl in front of her, fish mashed with rice, a spoon tilting in her waxy hand, to her mouth, shaking and spilling, then gagging, they rush with the pan, pure bile, poured down the toilet, she rests, let me sit here and watch, just watch, you two go ahead, and they can only eat a bit, for ceremony, putting her back on the bed, then she sleeps, then Ito washes Daisuke, puts him in pajamas, he sleeps, Ito cleans the dinner, smokes a cigarette, the night is sharp and starless, he opens the door and leaves, so quietly, down the street, to Flower Farm, where Xiu-Xiu was waiting. Lying in a hot bath.

Ito coughs, looks at Mariane,
Cancer, he says. Very bad.
Are you with me, Ito? Seems like you drifted there. Yeah. It isn't pretty, I suppose. That's what he was dealing with, so naturally he's spent, pretty ragged out and the waitress says, *are you still plumbing?* Her hair was kind of mayonnaise-colored and frizzy, I remember and he says, "*I get out for jobs, here and there. When I can get a nurse*" and he glances over at me over his coffee. Hurt, hungry eyes searching for warmth, so I ask him if he's going in the direction of Charlotte and he says, *sure, sure I'm going up that way,* I do think that was maybe my prime physical time, I really had it going on, so to speak, so I get in the cab of his truck, he paid my bill, and it doesn't take long for him to paw me up, he's crying and kissing me, just says, *I'm really sorry, I don't know myself these days,* so I let him and I guess at this point I was beginning to think this is what would always happen, I didn't stop or start, just flowed.

He brings me to his home and I guess I could stay there, he says. I can use a nurse, Lord knows, if you're willing, he offers. I see his wife in the bedroom, no hair and just as tiny as can be, just a heap of bones, she smiles at me and calls me Clarisse, her niece, he says. I want a home with curtains like they have, frilly and see-through. I mean, how'd she know how to make those things or where to buy them? So pretty, sheer like ballerina skirts.

<u>Three quarters of a bottle of Chivas, six large bottles of sake (accompanied by dried wasabi peas, some roast beef on a plate) Ito gets up to pour more sake, realizes the bottle is dry, swaying, tripping slightly, he says he will go downstairs for beer, does she want anything else? She says some Marlboros would be good, and maybe some Twinkies, does he knows those things? They're kind of yellow cakey things with frosting, no, not candy, a cake, just ask the guy, he'll know, Ito nods his head.</u>

Ito leaves and the apartment has a strange, buzzing sound. No ticking of clocks. Mariane goes to the window, still dark, just the beginning of dawn and some people are walking rapidly in their work clothes, clean, crisp, their hair newly washed, she watches Ito, a black shape, swerve in the walk, obviously drunk, she watches people turn their heads, she feels her head spin, she lays it down on the sill, the metallic smell of city dirt in her face, she falls asleep for a bit.

Ito has his hands in his pocket in the elevator, hums a bit, to an old tune ("Sayonara"), fingers a few quarters in his pocket, wonders again why they took her baby, then realizes it's not hard to imagine, Mariane with her drunken babbling speech, albeit charming, and the sake incident, it all seems clear to him there is a deep problem here, wonders if there is a possibility of sex with Mariane, thinks of her on the couch, he has followed the line of her thighs in her leggings as she tells her story, he has waited for her to shift on the couch, and catch a round suggestion of breast, he falls back against the wall for a second, his body giddy with drink and sexual longing, the lobby is dark and smells like vacuum cleaner exhaust, he notes that different smell of this country again, sweet, candyish, fatty.

The dawn is cold and vague. He sits on the concrete bench outside. He is drunk, swirling and the air is wet and light. He smells spring. He sees the 7-Eleven at the end of the street, rises, and he laughs a bit. *It is spring.*

He runs to the street where he sees a cluster of cabs, runs in front of a crisply dressed woman whose hand is outstretched. *Taxi, taxi.* The woman makes a disgruntled sound as Ito leans in the window, laughing a bit, maybe as drunk as he's ever been, and says excitedly, *Fulton Fish Market,* which comes out simply as:

Fool unh Hish Mahhk.

What? I don't hear, says Renton Fubela, a native of Nigeria, clad in an Old Navy zippered pullover in a brassy hue of yellow-vitamined piss, leaning across the seat, squinting, to take in the disheveled old Chinese guy who appears quite inebriated.

Fooool unh—

Listen, my man, just get in.

Ito does so, and collapses on the warm, soft vinyl, a piped-in voice talks of seat belt fastening, and tinkling from the radio comes some music, Soca.

OK, OK, say this again, man.

I say: *Foool dunh hish maaahkah*—

Fulton Fish! Fulton Fish Market! Now I got it, OK, sir!

Ito's head reels around his neck, loose and discombobulated, while Renton's smile gleams in the rearview mirror like a splash of white paint.

OK, OK. Hey, mister.

Ne?

Are you from China, my friend?

No, no. *Jah*-pan.

Japan! Yes sir! Fine ladies in your country. Know how to treat a man, am I correct, sir?

Uh, yessss.

Unlike the American women I encounter. Like Nigeria, humble. What you do, buy some fish, my man?

*Hi*sh.

You been out having a party, right? Dancing or something?

Just. *Drink.*

Well, you get some fish and cook it up. Yessir, here OK? By the lamppost? Hey, you know what you do, my man? Get that fish and fry it in cornmeal, fry some onion, peppers, put it on there, all over, some lemon juice, it's good, I tell you! You try.

No, no. I eat raw.

Raw? Are you crazy, sir? Raw?

It's the dawn and the market, Ito's arena, is in full gear, prime time, five o'clock, the best fish lying in ice, it is now spring, if he is fast he will find the perfect pearly Bonito, harbinger of spring in Japan, *Katsuo,* like his name *Katsuyuki,* he will prepare it for Mariane, she can finish her story, they can eat Bonito tataki for breakfast, and then, they can make love, Katsuyuki Ito rages with excitement, laughing, the taxi driver says, *happy, huh, buddy?* and he says, y*es, yes, happy,* the taxi driver shrugs.

Ito watches people milling in the early morning, he lights a cigarette, the streets whirl by.

chapter eleven

Menu:

Skewered Sashimo

Flesh Sashimi

Rice Soup for the Infirmed

There were approximately thirteen of them at the Flower Farm, including Xiu-Xiu, and she was the only Chinese and there was one Korean, name of Linda. The girls were referred to Miyakosan, the owner. She sits in the back office room, a pale peach rectangle with a pastel-flowered couch, a glass coffee table and a poster of the cherry blossom festival in Japan. Miyakosan had always fantasized about being a geisha, in fact she likened her career to that of a geisha, she demurely referred to payment in a poetic fashion, *That will cost 100 petals,* instead of yen, and the men who frequented Flower Farm came to smile and appreciate this archaic tendency for its delicacy and poetic nature, and she would serve sake in each small cubicle, or bean cakes, and sometimes, if they paid extra "petals," sashimi would be brought in for fellows staying a night, or Fox noodles with fried tofu, and once in a while, occasionally a man would look down, cough or stammer, and request her services, and she would have to say, *oh,* she would giggle, *I am retired, but thank you. You are being kind, but I am an old chicken. But you look through the book,* and she would hand them a handwritten tome of rice paper and silk, with pressed flowers, and point out each girl's picture, with their flower names, even though the men would insist, *you are still quite lovely.*

Sakura (Cherry Blossom): Is young and full of life. Will customize your night to the fullest guarantee of ecstasy!

Sakura loves men and knows what is their secret fantasy and wishes and is also known for her delightful sense of humor and grace. Room 4.

Barako (Rose Blossom): As the youngest, I need you to guide me! (They would look again and again to the picture of the woman in white cotton panties and bra, with pigtails in red ribbons, licking a giant, rainbow lollipop.) I am just a girl and like men to help me learn! Let me be your little girl for a pleasurable experience of the highest order! Room 8.

Yuriko (Lily): I am ready to punish you for your bad, bad actions. You have disappointed me on many levels. I am afraid I will have to teach you a very painful lesson. Yuri is cruel, and men like you will find out how torturous and wonderful that can be. Room 7.

Xiu-Xiu did not use her real name, but instead went by *Momoko* (Peach Blossom). She wore, in her picture, a Chinese dress and red lacquered lips, her hair in a bob. It read: I know the secrets of Chinese love that will drive you wild. I can do things with my feet you didn't know existed! I am known for my skillful ways, my artful tongue and I long to hear the cries of your unbridled passion. Room 5.

Men who were regulars with Xiu-Xiu, and there were many, could call her Momoko or Xiu-Xiu. After the first few sessions with her artificially Chinese poise, she would relax and walk in her platforms, or her mini pink dress trimmed in fur, with her Tokyo countenance and the men would accept it all, like the chamber of commerce director, Takichi Omori, who came dressed in his somber blue suit, a stack of cards in his pocket, who bowed succinctly at the door, who greeted Miyakosan with great respect for a customary ten minutes, drinking from the tiny ceramic bowl of tea, talking of the weather and the upcoming festivals, or the news, and then, Miyako would say, *OK, now please,* and escort him to room 5, where Xiu-Xiu waited, he would knock politely, and Xiu-Xiu would say, Come in please. Omorisan would enter and say, how beautiful you are today, and she came over to him, wearing her red sheer baby-doll gown trimmed in marabou, kiss his cheek lightly, and she would loosen his tie, and soon he would be down to his pale, tendony body in his black socks, she would escort him to the bed, and lie across him and do nothing, for Omori was impotent for years, but Xiu-Xiu would lie draped on his chest, and he would would clasp her buttocks and he would sleep for a few hours and then awake, hungry, and the sashimi would be called in, Miyakosan would enter with a lacquer box and redwood chopsticks and Xiu-Xiu would lie on the floor, removing her red gown, and sashimi would be arranged decorously on her pubic hair, and a small bowl with wasabi and soy in her palm, and Miyako would leave, and Omorisan would eat the sashimi, nonchalantly, with politeness, finish quietly, thank Xiu-Xiu as he would rise and dress and then he would leave *400,000 petals* in the bowl and say, next week, then? And the door would ease shut, slowly.

In that time, the sweetest time of his life, Ito would rise at four, bathe in the boiling hot water of his bath while his wife prepared his breakfast of broiled Sashimo fish, three tiny silverish fish skewered by three bamboo sticks and broiled in her tiny hibachi, accompanied by a heap of rounded rice, sprinkled with sesame seeds, a bowl of murky miso soup, green tea and pickles. He would wear his old *yukata* and eat silently, mumbling an occasional something to Tomoko, sometimes he would reach and pat her hand, *good breakfast, okaasan,* and she would smile, and although they had not had intimate relations, as she put it, in many years, they dearly loved each other, she would massage his broad neck, kiss his ear on occasion, Ito could trust that this woman would care for him. She would be there at all times, but he had been mistaken thinking that. He had not counted on illness or death. He had supposed they would die in old age at similar times. He had not supposed she would be fifty and fade immediately in a few rapid months, that her body would become littler and littler and just cave in, an implosion of bones and sunken capillaries.

After breakfast, he would drive to the water and buy the fish, filling his little wagon with slabs of hamachi, maguro, sake, hirame, tai, pink and pale white shimmering slabs, curling red arms of octopi, wooden boxes of gleaming mustard-hued Uni, socklike squid with flapping legs, baby clams for pickling, giant clam oozing live out of its shell, platelike rosy scallop shells, chewy red clam and ark shell, and a vat of squiggling eel, their eyes beating into the sides of the bowl, electricity coursing through their flesh, lifting it all into his small green wagon, with its dent on the side from tagging a seafood truck on just such a morning, Ito would get into his trim little car and drive out of the wet mist of the seafood mart, bumping along the streets back to his neighborhood, to Okara, his restaurant, careen to the back entrance where three men wait, holding cigarettes the way teachers hold chalk, the kitchen chef and two helpers, they politely greet him, fling the cigarettes to the ground and all grab a box, he unlocks the back door, the lights flicker on and he puts water on for tea, slaps his hands in the brisk air, it may snow soon already, says one of the fellows, not unusual to have snow so early in fall, and he washes his hands and coughs, gets the younger to sweep and make rice, the cook makes miso, makes tempura sauce, makes soy blend for the sushi bar, cuts daikon into long papery sheets, and Ito, only Ito, cuts fish.

He has five expert knives, a long thin one for fillet and a squat hacking knife for the severing of flesh, and he whittles the carcass of yellowtail down to a few oily bricks of perfect flesh, and he saves the bony jaw, with its pocket of tender flesh, to be broiled for the employee meal (*hamachi-kama*), and similarly, slices down the blood red transparent flesh of the tuna, tossing the blackened lines of oil and always never ceases to marvel at the perfect red slabs he creates, sometimes the natural beauty of the world catches Ito unaware and he is taken aback, at this moment, the leafy air of autumn brushes in, Jerosan boils daikon in miso and Ito feels nostalgic for his youth, he longs for the warm touch of Xiu-Xiu, for the tastes of autumn mingling in his mouth, poetry dances in his head:

> *When dawn arrives*
> *The sky is misted over,*
> *And in a moment*
> *The world takes on*
> *The signs of autumn.*

And he says it out loud, and the older smiles, and quotes his own poem from Sansho, and the younger, washing rice, says nothing, thinking of his own band and his handwritten lyrics in his notebook in his bag, but he is silent, and washes rice. Years from now, when he is old, he will be cutting rice then, he will smell fall, he will remember Ito and his nostalgia for fall's bittersweet coming and he'll remember his bleached spiked hair, his girlfriend with her thirteen piercings or the red broom he uses every day or the small crouch spot for peeing in the bathroom or the particular smell as you enter the back door early in the morning, or not, maybe he won't remember any of it.

In Japanese, Ito can be talkative at times, he turns towards the young one washing rice, to whom life is fragile and simple (whose girlfriend said last night *let's go in one of those karaoke boxes and do it against the wall,* so they did, right in the middle of the street market, they rented the karaoke box and the disco lights twirled, they were alone in there, with just the instrumentals strumming "I Did It My Way"), Ito says, pointing to the yellow-haired one with his knife,

Ha, this guy here thinking these old men know nothing about life (come to think of it, the yellow-haired boy thinks, Why didn't we use a condom? What if)

Did you know, for example, my fine young fellow, continues Ito, that sushi used to be a throwaway thing? Just rice to preserve fish and pressed in blocks, and some lucky guy gets too hungry and eats up that rice, then we wise up and put them together, and it used to be fermented, too, like they do in the country, layered and layered with vinegar, and pressed down and left for a while? (Will that karaoke box be available tonight? Should I call them?)

Lunch hour is almost upon them and Ito scurries to the front, layering the freshly cut seafood in small piles with bamboo leaves in the case, and some people trickle in, some regulars, and he greets them with his loud *Irrashaimase!* his welcome, and they greet him respectfully, and sit down, washing their hands with the scented cloth that smells of delicate lemon, and one of them inquires about the best of the day, and he recommends the tuna, only today it swam in the deepest black water of the Japanese Sea, and they order that, and others, and he slaps his pink hands and plies the ruddy strips of tuna with rice, in the perfect, exacting *seventeen movements,* and the customers know the special vocabulary for the sushi bar, with its own words for soy sauce (*Murasaki*) or ginger (*Gari*) and the bill is always called *Oaiso.*

Finally, the last of the fish is sold and Ito's day is over, the sushi bar is washed and fish wrapped, boxes put away, the case shined, and Ito goes home, washes himself again in the broad wood bath, scrubs down, puts on fresh clothes, kisses his sleeping wife and child, strokes his cat, Saga, and walks out in to the night, Tomoko hears his key turn and knows he goes to a whore and is grateful, secretly, in her stomach, there has been a dull, dull pain for a long time and she is scared, she pats her son's arm and prays silently.

★ ★ ★

Five times a week, Ito would come, the old sushi man, the others would say, *Old shokunin here,* they could see him coming down the path (his house was only seven blocks away) exactly on time 11:35 P.M. every time, late, after work, when wife is asleep, they would say, and Xiu-Xiu prepared, douched after the man before (a metro ticket taker, a skinny man with sour breath she didn't care for) or on Wednesdays, Teru, a man of the mafia, with tattoos, quite a good lover actually, who took his time and caressed her, a man who said he wished to marry her, but she wasn't interested, a man who said, if you need anything, ever, I'll help, just call me, he wore purple underwear, he had thousands of women in his time and claimed Xiu-Xiu was the best, he watched sports channels while she sat scratching his head, of all, he was the most normal, just a simple relationship of straightforward sex and cuddling, hanging out, discussing politics or sports, I can't get a date except with a skank, he said. Girls are scared of me, and their parents forbid it.

But Xiu-Xiu knew he was a little in love with her, a little tender. He'd pop in and say, he was just driving by. Sometimes he'd kiss her eyelashes.

It was Itosan, the old sushi chef, who often claimed Xiu-Xiu knew him better than anyone, that Xiu-Xiu saw his bare self, in every sense. She would laugh, come on. What about your wife? And he would just skirt around that, like swerving a car as a rabbit dashes out, just ignore and continue, and Xiu-Xiu always wondered, what is his woman like, typical Japanese housewife? She fancied Terusan was in love with her, and she fancied Ito was also. She figured his wife was his partner, a companion.

She figured he felt little for her. But since that day that his wife died, she knew better.

The African taxi driver, *Mr. Fubela,* lets Ito out on a black street with fires in cans every few feet, trucks barreling through.

Ito pays five dollars, and the taxi zooms off. He stands and watches the scene. Smoke trails through the sky like ghosts and burns his eyes.

It is like a crematorium.

As she got weaker, Ito noticed his son, Daisuke, got stronger. He was adept at hooking up the tubes, cleaning them, washing them with alcohol and flooding them, he learned to hook up an IV, tying the arm for a vein to bulge, palpitating the purplish quiver, sinking in the deep needle point, wrapping the white tape, but after a while the veins were sinking, and flattening, towards the end they were impossible to find, they hooked it on her head, on a shaved spot, then came the machines, the oximeter, which bleeped through the day and night, Daisuke would dust it, polish it, as if were an extension of his mother, Daisuke could make a very good version of rice soup, he kept pots of it on the stove and Ito would watch him spoon a small ladleful into a bowl, blow on it and add a spoonful of miso, patiently wait for it to cool and feed it to his mother, while Ito refrained from eating, drinking a beer, paralyzed as his son of thirteen became stronger than him, he would say, *I go out now,* and Daisuke would just say, *sure, sure,* never a complaint, he had been taught to do so, to show respect, he would go in the street, turn left twice, up a few blocks, past the nursery, past the tea shop, into the seedier area, to the Flower Farm, the small, unassuming door, knock, say his name, hungry for Xiu-Xiu's live body, warmth, for some noodle soup, for tea, for the perfume of her body.

Ito ate noodles, Xiu-Xiu massaging his neck. The noodles were thick and white, like worms, wrapped in a bowl with crunchy bits of tempura. Xiu-Xiu wore a pantsuit with bell-bottoms, her hair in little bow clips. Another woman walks in with a portable phone, her face is bandage white with drawn brows, *Shokunin's son is on the phone,* she says, *a little boy.* Ito doesn't hear her at first. He does not know how Daisuke knows the number. Daisuke says the doctor wishes to speak to him. The doctor is quiet and respectful, he says, *your son summoned me because your wife, Tomokosan, would not respond.* He couldn't get a vein. I cannot get a vein, either, I am afraid, Itosan.

Your wife. Your wife. Is it possible you could come here quickly? It is of the gravest importance. I am sorry. She is in a coma. He hangs up.

They cannot get a vein, mumbles Ito.

Nani? says Xiu-Xiu, *what?*

They cannot get a vein.

Vein, *desuka?*

Ito, in these four years, has never mentioned that his wife has cancer. He has never mentioned his wife, he has talked of his father, his mother, his childhood, his likes, his preferences while she handles his penis, his favorite foods and dislikes, his work, his admiration for her skills and her body, but never, never Tomoko.

They cannot get a vein, he says, slamming the glass door, running out in his slippers, the cold wind rushing in, the ladies whispering, even Mr. Hijigi in room 2, mid-ecstasy, heard the rushed word, *vein.*

He runs through the street, huffing. When he gets there, Saga the cat makes a run for the door and he lets her go, out in the snow, no patience to follow her, his son comes over to him and says, *Otosan.* He holds his icy hand. *Otosan.*

The doctor is standing up.

Very sudden, Itosan. Very sudden.

Tomoko lays on her bed. A funeral kimono draped over her. Her face, pale and taut.

Otosan, can I go outside? asks Daisuke.

Why? asks Itosan.

To play in the snow.

Snow?

Ito walks over to Tomoko, and falls on her body. Her smell is still fresh. The doctor is talking, steadily, about traditions, rituals, funerals, cremation, the boy is talking of the snow,

Otosan, I want to make a person out of snow, I have a carrot, two chestnuts—

The doctor interrupts. It is recommended, after the bathing, that I send for Tachibanasan, that we perform the ceremony of cremation before too long, you see—

Otosan! Otosan! The snow will melt!

I do not understand, begins Ito, why a vein cannot be—

A cremation must be—

Otosan!

—why a vein cannot be found.

The cremation is simple and traditional. Her bones, clean and flame-scorched, are kept in a jar on a red cloth. They eat the simple vegetarian food of mourners. A few relatives, his sister come. They are respectful. They give money.

Ito sits with Daisuke.

Daisuke.

Otosan, can I, can I—

Daisuke, they suggest, this is hard to say. . . .

No. Please.

Listen please, they say, it will be better if you live with your aunt. Family situation, now, has changed, I feel I am not *proper*—

No!

Please, son.

No. No.

(Isn't no the worst word when you know it means nothing, when it is powerless, when it only has the sound of a puff of air?)

Ito packs his bag, Daisuke's small *Twisted Metal 2* pouch with his books, his large duffel with his clothes, and when the aunt comes, they all speak in hushed reverential tones, *Does he need toothpaste? What about the quilt?* and Daisuke sits on the mat, his eyes ahead, he eats a box of small seaweed crackers, and strangely, Ito doesn't feel torn or anguished, he feels rather solidly locked up in reality, as he sees it, What kind of home would I make? I cannot cook for him (although he does this professionally), I cannot wash his clothes, bottom line, I am not a woman, he thinks, and can't nurture him. It is something he has never done. It is not possible, he tells himself. In the layered way people build reasons around an act *that is not right,* and because Ito knows deep, deep down this is not right, he repeats silent mantras to reinforce the rightness of his thinking, *It is better for him, I am not fit* (whores at night), *I am probably a bad influence, he will be better off.*

When Ito says good-bye to him, he pulls an invisible draw-string that people do to buck up. He pulls it tight. His mouth is a slash. His eyes dry. He shakes his hand. Good-bye, son. I will call soon. Please take care of Saga. I will send money soon. Thank you. Good night. Please watch the ice on the step. Good night.

chapter twelve

Hey! Squint, through the fires. The men in black, in shades of gray, rubber boots, hooks in hand, shouts, wet pools of melted ice, loading, unloading, *hey!* backing up trucks, *beep beep beep beep,* the smell of burning plastic, *hey!* the smell of ammonia, of fresh wounds, the sound of gravel, ice, engines, muffled lights, *Hey! Hey! Hey! Move outta the way! Mister!*

Ito falls forward slightly, trips, his cigarette burns his hand. *Ya deaf?!* A man on a motorized cart jets by him, laden with heavy boxes of Atlantic Fresh Rockfish.

Off the Izu peninsula, the squid boats glow with multicolored lights, like jewels in the black sea. The fishermen use them to attract the squid and other fish. Astronauts in space, orbiting the earth, report that the whole of Japan, the entire island, is ringed with the shimmering lights of their boats.

The squid lay frozen in blocks, white ice across their saclike bodies.

We got good squid, today, ten a box. Ten a box.

No, no thanks.

Ito walks along the grimy open-air mart, past the piles of ice, to the tuna tent, fog from the refrigerators pouring out into the street like an eerie horror flick, entering a large space with men shouting, heaving the large white bodies of the dead fish around.

Excuse me, Ito asks a large blond man with a red face, Bonito today?

What's that? We, uh, got tuna, here, you mean, you mean, oh, *Bone*-ita. Skipjack. Ask Telly there, he points to a dark-eyed man in an apron.

Hey! Hey, Telly! Bone-ita, you gots? the blond man yells.

Ahhh, yeah. Just a few. Sold a lot already. Let's see.

Ito follows him to a pile of metallic blue fish, small eyes gleaming,

How about this one, how much?

That? Fifteen, old man. fifteen.

OK. OK.

He pulls out a roll of bills, hundreds, twenties, fifties, and peels off a twenty.

Whoa, fella. I'd watch that roll. You know? Can't be too careful, you know what I'm saying?

It's *OK, OK,* Ito says, slightly embarrassed, laughing a little bit. *No problem.*

Big problem for you if you get rolled, bud. Watch yourself. Especially when you're juiced like that. *Shit*—

No *problem,* Ito is angry now, he grabs the fish wrapped in newspaper, throws the man a twenty and doesn't wait for change, stumbles off, tripping slightly, the lights spinning in the cool dawn, he skips out to the street, carrying his bundle, he is eager to get back, he needs to get beer, cigarettes, Twinkies—

He finds it amusing to say it over and over, *Twinkie, Twinkie,* as he walks in lower Manhattan, the trucks with grimy teddy bears tied on in front barreling through the city, congesting in honking piles as he reaches Tribeca, he stumbles along, completely lost, smelling like a stinking fish, sitting on a curb for a moment, some-where, on some damn street, completely lost, and Ito finds that the roll of money is gone, lost somehow, the money roll from his pocket gone, he checks and rechecks, but, somehow he's dropped it on the way, or someone picked it, filled with adrenaline he pats his pockets for the outline of the roll to no use, he scans the curb, the sidewalk, the people's faces.

Ito begins to cry.

At first, just a few drops, then his face is twisted and wet with tears, dripping onto the fish, he sobs in his fishy hands, sobs on the Bonito, people stream by not looking at the Japanese man crying on his fish, loudly, assured he is crazy, *another one, don't look, God forbid,* not realizing Ito has never cried before, never, these tears are as odd and strange as a stranger's skin, people walking by see a drunken man sobbing on a fish and Ito, sobbing on a fish, is gasping (like a dying fish) for some kind of salve, for his ineffectual tongue, for words, why is he crying, no one knows, but in his mind the images of pain float like ripped paper in a watery eddy, scraps of his remorse, his utter sadness about the money (Yoshi gave him for the week's supply of fish), for Tomoko (his beloved wife, he could not help and seemed to not care, but he cared to the point of paralysis), for Xiu-Xiu (a woman he loved, who left him without so much as a note), for the poor Chinese girl he was stalking (he knows she is not Xiu-Xiu, now he knows, it's becoming clearer), these images give him great remorse, moans and sobs heave out of him, so much pain packed into a single small capsule of space, his heart, chomped down and swallowed, eaten, smothered, covered, lied, disguised, he cries, he cries, for his son, Daisuke (whom he loves and misses sorely, whom he *abandoned,* and he introduces that word and feels the saltiness of its weight), crying for the years of hard work and coldness in the restaurants as a boy, the cutting of clammy fish, the people behind the bar who would eat the food and look at him as if he were some type of icon, some figurine. Tears, wet streams down his face, and Ito even feels pain for the stiff little Bonito in his hand, wrapped in the blurring newspaper, which days before sailed through bluish currents, majestically, and now he lies dead, covered in a man's tears.

And then the last image of Mariane makes him sob again as he feels bathed in such squirmy pity for the woman, for her delicate dreams and hopes, her baby, that this baby, this baby, her dream, her salve, was no baby:

If Mariane is in her forties, this baby is long gone, long down the road. There is no plan, he realizes, anymore for Mariane.

The baby is all grown up.

In his head he sees her baby, but it's Daisuke, wearing a *Death Battle II* T-shirt, his face without expression, his eyes looking down, his foot twisting on its toe, watching his father leave.

His head spins. He is tired and weary. He's been keeping himself up for a long, long time. Ito attempts to stand, but then his foot catches on the edge of the sidewalk, he does a desperate half-turn, he swipes for the street lamp pole about two feet away, but he misses, hurling him towards the ground, his head smacking the cement with a snapping crack. His eyes fly up in his head and the images that spin are tainted, blurred bits of a surrendered subconscious, nonsensically sewn together by liquor, pain, damage and fear.

Ito is *out*.

Of those who step by his curling hand, halfway across the sidewalk, a long oblong newspaper-wrapped package an inch away, a man whose mouth gapes in a beige O, hair slanted to one side, shirt stained, underneath a purplish spot of hematobic tissue, in this junction of Ito and others, the thoughts are:

Good God, a fucking drunk/ *Poor Guy, I really need to help these*/ Funny, you don't, what's that package thing?/ *I hope Sandra's not dealing with Baxter 'n' them before me, because*/Jesus, these homeless/*I wonder if that coffee shop there*/I'll have to call Stewart at nine, Terry at ten/*No more! No more!*/Ugh. Is he dead? Nah./*Mierda! Mierda! Yo lo siento*/Is this guy OK?/ *Where's a taxi when you need*/ I'll try it with him one more/

Over his hand, move:

An American woman in a black suit, a cell phone in her hand. She wears a gold bracelet.

A Chinese man, thirtyish, carrying a briefcase, to work as a manager on Broadway.

A Chinese woman, forties, hurrying, to work on Broadway.

A Chinese man and boy, carrying boxes, going to his office.

An American man, in jeans, mumbling to himself, walking to work breakfast at a restaurant at the corner of Canal and Lafayette.

A German man, who got fucked up last night, woke up in a strange apartment in Tribeca, and is wandering, lost.

A Vietnamese man, of low intelligence, who works in a duck shop and lives with his mother, who stops and speaks to the old man.

Sir? Sir? Are you OK? Hey, hey, buddy.

He heaves him up on his small shoulders. He smells a wave of fish and sour liquor, and the man sees the bloody spot.

You need help. I help you.

He walks down the street, dragging Ito, supported on his shoulder.

I'm gonna help you, mister. Maybe my mother'll be pissed, but—

I'm gonna help you.

chapter thirteen

Menu:

Persimmons

Chestnuts

Udon Noodles

Blood

The worst of it:

In his concussion, Ito's brain lays suspended in a Jell-O mold of clipped old memories and muffled voices, jettisoning him across oceans with the speed of blood currents to sometime before he came to America.

He doesn't know Sugibar or Mariane or Yoshi yet. It is the fall and he remembers walking through the streets smelling fall things, green Japanese pumpkins, smoky fires, stews cooked with sweet sake resin. It is one week after Tomoko has died. His house, always cold, causes him to work more.

With his head wounded now, on an early spring morning in Manhattan, Ito is carried by a man through the streets and his head is wrapped with a blanket of those comforting smells. He tastes chestnuts and smells them roasting. He hears the street hawker selling roasted sweet potatoes and tastes the crisp orange skin with chili powder. He feels the powdery skin of persimmons and sees the translucent orange clarity of their flesh and he is eating one right now, gnawing around the pit. He then eats a fish-cake stew, in Bonito broth, and doing so, he feels the shadow of Tomoko in his kitchen cooking it, he hears her talking, softly about winter coming, he is blessedly free from the pang of knowing she is gone, he is totally in the grip of his selective memory. Then, just as quickly, he is at work, appeasing the fall-inclined tastes of the customers, spending hours cutting, slicing, searing squid sashimi and placing it on a plate with pine needles. It is a Sunday, then, and Ito asks for a day off. His boss agrees.

Mr. Hijigi (the same who incidentally heard the word *vein* flung in the air when Tomoko died, when Ito fled the Flower Farm after the doctor called) goes to the Flower Farm every Sunday and has taken to visiting Xiu-Xiu. He says, *I would like to visit that pretty, charming Chinese girl, please.* He enters and the familiar smell of browned sugar is there and he doesn't notice the frown on the owner, Miyakosan's face but as he begins to hang up his coat, she cuts him off—

So sorry, but I don't know where Xiu-Xiu is. She's left. Nobody knows. Maybe you can try Yuri—

She's gone?

She's gone. We don't know where.

A new girl with bleached gold hair says, I think that mafia guy took her away. The man with the perm. I think they marry, maybe.

Marry!

Miyako said she saw them together. She say so. Mr. Uno was Xiu-Xiu's last customer. Then she goes to get noodles for lunch. But she doesn't come back. He snagged her at *udon* shop. They say they want to marry. But sometimes they sell them to Saudi Arabia for big money. I say we boycott *Yakuza* here. They do no good.

This story was not true, though the rumor persisted.

It was not Terusan she saw as she walked to buy noodles, that fall day, skipping down the street, in a long pink dress of velvet, her face dark and unpainted, thinking of a soap opera she favored, and the actor Tim, of whom she was fond, it wasn't Terusan she saw near the *udon* shop, by the cedar nursery, it was Ito.

Itosan. What a surprise.

Hello, *oh,* Xiu-Xiu. You look very nice, so very nice.

Thank you.

How about a ride? Is it possible?

Oh, oh, thank you, but I am just buying noodles. You know, lunch.

Oh, I insist. Please.

Well. Can you wait for my noodles? A few minutes?

Of course.

Then she got in his little car, filling the car with the warm paper bag and tempura smell, adjusting her tiny frame in the front seat, her pink dress.

OK, just back to the shop.

How about drive, one minute.

Well, OK. A little bit. I'm, well, not really *working* right now, though.

Of course.

So, it was the suggestion of thirty thousand yen, flat out, in crisp bills, no cuts taken for the Flower Farm, that brought Xiu-Xiu to his house after that, she brought her noodles in the door, as Saga tried to leave, she took off her platforms, and then Xiu-Xiu was hit with the disinfection smell of death, the burned ashes and incense smell, the dank, sour smell of a lonely old man's house, and she knew it well—the tiny plug-in heaters dragged from room to room, the ferocious hairs that grow in their noses and ears, the smell of old sour convenient food.

She stood cautiously.

Let's eat first, *ne?* Ito said, plugging in a heater.

Oh, good. I'm kind of starved.

He scurries over and grabs her bag, sets up a table by the fire, places the plastic containers out, gets his supply of chopsticks and bowls, goes to the fire and throws some hunks of cedar in, brushes his hands and then Ito and Xiu-Xiu sit awkwardly on the folding chairs at his little table, and begin slurping the noodles quickly, chewing the pink chunks of fried shrimp and not talking, from time to time he watches her in a quick glance and feels eager and happy to know he can take the dress off whenever he wants, he can do whatever he wishes to her, it is a good feeling, he reaches his hand over and caresses her thigh, she smiles, he slurps a noodle, he pulls her dress up her thigh and rubs her, *over there is the futon on which Tomoko died, she breathed her last breath on that bed,* ignoring that thought, he stops eating the noodles and uses both hands to pull up the dress and she says, *I would prefer bath first, if it is OK,* he doesn't listen, her underwear is exposed, small deep pink velvet also, and he spreads her legs across the chair, until he sees the tiny triangle of her crotch, her dress hiked up, she is still eating, and she stops, *no, no, continue, ignore me,* he says, so she does (*thirty thousand after all, she is thinking*), he pulls off her underwear, it is difficult and catches around her knees and hips and he throws it (Saga plays with it) and spreads her legs again and sees the full inventory of her sex, as she eats, he watches and he unzips and pulls out his penis and slowly rubs it, *over there on that bed, Tomoko became a skeleton, eaten away,* faster, faster he moves his hand up and down and sees the small bivalve delicacy of Xiu-Xiu and the neat, trimmed carpet of her pubic hair, he pumps hard with his hand and she finishes her noodles and takes her chopsticks and spreads herself, with a slow delicacy, as if she is softly dissecting a flower, and the vulgarity of this appalls him and *that bed, that bed of death, that Tomoko lay in,* he stands and picks her up and the chopsticks fall down, he picks her up like a child and carries her *to the bed, where his wife lay dead for days and where she took her last breath, and, incidentally, where she fed Daisuke from her breasts, where she and Daisuke slept all of the boy's life, this bed is where he takes Xiu-Xiu, the bed where actually Daisuke was born, this bed was where the ball of his head first appeared, where white sheets and towels were spread and she pushed until her face was almost black, and the fluid gushed out, she pushed and Daisuke fell out in a tumble of wet limbs, creased and cheesy,* he took Xiu-Xiu there and lay down and she sat above him and he closed his eyes and she moved in her special way, with tiny gasps, and Ito groaned.

Coming towards the peak of his orgasm, half lost in the union of his flesh with Xiu-Xiu, and torn between interfering thoughts of Tomoko, *her dull cotton nightshirt,* for example, *and the way it hung on the hook by the bed, its floppy fabric,* and Xiu-Xiu, back and forth, back and forth Xiu-Xiu's body above him, impaled on his penis in his own home, the dusk is settling and his house is growing shadowy, Xiu-Xiu is bucking more, he is speeding forward, *Tomoko lying damp on the covers recovering from her bath, warm and small,* he tries to shake off these memories by shaking his head but they fall back in his head, maybe her *ghost* is in the room, maybe he has shown too much disrespect in this act, it hits him with an anesthetic rush— *this is inappropriate.* But it is a thought felt too late, he can't stop, he is looking at Xiu-Xiu's body (opens his eyes to see her twisting stomach with the tattoo, closes them again), but he thinks of his wedding to Tomoko—

Was it the fall? Yes. October 22nd, thirty-two years ago, he remembers the pale white flounder sashimi in the red lacquer bowls, pouring the sake and spilling some on the green kimono, he remembers the dark, flat faces of her parents and the row of relatives, he remembers the Shinto priest smelled bad from his mouth and had a mole on his eye, he feels the tininess of Tomoko's hand in his under the starched, white covers of a hotel. They did not make love that first night. It was three weeks later. It took three weeks for Tomoko to relax, for Ito to work himself in her without pain. After it happened, he held her head. When he did, wet leaves were slapping against the window. It was raining that fall night.

Pale white bones, pale white flesh, her hands the color of raw cotton in winter light, holding the sheets in her last days. In her healthy days, her thin mouth, moving with cackling laughter. A picture he found of her in a dark blue school uniform with dry, dusty knees. *How I enjoy a dance hall!* he heard her say once to a friend on the phone. A dance hall. He did not know she had even been to one. Had she danced with other men there? Had she kissed one of them? Ito pulls his thoughts away to Xiu-Xiu, he pumps more arduously, but it is too late, he feels his erection fading.

He doesn't hear the door open, left unlocked, and Saga's loud meow of recognition because he is lost in the feeling of skin against skin but he feels Xiu-Xiu drape across him and it is an instant where he thinks *how lovely, she is overwhelmed* and another instant where he realizes something is wrong, feels the oily warmth of gushing blood, feels the violence of her movement and he sees as he opens his eyes *his son with a large poker from the fire* and he feels the smacking thud as Daisuke pounds it into her skull, Ito screams, *no, my son, no!* and Daisuke is crying, *My mother! My mother! My mother! My mother! My mother!* Xiu-Xiu is moaning and gurgling now, Ito pulls himself up and holds her, *Xiu-Xiu!* and Xiu-Xiu is still and bloodied and Ito is frantic, groaning, not knowing what to do, he checks her pulse (it is gone), he looks in her eyes (her pupils are doll-black and zoned out) and he knows she is dead, gone, the bed is red, his penis is lying out of his pants and the boy, Daisuke, is standing and not moving, not speaking, splattered with blood.

The two, the father and the son, sit on the bed, on opposite edges. Ito holds her head. Daisuke speaks softly, high-pitched, holding the poker:
Otosan. Otosan.

Otosan. Otosan. Otosan. Otosan. Otosan. Otosan. Otosan. Otosan. Otosan. Otosan. Otosan. Otosan. Otosan. Otosan. Otosan. Otosan. Otosan. His son speaks as if in a praying chant, slowly with cadences. He rocks from front to back, and as he does so does Ito, and Ito doesn't think, *she is dead* or *my son has murdered,* in this moment Ito thinks of things he wishes to buy for the house, *eggs, toilet paper, flypaper, beer,* he thinks of his empty refrigerator, running through its contents, *miso, plum pickles,* forcing himself to think of the list through the dull chant of his son's voice, *Otosan, Otosan,* buying time for some conclusion, hoping the reddened head of Xiu-Xiu will rise and say, *Oh, Itosan, I feel funny,* some squeak of her voice, some peep, so he may assume a heroic poise and save Xiu-Xiu, save his son, he bides his time, he shifts to a list of gardening tasks, *trim pine, mulch berries,* but the son's voice is higher and higher, the wind outside is picking up and rattles through the eaves, the smoke of his fireplace increases as the embers die out, and then Ito returns to the presence of dead Xiu-Xiu, his beloved.

Help me, son. He grabs his arm and pulls him up. Help me here.

Rolling Xiu-Xiu in the futon, they are silent. One only hears Ito's heavy breathing as he struggles with the awkward mattress, wrapping it around her. His strategy is to think of her as a carcass, as flesh, as a particularly large harvested tuna, in order to maintain some calm. He drags his eyes away from her pink dress, her rouged lips, the more human aspects, and focuses on the bulk and its disposal. He grunts to his son, *in the drawer there, top,* and Daisuke comes back with rope. (He is smeared with what appears to be dark purple spots, dried blood. He wears his new *Shaian Rainstorm* T-shirt, Wrangler jeans, and blood-spotted Nikes.) They wrap the rope around and around the futon and tie it securely, Daisuke leans against it and starts crying, little snickering sounds, *Otosan, Otosan, Otosan,* and Ito stops, stands still, *Quiet! Enough!* and Daisuke stops, wipes his nose (further smearing with blood), *go, go, go, wash now, go,* and

Daisuke obeys, runs even, and Ito goes to the kitchen, runs cool water, and scrubs his arms. They both scrub off her blood with soap and scouring brushes and Ito tries to ignore Daisuke's moaning, *mmmwaa! Otosan, Otosan,* and the buzzing quality of the fear present in it, he ignores that and thinks of the best plan of action, *what is reasonable.*

In the car, his son is suddenly a motormouth and Ito notices he has a large smear of blood on his forearm, the boy is blabbering—
Otosan, did you know, that, *mochi* feels like skin? I mean, just like skin! It's weird (and he has a packet of green tea *mochi,* a pounded rice delicacy, he waves around) and it's chewy like skin, not that I, not that I, not that I, oh, oh, oh, oh did I tell you I got a new game yesterday, Aunt gave me it it is Death Battle Peak 5.0, and, it is ruthless. Ruthless, oh look, there is my school over there, hey—
Aaah, shush! Come on. Be quiet. Look what's going on here. Oh.
Pay attention.
It is dark, they are on the old side road by the river, the car stops and they get out and have to pull out that futon again, both guys, they have to push it in the river over the bridge and there she goes. Down in the water.
Ito has some instant wipes in the car. They wipe the last traces of her blood off. Ito drives Daisuke to his aunt's house. He lets him out and they don't speak.

That is the last time he saw him.

chapter fourteen

Menu:

Lemonade and Vodka

Mountain Rhine Wine

Baby.

Sounding like a far voice in a back cave, so gentle and soft, and Mariane melts on the word and falls into the sweet, creamy memory of her baby's smell, the sugary milkiness of it, the pinkness of her skin, her red gums, her arms roped with fat, the feel of her little mouth on her breast, patting her downy head, telling her she is a *good little baby, Mama's best little baby, the sweetest in the world.*

Mariane is lying on the sill in Ito's apartment, 5:01 A.M., her nostrils expanding with each breath, her hair covering one eye, right hand crunched under right cheek, mouth contorted with a slight drop of drool gathering at the edge of her lip, the slight warm lemonade odor of a *lush* seeping from her person. The apartment dark and soft, like felt, sake bottles askew on the tables, sour cigarette butts mashed into a plate.

At first as she sleeps, her mind buzzes with snippets of the day hemmed together with surreal, vaguish results—Yoshi, talking about horse races, the restaurant a different shape, much larger with extra rooms, then *anxious, anxious,* people gathering at the door, hundreds of them, demanding seats, the sake machine pouring without control, waiting and waiting for sushi that never gets made. She quivers slightly with these nervous dreams, breaks their rhythm by shifting, then another starts. She shakes her head to the other side, exposing the bar lines of the window on her right cheek, falling into deeper REM. Her mind settles like a cool, dark lake, her dreams plunge to the bottom, to old memories buried in synapses and limbic coils, dredging with chunks of forgotten, despised smells, words—sharp, unpleasant things.

She smells Raleigh, North Carolina, the wafting warm air of summer, of vinegary barbecue, sweat tinged with sugary deodorant, pesticides, the iron smell of red dirt. Feels the plain, flat sun of the backyard on her face. Smells Carl, her husband, old Carl in a short-sleeved madras shirt, Carl of Vitalis smells and cherry pipe tobacco, herbaceous, greasy Carl. Hands in his back pocket, slid in upside down like pieces of toast. Her body feels lighter in its youth.

It had been sixteen days of living in the rambler on Hillshire Drive that was dark and over-air-conditioned, decorated in old colors of cheddar cheese and brownish orange, with piles of Lawrence Welk records, and a smell she hated, especially out in the kitchen, like sour old sandwiches made of mayonnaise. Carl said she could just help out, for room and board, shop at Piggly Wiggly, vacuum and such, keep the place up. When he was around, he got too close and would hug her, smell her hair, rub against her and she could feel a hard pellet in the middle of his body where he moved in little pumps. He'd kiss her against the refrigerator, no tongue, and squeeze her titties, and then pull back, *I'm sorry, I'm sorry. I gots to watch myself, sugar. Janie up there and all.* One day he said, in his hot breathiness in her ear, on the couch after TV, *you done it before, girl?* No, she said. *That's good, that's real good to hear. I'm gonna wait till it's proper. The proper time.*

I always knew the ways of old men. I knew they had to pee more, and were slower. I loved the way Carl was happy to hold me and smell my hair. Called me a Barbie doll. I was living the life of a princess. At night I slept in the guest room and Carl slept in a cot next to Janie, his wife, because she was getting more and more fragile and he cried a lot, that man, hardly had any strength left or anything. Carl worshiped my sixteen-year-

*old self, grilled me steaks out on his patio and even fried hush puppies, too.
I never knew a man could cook.*

I begun to think, I was happy.

Sixteen days of living there, nursing his wife with the paper
skin and the eyes faint and glassy and gone, her arms like bent twigs
she'd move around to wash under, placing a bright blue *chucks* under
her nonexistent ass, peeling off her heavy diaper full of urine with
a vegetable smell, like asparagus, washing her down, then feeding
her a few bites of tomato soup, Carl'd come in and pull up the blinds,
how ya doing, Missus? how ya feeling? Her glassy eyes just staring at
the wall.

*Do you love her much, I asked him later as we ate a dinner of ham
and grits.*

*Oh, yeah, something awful, back then. I was doing journeyman work
in Raleigh and we just got married. She was a sweet thing. And then, I
don't know.*

He sighed and held her hand.

*Then. Things just fade out between us. Something just died. I sup-
pose because she had a miscarriage.*

Oh, no. Poor Janie. What happened?

*I don't rightly know. Things were all good and we had painted the
nursery. She started bleeding, "spotting" the doctor said, no biggy, but then,
like clumps start coming and, you know. It's all over. She goes to the hospital. She got mad at me, like I did it or something. I mean it. Things were
never the same.*

Never the same?

*After that day. It was one those summer days in June, hot as hades.
I'd set up one of them pools out back. I was in Fort Lynn that day, rigging
a mall. Big job. Janie's sister tracked me down and said the baby was gone,
but she was doing all right at the Methodist hospital. So I finished setting
the concrete. I was just, you know, being practical. I'd have lost us two
days' pay if I left right then, and I figured. Figured it was gone. Too late.*

Janie in tears when I walk in. After that, she just kind of faded out. We didn't have no more kids. Through the years, I just didn't feel nothing for her, pretty obvious she felt the same. Like living with a ghost.

Sixteen days of washing her sheets, vacuuming the house, cooking grilled cheese and scrambled eggs for Carl, putting Queen Anne's lace in vases around the house, wearing Janie's housecoats wrapped around her waist with Carl's ties, sitting by Janie reading her *Redbook,* looking through her closet and finding her old yellowed wedding dress, wearing her pointy pumps and looking through the pocket-books and the drawers of makeup, old brass tubes of lipstick with red hardened lumps, boxes of sweet-smelling powder, and last week she found a box in the far corner of her closet, a red one tied up with rubber bands, pushed under her shoe boxes, Mariane opens it and finds a pile of letters, about fifteen or so.

Janie my Love. I can't wait to see you honey. I am dreaming of your sweet smile, my darling. I may be coming through town next week for work and see the family, I will plan to meet you in the usual, though I will call. Love you always, Jimmy.

Dear Janie, Last Tuesday night was the most glorious night of my life. I can't wait to see you. June is leaving to visit her mother in Florida with the kids I will be in town on business for one week—

Mariane takes the letters out and stick them in the middle of the trash, then bundles it up and flings it in the Dumpster. She doesn't tell Carl about them.

On the sixteenth night it finally happens, she dies, late at night, they could hear the machine beeping, waking them up, a big loud *beeeeeep,* Mariane said, wake up, Carl, wake up, he looks around, groggy and she said, call the doctor, Carl, she's gone. There she is in the backyard the next morning with Carl, watching the ambulance drive away, he in his madras shirt, smelling of Vitalis, smelling the red dirt, the ambulance slowing driving away. Carl was crying, pulling his hands out of his pockets to wipe the tears that were sliding into the creases of his face. *Well, that's that. What do you know. That's that.* When the people come and the funeral happens, Mariane stays home and cleans. Carl goes to Piggly Wiggly and buys onion dip with vegetables, chicken wingdings, barbecue and slaw, and ice tea to bring to the funeral home. Mariane goes with him and sees Janie in the white oak casket lined in a poly-blend sateen, sees her hands so pale and bony. Thirty-three people come and drink tea and white zinfandel in plastic cups. Mariane isn't feeling so hot, she leaves early and Carl smiles and says, *you go on, hon.*

When he comes back, she's sitting on the bed. He comes over, smelling of bourbon, and lies down. He closes his eyes, covers them with his hand. *Oh, Lordy. Shit,* he says. You want some ice tea, Mariane says. *No, ma'am, I don't.* He turns to her. Mariane is wearing shorts she bought at Wal-Mart and a halter top. He reaches over and undoes the tie around her neck. He pulls down her shirt and her breasts bounce out, pink, puffed areolas, young and soft. *Carl.* Hussh, hush, he says. Don't speak now. *But Carl.*

The room is dark and the air conditioner is on full blast. He undoes his shirt a bit, unzips his pants, pulls down her shorts. Not knowing what to do, she lies there. Carl pulls down her underwear, pulls her legs back, saying *alrighty, alrighty,* in his cool, soft whisper, *just a bit, just a b-i-i-t,* he pushes himself in, she feels a momentary pinch, but really not much, mainly his sharp hipbones ramming and gouging against her, just when she shifts to accommodate his weight, he lunges up *Goddamn! Goddamn you sweet, sweet child!* and he lays his sweaty face on hers, mumbling things, smelling of fried chicken, salty tears, bourbon and cherry tobacco.

Honey sweet baby child, he said to her that night in bed, *how the hell did I land you?*

Shortly thereafter, Mariane became pregnant, as they used no birth control. She was unsure, scared, sick quite a bit. Carl was pleased as could be and they married, a simple civil ceremony in the town hall. Most of his friends grew scarce in disapproval. Mariane became a full-fledged *housewife*.

Carl said, *you can count on me, sugar.*

Carl was getting a pension, so they had adequate money. Mariane cleaned and cooked and made chicken and dumplings, biscuits and gravy, all his favorite things from a dirty, yellowed index card box of Janie's in the kitchen. It had been passed down by her mother. Tomato aspic, fried chicken, she cooked and cooked as the baby grew, as her stomach popped, and Carl painted decoys in the garage, beautiful gleaming ducks they had on display all over the house, and he'd play golf a lot, too, and then, when he was home, he'd nap a lot. On the couch, his mouth gaping. She'd say, let's watch *Saturday Night Live* and she'd fix some popcorn and she'd be laughing at Dan Aykroyd and Carl, Carl wouldn't last a few minutes, gaping mouth, snoring, what she started to feel was, *Hell, I'm alone here. With an old man. Eight months pregnant.*

She was getting lonesome for her mother. Mariane called her up and her mother cried and begged her to come home, said she was sick. Mariane asked Carl if she could come to them, and he said *no*. He'd had enough of sick people and that was that. *Go down to her for a while.* So, OK, she'd do that but she wanted to wait until the baby came. Her mother said OK, honey. She asked, who is this man you've gone and married. And Mariane just told her, Carl. She didn't seem to have much strength. Mariane didn't ask a lot of questions. It was her liver, her mother said.

But about a month later, her mother's landlord calls and says she had a heart attack on the lawn last night. She's at the morgue. Mariane's crying, and Carl arranges for it all, the funeral, and as she's packing to go down there—

Bright liquid, yellow as Gatorade, spills down her legs, through the panty hose, on the cream-colored carpeting. Carl picks her up, *you ain't going nowhere, hon.*

Mariane has the baby. Sweetest little red thing. They call her
Daisy.

So afterwards, Mariane really gets into the Mom thing. She
buys the baby all kinds of things, monitors, swings, soft teddy bears,
frilly onesies, little hats, white lace booties, pushes her around the
neighborhood in her stroller, but she admits she was getting a bit
tired, even the lawn guy named Bobby noticed it, it was hard work,
cleaning, feeding, reading books to her, bathing her, she got a bit
run-down, as anyone would in that position.

*I was lonesome, tired, baby crying and feeding all the time. We hired
a lawn guy named Bobby Baxter and Co. to lug some stuff, burn some
weeds, cut, bush-hog. Kind of a red-faced, bullish guy, with a hard, lined
neck. Shaved blond head that looked fuzzy. He rode, standing, on a big,
industrial mower and drove a big-tired truck that he quickly parked on a
slant. I'd give him lemonade and one day he said, when Carl had made it
clear he was heading into Raleigh for a few hours, hmm, wouldn't mind a
bit of something in there, you know. Bit of what? I said, Oh, you know,
something spice it up. Juice it up. I looked at him kind of dumb. Liquor,
woman, he said laughing. So I laced it with a bit of vodka Carl kept in the
living room on a tray along with some Wild Turkey and half a bottle of
cream sherry, and he sat back on the counter, his big legs spread apart, and
sipped it, said, ah, that is good, yes, that is tasty but then Daisy started
crying on the monitor, I went up there and rocked her and I was aware he
could hear all our sounds. When I came back down he said, bet you need
a break too, hunh? Young gal like yourself, so I had some spiked lemonade, too. And we sat at the metal table and just drank like that, joking
around, told me he'd been working for two years on his own, slugging away,
girlfriend does his books and then I reload his drink and he stretches, musses
my hair up and heads out to mow some more. But I was kind of shitfaced.
I fell asleep up next to Daisy. When I woke up, Bobby was gone and it
was almost time for Carl to get back.*

Next day, Bobby says, hey, while I'm out in the backyard, hey, beautiful. I could see him sweaty through the awning of my hand, how about you, he was whispering secretly, how about you top off this thermos, eh? Add some poison? So I went in and while Carl was napping, loaded us down again, and I laughed and laughed with Daisy in the wade pool while Bobby drove round and round, waving at us.

But then he was finished, the yard looked good, so he stopped coming, but I got used to the lemonade. Every day I snuck a little, added a little water to the bottle and it seemed to expand the day, to speed it forward, to add more fun. Then, nights, Carl and I start drinking wine with dinner and I just kind of continued through the night, Almaden Mountain Rhine, in the jug. Laundry lying in piles. The house unvacuumed. Start buying TV dinners, and slacked off on cooking. Most days I'm kind of happy you could say, dizzy, buzzed, kind of floating. Drunk as a skunk, baby crying. Carl says to me, are you sick or what? What, what is going on here, woman, the baby, the baby and one day he says:

Goddamn, you're shitfaced.

And I said, what?

Yes, you are.

One day I realized Carl, that sweet man, was being rather nasty and mistrusting. I don't think he realized how hard it is to run a house and take care of a child, especially at my age, and some secrecy between him and his sister-in-law developed. I'd catch him on the phone and he'd look shifty and hang up quickly. Or he'd frown and say, you OK? Hunh? and I'd say, sure. Maybe they were having some kind of affair, or maybe they were plotting against me, or maybe she poisoned him against me, I don't know, but one day I dropped our dinner by mistake and he said, Oh, goddamn (it was a platter of fried chicken), goddamn it to hell, you drunken thing, you god-damned drunk-en thing. Now I may have had an inclination to a glass or so of Rhine wine, that was my fav, you know, but come on. It was a stressful life. But that was really rude. Really pushing it.

Goddamn! You're a damn drunk. Tending a baby and be drunk! You ought to be ashamed yourself!

I am not! Liar!

Oh, hoo, woman. You reek of liquor all day. Going through three jugs of Rhine wine this week.

So hard to get up in the mornings. Carl was a good daddy. Carl got up and fed her a bottle. I was heavily involved in the lives of the soaps, Luke, Laura and General Hospital *became the main interest in my life, I imitated her makeup and clothes and spent hours drinking wine, wondering about their lives and problems and admiring the clean, glossy interiors of the show. And I'm starting to have a problem, because Carl says only one jug of Rhine wine a week so I would like to get some vodka somehow, but being underage that is a problem, so I found Bobby's card on the refrigerator and called him, and his girlfriend answered and I told her we needed some work done, but when he got on the phone, I came right out and said, I'd like you to buy me some vodka, I'll pay of course, and he says, sure, girl. You got it. So we go to a tavern for lunch, he has a Reuben and I have onion rings and a whiskey sour (his suggestion) even though I'm seventeen, Bobby says, Hell, yes, she's twenty-one, Denise. She's married and all. You see her baby there.*

Then Bobby buys me a thing of vodka later, while I wait in the car with Daisy, feeding her a bottle, he comes out gripping the paper bag, says, here you go, and drives in silence for a while, then says maybe there's something you can do for me, he says it quietly. See, thing is, I do believe I have a little thing for you here, I believe I've gotten a little sweet on you, you know? And I-I can't stop thinking about you, like, all the time and basically, it means, that basically, a-a kiss would be quite a fine thing, just a little kiss?

Can I please just kiss you, Mariane?

We stop by the field, the baby is sweaty, it's a hot day. He reaches over the gearshift, across the baby and his dry lips brush mine, just quickly and lightly, and I say, OK, and he says Okeydoke, thanks, thanks a lot.

That meant a lot. Anything I can do in the future to help out, just holler. He drives me home, Carl swears at me as I come in, takes the baby, the vodka drops, crashes, smashes on the floor, baby crying, yells this crap gonna stop.

Imagine my horror to know Carl and the sister-in-law have plotted against me, getting the police involved, child welfare services. She came by in the morning and came in all official and picked up Daisy and Carl had packed a bag of her stuff, and I started screaming and Carl held me back and said, please, come on now, Mariane, things just a little out of hand for a child here. Just a little too crazy. And there was nothing I could do. She drove off with her and that's when this woman Loretta came by, a pudgy lady in a pale blue suit and a clipboard, she took my blood pressure and even a blood sample and Carl said, here's the deal, sweetie. I love you. You know that. But I can't be allowing this kind of crap in a decent home, and messing up my baby. Lord knows you are too young. But we're going to work this through. That's right, Loretta chimed in, you can do it, you can walk from this, child. We're going to fix you up, he said.

You're going to rest it out a bit, at a nice location up the road near Charlotte, and then, then, when you get a grip, you come on back. I know you been drinking like a fish, whoring with that damn lawn monkey—

And he went on and on and she drove me down the road. That day was the last I saw Daisy. When I got to the hospital, I went down the hall and entered the side stairs. I went to the laundry room and left through the exit. I hitchhiked to a gas station and called Bobby. I wasn't going to stay there for three months. I could fix things myself. Bobby drove up later and we went to an Econo Lodge. He bought a bottle of champagne. He listened, sitting in a chair as I cried my eyes out on the bed, and told him everything, drinking champagne from little plastic cups. Then he came over and kissed me slowly, saying, goddamn, you are the sweetest, poorest thing and he took my clothes off, one by one, and we made love on top of the bumpy chenille covers. Then he called up for more champagne.

We can go to New York, he says. I got a connection there and we can fix you up. We'll get some money real quick and hire a crack lawyer who'll get your baby back quick and you can get custody from that ol' fart. Get ourselves hitched, make some more babies. Blow this fucking town, get ourselves hitched, get the hell out.

I just want my baby back.

Don't worry about that. That's the first thing on the list. One week, two at the most.

We had a lot of fun together, Bobby and me, kept saving money, I am still saving money, but so many things get in the way, got to get the right home set up, because I want to do it perfect this time, nursery and all, the right crib, have you seen those round cribs, those are so neat, want to have a closetful of little clothes and such, need to work, need to play, have a little fun, too, to take my mind off, the sun goes up and down, I miss the weight of her in my hands, that sweet baby smell, I hope she hasn't lost that, like milk and butter cookies and salt, oh, my girl, my Daisy, not too long now, soon, soon—

Mariane wakes up in a sweat.

The room is lightened, chilly, buzzing from the refrigerator, smelling of old smoke and her face is sore from sleeping on the windowsill.

For how long? And where the hell is Ito?

And my drinks, and my *Twinkies?*

chapter fifteen

Menu:

Vietnamese Sausage and Bread (*banh mi gio*)

Scottish Shortbread

Jasmine Tea

Ton is scared. Ton is hungry.

Ton is sore from carrying the old man.

He rubs his arms and then gets the medical kit they keep in the closet, *quick, quick, quick.* You can hear the shuffle of his feet, *scuff, scuff, scuff,* running around. *Bang,* he knocks a tin box of shortbread cookies from Scotland over. It's early, early morning and his mother is already gone for her cleaning job in the hotel and she left a thermos of hot water for tea and some French bread and sausage on the counter and Ton is *hungry,* Ton is *scared,* and his mother will be back, and why didn't he think of that when he dragged the man here. *Why forget about Mama?*

Scared. The man, Ito, is sprawled on the couch. Ton wonders if the man is going to need a real doctor. He crouches next to him and prepares to bathe the bloody part of his head.

Hungry. He dunks a cloth in warm water and liquefies the blood on Ito's sticky hair and rinses, again and again. Ito moans slightly, his eyes showing whites.

Ton is scared, *scared, scared* the man might die on his couch, might bleed all over the place and his mother might yell, he doesn't like it when his mother yells, and he starts whimpering, sucking his fingers, yelling in Vietnamese *don't die, don't die.* He walks on his knees over to the altar of his ancestors and lies prone and thinks, to them, please help this man and me, please don't let her get mad or him die. I am only trying to help. I mean well, I only.

But then, he hears her light padding step, the key in the door. He jolts himself back and whirling with fear thinks to hide Ito, he skitters over and grabs his legs, knocking down a vase in the meantime, pouring stiff daisies all over Ito's knees and water all over the blanket, he pulls him off the couch, halfway, leaving an unfortunate smear of reddish brown across the top, and then just throws a few pillows on top of him, he heaves and whines, the door opens and she is there, putting down a package and spinning around, screeching, *Ooooo,* her hands at her head, *Oooo,* her cheeks, she stares at the scene in front of her, *Ooooo,* her son, slightly bloodied, and an old man, obviously injured, half on the couch, half off, the particular high-pitched smell of Ton's fear sweat in the air, a smell she dreads.

As his mother, she has come to know well his blunders at hiding things, his pitiful attempts, so she is expert in picking up the bump in the bed, the pile of pillows against the closet, the huge pile of crisp paper towels in the trash in his desperate attempts to hide from her small eyes as dark and shiny as crickets—to hide *Penthouse,* to hide the sperm-soaked sheets, to hide his underwear full of feces, to hide anything at all which uncovers himself, which when found is flung in disgust and ranted over, *this is a dirty thing, this magazine,* until he sits on the floor and cries and she will stop and say, *we have to be more strong next time,* but notice there is always a next time, because you can't take something away from a person without replacing it with something, you can't leave a gap, there will always be his hidden, scurrying acts of rebellion and her oniony face contorted in anger.

Ooooo, she is whining, she sees this man, her son, *Oooo,* and flashing through her brain in the Vietnamese dialect of the Phan Thiet region, her thoughts gel in panic—

Oh, no, *no, no,* I think this will happen *my Ton* oh no *violence* I'm always worry that his side will show *to kill* hurt people gets *so angry* sometimes he must've he must've tried to kill this man that time with that girl *so hard to protect him,* I try, I try, Oh, no, *OH, no,* this bad he beat up old man, *for money?* For money? Just angry? I always say, I know, he can't handle, *can't handle,* can't handle.

Her thoughts are whirling around like this, kalunking in her head, she's got her arms outstretched and she's only whining slightly, she's unwinding, unhinging, the mother of a *troubled child,* a child who is different from the rest, knows this so quickly, as quick as thought, but is shrewd to hide, to cover the signs, to give the benefit of the doubt, to justify and explain, she has cleaned and covered and hidden Ton's indiscretions in every way, in order to prevent the worst horror, someone putting him away, where he would be beaten, or mistreated and taken from the only one who loves him, so concerning the *rape of that young Chinese girl in the restaurant* years ago, she was quick to blame the girl and move on, get him away, although he insisted it was *love,* and she was careful to home-school him, lest others think him an idiot and put him in an institution, and when the women at the church told him she should get special teacher, she laughed and said, *Oh, you don't know about it! Ton is getting a special tutor because he is gifted musician, like a special gift he has.* Which was not true, but she hoped it was, and she really felt, if she kept him safe, he would one day reveal his special gift. She had heard of this happening. She had articles cut out from papers of idiot savants who surprised their parents by playing Mozart by ear. It *would* happen. She believed in the power of will, of prayer, and now as she whines and flails, her mouth opens and gushes out,

TON!!

Ton lurches around, crying, *Maaa!*

She rushes over to him, whispering in Vietnamese,

Oh, my son, is he dead? Ooo, this is mistake, don't hurt people, what happen? Ton? What happen?

Mama, I find him hurt on street.

No lies, Ton, no lies.

True! Mama, he was hurt.

She smacks him hard, Ton! You hurt him, he is old man! Oh, trouble! Is he dead?

Mama! Maybe he is dead!

Ton had long ago learned he had a guilty face, that a sickly smile would creep across his face whenever she accused him of something and that it made him look guilty as hell, so he gave up trying.

She leans down to the old man's chest.

No, son. Thanks God. No. He is alive. Go put water on!

Mama! I didn't do it!

Go! Put water on. I make him tea.

She cradles Ito's head in her hand.

This old man been drinking! You attack drunk old man. Only cowards do this.

Mama! I don't do that! I only—

Water! Water, damn it!

He runs to the kitchen, the fluorescent light flickers a few times before it comes on. *Poor old man,* she says. She straightens him, and heaves him up on the couch, attempts to, and Ton runs over and helps her, she grabs the cloth from the table and lays it on his brow, *get me new cloth, here, Ton,* and he runs off, and she gathers up Ito's head, *and the cleanup begins,* she starts singing, a low soft voice she used when Ton was a baby, a voice she uses when he has a fever or a toothache, low, quivering, in an old version of her language she sings an ancient rhyme, *when I was on the river, long ago in my youth, I re-mem-ber the birds of prey, high in the summer sky,* then she stops and yells in a long spewed sentence, *You are bad boy to hurt old man, bad boy bad boy bad boy!* She has tears now because she remembers Ton as a baby. He was a good baby, she thinks. This man do nothing to you! He is drunk old man!

Mama, I don't.

Lies! Lies!

Ito, on some far, translucent level, begins to sally forth, to open his mind, to recognize again the signs and symbols of the day and time he exists and operates in, but at this moment he swings in a light haze of senses, the smell of blood around our face, indeed *the* first smell, blood, and it contains its own imprint of identity and fear and death and birth, as if he was reborn through blood again, his mind had left off before in the sad haze of a remembered murder, committed by his son, and he slowly awakes now, to the smell of his own blood, calling forth not only that day he rolled Xiu-Xiu into a futon, but the moment he was born from his mother's bloody portal, and now another time, mid-childhood, holding his father's hand in the icy, gray fog of Kariba Mountain, sitting so still his legs lost sensation, acorns burned small holes in his buttocks, pins and needles cascaded through his small thighs, he slept, he woke, he heard the scratchy sounds of animals as they woke, predawn, in a fog of microbial dirt and sootiness, bark, leaves crushed into mush beneath him, the unexpected lurch of his father's body, the *sw-ooookkuh* of his father's arrow and the little bleat of the deer, crunching down into the leaves, scurrying through the crisp floor, finding the animal, a stick from its chest, straight and perilous through its heart, still beating, its eye as terrifying as a sliver of mashed liver and the way it flattened and lost glossiness as the father sliced the neck, fetched its heart in his hand and made Ito eat it, made him drink the blood, the smell of old nails, the smell of mildewy rainwater left in a pail, the turnip crunch of the purple heart, blood smells mixed with the incense from the altar in this boy's house, reminding his mind of Tomoko's funeral, the smell of no blood, veinlessness, of palehoned bone hunks and ashes in a jar, next to her smiling picture, taken at one new year, a picture where who would think, *this picture will accompany my scorched bones,* the incense and blood, two odd mixed scents pull him up from the backwater of sleep and damaged nerves, his eyes flutter, hot tea seeps in his mouth, the bitter taste of jasmine and he awakes foggily to a seesaw cawing of Vietnamese, the angry hot eyes of the mother and the frail bleating of the son from away,

Oh! OH! Waking! she says, man is waking!

Uhhh, says Ito. His head is dizzy and saliva floods his mouth.

Drink tea. Drink this, I so worry. Worry. You very sick, man. You sick and I worry, you feeling better, feeling better?

★ ★ ★

Wh-wh-, says Ito, and he gags, splashing tea down his front, some on the woman.

Oh, get me a cloth, Ton.

Ton, like a hulking ape, comes running, sniffling, with a roll of paper towels.

Not *whole* thing, you.

Wh-*where.* Where?

With his strong accent they hear a loud forced emission of air, *W-W-WAIYA.* Mother and son look at each other.

Where?

Her face unfolds with some recognition of the sound.

At my home. You at my *home.*

Mama! I found him! Ton says in Vietnamese.

You found him nothing, she says to him, and then falls back into her vowelish dialect and the boy answers back, chopped fragments of Vietnamese feline sounds and wooden blocks of English, strewn together in an odd macramé of soft and hard, and Ito's eyes are open, he sees the mother's worried hawkish eyes, and the boy's guilty pleading words and eyes and gains a sense, accustomed to piecing together fragments of unknown language with visual signs to understand, he gains a sense that she thinks the boy did him some harm and he wonders if he is in a perilous situation, his mind grasps some explanation and he sputters over the looming space in his head, he remembers the taxi driver and his comment on American women, then the fish market, he remembers losing his money and feels a huge surge of shame, for it was Yoshi's money, one thousand dollars for fish for two weeks, remembers sitting on the bench in his sadness, and then does he remember falling or did someone hit him? He wonders if he should get up, if he can, then suddenly he remembers Mariane, at his apartment, the fish, the Twinkies, waiting for him.

Where's his fish?

★ ★ ★

W-WAI-ya! he spits out in a burst of throbbing pain.

They both spiral in his direction, arguing stops.

Where. My. Fish.

Ha! Fish! Old man ask for fish! she cackles.

Mama, he had a package in his hand, smelly package. Wrapped-up fish. It dropped somewhere.

My Bonito, Ito whispers. First of spring.

You can always get more fish, fish cheap. You almost die, more important.

She gets a warm cloth, wipes down his head.

I clean, I take care. Old fish not important. Living more important.

Mariane.

Who Mariane? Your wife? I call for you?

Oh, yes. Call for me, please. Call this number 998. Uh, ah. Take easy now.

9–9–8, uh, 4–4–5–3. Sorry so much trouble.

No problem, no problem

She runs to get the phone, fear dripping down her spine. If her son could attack people now, it was a problem. She had to make this man happy. What if Mariane child welfare lady? What if she is policewoman? She brings the phone.

Just tell number, I ring.

998

OK.

4453.

Good. Ringing. Ringing. Here.

Ring.

Ring.

Ring.

chapter sixteen

So, let's back up a bit and go over that singing-in-a-band time, that time when Bobby Baxter and Mariane are in New York City, she's left her baby in North Carolina, when they live on a fourth floor walk-up on St. Marks, a dusty step surrounded by Jamaican Rastas hanging at all hours, booming music, and the teenagers clustered there, too and Mariane has to edge by them daily, the same ones with friendly faces, the young girl with her oily ringlets and wet, red mouth, smoking a cigarette, a crisp, navy blue polka-dot stroller by her side at all hours with her tiny baby, Joey *Joon-ya,* Mariane has to edge by this and mumble, *hey,* at all hours, let's say an average of about 4:40 and 5:35, that bad time for Mariane, that's when she would slink by the kids, *how ya doin',* and what is notable is how she shut down part of herself in reaction to that baby, Joey Junior, how that part of her mind was temporarily draped in a black cloth, with the helpful anesthesia of alcohol further dampening these sentiments, how she never poked her head in the canopy of his stroller and said, *aww, how cute!* as everyone did.

After all, she had left her baby a mere two weeks ago while still breast-feeding, at the clinic they gave her medication to dry them up, but that throbbing rush of tingling still occurred when she saw a baby, any baby, or thought of them, that letdown of milk was happening without her control, her breasts would fill with pins and needles as they engorged and dripped through her bra, and this would happen as she walked by Joey Junior, smiling to the young girl, his mom, pretending she didn't notice the baby, but her eyes had skipped over the far dark rectangle of the stroller way back two blocks ago, and she had trained them to look at the shop windows, but it was too late, the hypothalamus needs only the tiniest grain of scent or a flash of image or the sound of a cry to bolt its command with the surge of prolactin, *Oh, fuck,* milk already dripped through her shirt, as she said, *Evening,* and slipped past them, Mariane would stroke her mind with sweet comforting words, as people who are used to doing this do, *OK, that's good, because you need to be ready for your baby,* because Mariane built her own papery lantern of excuses, reasons. Whereas Ito suffered between the contrasts of what he thought and what he said, Mariane only allowed the words and thoughts which contributed to the fast-advancing euphemistic world she allowed, Mariane kept herself in a modern playground of fun, of having a good time, words like, *party, drinkies, fun-loving, good times, living life to the fullest,* these were allowable concepts and she ignored the sounds or possibilities of *problems, fucked up, dead end* or *alcoholism.* In fact, Mariane had long rationalized that her drinking was a fun pastime as she gathered economical strength and not the actual eye of the storm, that it could be abandoned when the proper substitute became available, such as wealth or fame, and that her drinking had a minor, fleeting presence in her life.

At this point, one could say she was at a beginning part of her addiction, and if analyzed by a physician in the protocol of the day, the C.A.G.E. methodology, another acronym popular in modern medicine, the first question being, *Have you ever felt the need to Cut back on your drinking?* and the second being, *Have you felt Annoyed when people criticized your drinking? Have you ever felt Guilty about your drinking? Do you ever take a morning "Eye-opener"?* Mariane would've scored a resounding yes to every question, yet she probably would have dodged, or stretched it a bit, or just lied really, and as she walked up the stairs to her apartment, where Bobby slept, light heaving breaths as she undressed, he'd wake up and look at her a few cold moments with his bleary red eyes from sleep, *Mariane, Hon? Dollbaby? What's happening to you, sugar? Didn't we come here to get it together?*

Bobby Baxter was a kind man, really, with simple aspirations, he hoped to create a little home with this forsaken young girl he'd taken up with, this young eighteen-year-old, with the pretty mouth and dark eyes, this slight thing with her pale, curvy hips and flower petal breasts, whom he'd taught to drink on hot North Carolina summer afternoons, just because he was bored and she was bored. He had been married before and that didn't work out, had a girl-friend named Sue, a big girl with blond hair, and they'd been off and on for a while, and he had a reasonable amount of work cutting lawns, laying mulch, planting bulbs, saw his mom and stepdad on Sundays in their small brick rambler by the lake, ate her green bean casserole with gusto, enjoyed a bit of sports on the TV with Bob, the stepdad, then would go home and lie down with Sue, they'd grapple a bit in the bed, and he pretty much led his life like this day after day, and was taken aback by *this young thing,* this pretty little girl in cutoffs with a baby and an old geezer husband, I mean *how the hell did that happen,* softest, prettiest thing, he'd mow the lawn and watch her breast-feed that baby, pull up her halter and that baby would suck on the nipple, pink and pointy in the micro-second he saw it exposed, and there's a whole world of difference in the way a man views that and a woman. Because if you have a baby, your body does a weird thing, it turns off your sexuality (that flood of prolactin again) and the baby at your breast, sucking, only creates a haze of beaming Mommy feelings, almost like an invisible wall comes down, but Bobby thinks, bet that's a turn-on, that baby just sucking away, bet she likes it, in the same way he imagines a woman likes a tampon up there all the time. Betcha she does.

And, yes, he liked to drink a bit, it was true, lots and lots of beer, really, with the occasional Lynchburg Lemonade (addition of bourbon) and, drunk on beer on the weekends, Sue and he would do it on the bed, before football, and after a while he substituted Sue's reddish face with the pale, blue-eyed one of that girl, that fine young baby at his job, floating on the incredible suggestion of moving inside her body. Bobby Baxter, actually, had fallen in love with Mariane, big time, but like love often can be, as a promise of what he could be, a shinier, newer Bobby Baxter, that this fresh young thing, who liked to party and whoop it up, just like him, unlike Sue, who tended her dogs and read mysteries at night, *oh, you go ahead, I got my tea,*— No, Mariane gave him an inventory of possibilities, even at thirty-three, he could start the whole *she*-bang again, and he fell for that. He fell in love with Bobby Baxter at eighteen, curling blond hair against his brown neck, before a permanent white crease developed there from the sun, before his shoulders were a mass of brown connected freckles, before Sundays were spent in front of a wide screen.

He would drink at her house and loved her tinkling laughter, and as he saw her life fall apart, he was gleeful, he was all too ready to pick up the pieces and ditch his life, to zoom off in his souped-up truck with this sweet-smelling girl at his side, leaving Sue pissed, his parents confused and leaving most of his clothes and things in the apartment with Sue (it was her place, anyway) and besides, he was going to get new stuff, taking this young girl to New York City to start something, and it was all cemented by the actual act of making love to Mariane, *the girl was fine and a sweet thing, no less,* she found a job in a restaurant quickly, and he did construction in Brooklyn, and he was off at six and would wait for Mariane to get back at ten, tonight he had made a pot roast with Lipton's onion soup mix and some wine, and the smell filled the apartment, he had paper plates set up, a bottle of some white zinfandel, even dessert from an Italian bakery (*Veniero's,* around the corner, good cannolis), and then Mariane didn't come home at ten, nor at eleven and on and on, the pattern this week, coming back at three, four, even five, trashed, he'd discuss it with her, *the baby, girl,* and she'd get all defensive, like, *I got to be ready for her, I can't have them take her away again.*

It was like she instantly fell in with a cool, slick crowd at work of people, some entertainers, who would go for a drink or two, in addition to the shift drink, and this produced a feeling of exhilaration which fed into itself, they'd move on to a club, and this was all new to little Mariane—A club!—In New York City, and to after-hours places, the night couldn't be long enough for her, it was a glittering stream of rush, from taxi to club to drink to laugh to the attention of the men, and basically, this particular night, of the pot roast, marked a certain turn taken—a certain fellow waiter, Carlos, had danced with her all night, and they had made out, first tentatively and then freely, and it was wild excitement, pure ecstasy for Mariane, in her mind, it was all fair substitute for the lack of the baby, this fast life, she began at this very point to push that baby into a corner of her head, for the time being, as Bobby waited for her, as Carlos and Mariane sucked face.

Bobby was offering up a new model of a home, with his concern and warm meals and aching caring, and Mariane had a heat-seeking need for disarray which skirted around that, and looked for the warm spot of dissolution. She came in nights in torn stockings, nights reeking of puke even, and Bobby was caring, she came in, after a time days later, reeking of men's sweat, and Bobby justified these things somehow, but it was when she came in one day, and said she was going to sing in a band that Bobby freaked, that he knew it was all over, his myth of Mariane as his wife, Mariane in a band meant explosion and disaster and he packed his bags, and she cried but, secretly, Mariane was relieved, *I can get her back, later, on my own, without Bobby Baxter.*

Going back to chaos, which is the main thing here, because Mariane cannot live a life without the juice of chaos, she doesn't feel fully comfortable unless things are fucking up, falling apart, at odds, if she had stayed in rehab they would've pointed this out, she would have come to realize that because of her upbringing—

★ ★ ★

You see, it was just Mariane and her mother.

And this is the mother we are talking about, lying in bed and not getting out, just lying in bed. Mariane, tiptoeing in with a cup of tea, made just the way her mother likes it, three sugars, milk, putting on the radio, Mariane is eight years old, Mariane makes her own lunch, breakfast, does her own laundry the night before (as her mother is out; Mariane is alone all evening).

But, it was more the lack of what was in, for instance, the living room: a mattress on the floor, decorated with a thready Indian bedspread covered in cat hair, a velvet raised poster of Jimi Hendrix, and a stereo. Oh, and a phone. Mariane was just kind of on her own, most of the time. I mean, she went to school on the bus, and that was its own world of pain, of course, because the girls in her class, Tammy, Carol, Denise, Theresa, to name a few, lived in the developments that had names like Exeter or Duck Pond, with green curved lawns surrounding brick ramblers as crisp as Legos, and fathers who actually barbecued, or called their girls endearments, *honey* or *sweetheart,* odd presences that seemed almost fake to her, theatrical, as if they came from a television show, and of course they had perfect rooms with pinkness and lace and stuffed animals and the fresh lines of recent vacuuming in the pale wall-to-wall carpeting, and even their own bathrooms, with electric toothbrushes, and Mariane dared not invite them to her apartment on the other side of town, with its little terrace that had a dried-out old plant, no father, a mother at work or "out," a smelly, dirty doggishness to the whole place that a broom couldn't, sweep as she might, rid the rug of (they didn't own a vacuum cleaner).

It was sad really, Mariane's desperate attempts to clean the place, but the rug was a dark brown, and had stains, and the dog hair wouldn't come off, and the cigarette burns, made by her mother, and the linoleum in the kitchen was permanently scarred by her mother putting a hot plate down, laughing and making crepes late one night, and Mariane tried, with new excitement, to fix up the place, even paint the wall with some beige paint she found in the closet, and her desperate attempts to dress like the girls, she kept trying, thinking she would get it right, but she made the attempt of inviting Virginia one day, who sat with disdain, stiffly in a chair, who called her mom to come early to pick her up, she pretty much dropped it then, just stopped pretty much doing anything, then the neighbor problem occurred, then she just took off, just out of the house, saying good-bye to her mother as if going to school, her mother in a big T-shirt, mixing eggs to scramble in a square Tupperware bowl, cigarette in her mouth.

In her mind, the thing became an issue of obtaining a certain level of cleanliness before she could justify getting the child. Until she had some money to get a brand-new spanking clean place, with wall-to-wall carpeting, and all the amenities, then she would be different than her mom. She put more emphasis on the place than the parenting, she started to believe that being poor was the problem from the beginning, that her mother just needed money and things would've been right, and this is how she will do it right.

Carlos said his friends Maxine and Billy were starting a band and needed a singer, and Mariane perked right up, Maybe I can do it? she said, and Carl said, well, that's cool, can you sing like Lydia Lunch? Or Lora Logic?

Yeah, she lied (*who the hell are they?* Mariane had sung along to Tanya Tucker back in Raleigh.)

Well, then, I can call them, he said kissing her neck, yep, it was true, Bobby Baxter, though still living with her, was out of the picture, because she didn't want a home. She thinks she does but she doesn't.

So later in someone's apartment, she is drinking whiskey sours, she wears black pants and a black shirt and they say what can you do? What's your deal? Well, I can sing OK, she remembers those singers' names she didn't recognize, she gets flustered and she stutters, do you know that song, uh, "Respect"? You mean, Aretha?

Yeah, that one. Well, yeah, but Motown? I mean, to just show what I can do, you know, it's just a demonstration, oh, oh, sure, and then she sings it, strongly, loud, growly even, it's really not bad, it shows potential, and they say, *that's good, alright,* they were a group of Upper East Side kids who were dangling in the dark, seedy side of music and downtown, hoping to get some type of burnished naughty patina on their gleaming pink skins and hopelessly shiny hair, just aspiring towards the fabled edge, to a certain point, of course. Alcohol, a few recreational drugs but nothing too committing, nothing permanently damaging. No needles, no pregnancies, no tattoos. And, as a jaunt between the world of Wall Street futures and Westchester Volvos, at this twenty-something stage a measured dose of darkness, in sterilized form, was called for. A lead singer of a nastier class could be provocative, earthy, because certainly Melinda, the lead guitar's girlfriend, couldn't be employed, there was the problem with bulimia and the hairband (and truth be told, in her schooling at Foxcroft it was Little Feat and Grateful Dead she preferred, though she never confesses). So, Mariane, discovered by a friend of a friend at her restaurant, fits the bill, and she smokes some bong hits with them and they just start practicing a few covers and say we have a gig on Saturday at a little club on Tenth Street, she says great and she's to meet them at ten o'clock, and then that day, at work, hungover, she feels shitty, she says she can't make it, and they get pissed and then she's on for Tuesday, but she cancels, they call a few times, but she doesn't pursue it, yet she always says, for six months afterwards, *yeah, I sing in a band* and people are awed, then she starts to say, I *sung* in a band, though she never really did. And she heard they cut an album and she starts to add that to her myth, yeah, they got a record out, *cool, you got a record? Yeah, yeah, it was pretty neat,* then she'd quickly change the subject.

I was with Bobby for how long now, let's see, let's see, I suppose, it was, it was, about a month or more or, hell, I don't remember, it's hard to keep up the odds and ends when you've got other things on your mind, thing is Getting Daisy Back is my, you know, priority, see, and I think the thing is with Bobby, I think he wanted to own me or something, like I was a package or an object, and I just felt, that, that wouldn't work, because, I, like everyone else, need freedom and he wanted to hold me down,

Mariane, I think we gots to talk here, because—

Huh, Bobby?

I think this drinking is getting out of hand, I mean one or two is fine and all, but it's all day, girl, all day and where are you, anyway? You work to ten but then you're out carousing all night—

Because you just want to sit around, watch TV. Can I help it if I meet people? I'm going to be singing next week, do you care?

But, Mariane. This is too much, what about our plan? We—

I'm working on my plan, if I sing, maybe I'll get famous and make a lot of money, I can't take care of her now—

The drinking—

You're just jealous.

I think he wanted me to be little Suzy Homemaker, and I couldn't because I was getting a career together, you know, I had friends in places and stuff, and I just wanted to have fun, and he was a lot older than me, so I think that's what sent him off finally, I think I was just, you know, wild and crazy and such.

I'm still going to check out singing, though.

Those kids I was hanging with then kind of faded away.

That happens. Shit happens. People come and go.

I mean, things are always changing, you know.

I'll go get Daisy soon, just got to be grown up myself, too you know?

I'm thinking of looking into voice-overs, because that's a lot of money I hear.

Voice-overs. That's the ticket.

chapter seventeen

Menu:

Oranges

Long Noodles

Ring.
Ring.
No answer, mister.

I don't understand you men not know where your wife be, how can man not know where wife is, in my time this bad, people say *she too wild,* you see I always said to husband, Husband, I'm going market or Husband, I'm going to doctor, you know. Get her to try this, OK? Because look, her husband sick in the street, drinking and she not take care now. This is no good. I had husband before—here you comfortable there, I get another pillow, Ton! Ton! Where are you?

Ton? Oh, he's in shower? *He's a little not too smart, you know? If he hurts you, he doesn't mean, he's just a little not too smart. I hope he didn't hurt you.*

Ton in the shower, speaks out loud to the soap as if it is Ling, he says, *I'm going to marry you and get away from this crap, this mother who bosses me, I hate it. Wait. Wait and see, I'm going to marry you and she can't do a thing. Not a thing!*

I said, I had a husband before but he died, yes, he died, he get encephalitis from mosquito, you know you can get this from a mosquito, huh? His head get big and it was terrible business, and I took care, but he die, mister, he die. That's right, sometime you can take care and don't matter at all, I took care when I was pregnant, I don't eat oranges, I don't eat long noodles, I do everything, but still I make some kind of mistake, because, she whispers then, *Ton isn't right, you know what I mean, he's not right in the head, it's big problem, only me and Ton in the world, nobody else, and I got to take care, and he took up with a bad woman, too, he takes up with a whore* and she tries to take away my Ton, tries to get my money or something, teaching him evil.

Ton washes his hair, *she doesn't trust me, thinks I am bad person, thinks Ling is bad, thinks everything is bad! She tries to stop everything good. I help some old guy who's hurt and she thinks I hurt him. I'm going to get away from her. Far away. Maybe soon, maybe tomorrow, I'm going to find Ling and get her away with me, because I can do a lot, I can clean and work hard, I don't need a mean mother! I don't!*

That woman just want things from him, don't care about heart, you know? I say to Ton, never! Never I'm going to let you go with this type. You can get disease. I know about disease. I see my husband head blow up, I see blood coming out. Then I get a messed-up son, I love him but this is hard for me. Hard for me. I work hard at the hospital cleaning, on maternity floor, I work for six year there, and I have to clean up a lot of stuff. Having babies make a lot of mess. Mister, you sleeping. I wonder, I wonder if he's no feeling good. Maybe I call my friend, Doctor Slingoff. He can help. Sometimes you hit head you can get brain problems. I. I. Better make tea. Get a hot cloth. Ton! Ton!

What!

Maybe I leave tonight, who knows, maybe I get Ling and go tonight, maybe we just get out and go to Graceland. Get married in the land of Elvis. It was Elvis who brought us together. The soul of Elvis got us together and I got to call up Ling.

★ ★ ★

Ito feels that rushing train sensation, big fast blood in his head and the flood of saliva in his mouth. His head dizzy, his body crumples.

Ton! Come here quick! *Old man not look too good!* Come here now!

chapter eighteen

Menu:

Twinkies

Kit Kats

Marshmallows

Beer

Ring.
Ring.
Ring.
H-, ahum. He-*llo?*
Are you miss your husband?
What?
I say, are you miss your husband? Where your husband, lady?

*Twinkies. Drink. Ito. Night. Her face crinkled from the hard edge
of the sill. Light outside. People walking outside.*

My husband?
A huge panicking bolus of adrenaline hits her chest—*Carl?
Bobby? And who the hell?*
This Japanese gentleman. He sick, lady. Your husband.
Oh. Oh. Oh. Ito, you mean. Oh, my goodness. Is he *OK?*
What time is it?
It eight-thirty, lady, and this guy maybe hurt bad. I take him
to hospital, OK?
Hospital? Mariane wonders what the hell is going on, is he
dying? Who is this woman?
He bang head, I put cloth on him, he, wait! He waking! Mister!
Mister! I find your wife, you speak here, here.

There is a rustling, crumpling of sounds, a long jabber of indistinguishable language from the woman, then a pause, then:

Mariane?

Ito? What happened?

Don't know. I go buy things. Get idea—*no more tea, please*—get idea to buying fish. Fall down. Now I'm here.

Oh, gosh, do you need a hospital or something? An ambulance?

I need, need. Go home, please. To talk to you, Mariane.

I am here.

OK, I go there.

Mariane rubs her face.

Come on then, I still need a Twinkie.

Sugar. In massive quantities. When Mariane's not drinking, it's sugar. Twinkies. Kit Kats. Marshmallows. She gets up to check out his stash.

Mariane had always been a snoop, from early on, she had liked to open things and peer in, at friends' bathrooms she would open the medicine cabinet carefully, so it wouldn't click, and peruse the contents, looking in the linen closet, even looking in pocketbooks, or men's pants pockets for some kind of clues.

After she awoke at Ito's, she was bewildered and stared at the empty place, its '70s-ish furniture and the dull masculinity of it all, the somber colors of black, gray and taupe, without any paintings or art. The room smelled of his body, warm, mothball-like.

In the semilight, she peered around the small apartment. In the kitchen, she opened the cabinets and saw strange Japanese powders and packets of hard noodles in rectangular shapes. The drawers revealed no forks and only one long, thin knife, with a wooden handle, the kind she'd seen behind the sushi bar, and a pile of disposable chopsticks.

There were no cookies, candies in sight. A few packets of sugar lay in the corners.

The refrigerator was barren also, but she found a silvery can of Japanese beer and cracked it quietly, letting the sharp flow of bubbles trail down her throat.

She insists on going with him in the taxi, Ton's mother, she wraps his head in a towel and he says, *no!* and she becomes hawk-like and says, *you listen to me, you want to die, you want to get infection,* and he is silent, she yells to Ton, Ton! Ton! and he answers sullenly, what? and she says *I take old man home* and he says OK (good riddance. I will call Ling now, go see my baby), *I mean help me now, Ton* and those vowel sounds go on again, and he runs over and grabs the man's arm, and she holds Ito's arm also down the elevator to the blast of cool air outside. They find a taxi and speed through the streets, his head pounding, her babbling on. And Ito thinks about Mariane, how he must tell her about the baby, that she's misled, that she's fooled herself into some terrible lie, that she must stop drinking, that she is killing and poisoning herself, he envisions holding her crying and telling her these bitter truths, telling her she has lied and stolen, and been misused, has allowed herself to be misused, and he feels a wave of sadness for her, tenderness.

They get to the building and the mother says, *oh, this nice place, you must be good worker, mister,* she goes in the elevator, and then they are in the door, and Mariane is there. They all stand awkwardly in the doorway.

Ito enters his apartment, waves them in. *Come in, come in please.*

Oh, Ito, what a night, hunh?

Mariane, I'm sorry.

Hey, I slept through the whole thing.

This lady, he motions with his arm.

Carol, she squeaks.

Carol?

I choose American name.
Oh.
Mariane, Carol, let's go to Sugi and I make breakfast.
Breakfast! You need to rest—
No, no. Come on.
He rushes to the door, his head wrapped in a bandage.
Come on! Breakfast!

Like children, they silently follow.

chapter nineteen

Menu:

Coffee and Cognac

Fried Rice

It was dark at Sugi's on this Monday morning, the day the restaurant was closed, Ito twisted with the lock for a while and then they all walked in and he pulled the shades and flicked on the lights, *here we are,* he said.

Oh, this nice place, mister. Nice place.

OK. I make coffee?

Please, said Mariane. She was quiet and sad, her head pounded. She looked at the row of bottles behind the bar and two thoughts mingled, and actually, fed on each other, the occurrence with Yoshi and the need for just a trickle of some liquor.

Carol was looking at Ito and feeling a bit scared, yet protective—*Does he want to get Ton in trouble? Does he know Ton try to kill him, but forget?* But at the same time, she was having fun, the poor woman works twelve-hour days, eats Oodles of Noodles from the same worn plastic bowl for years, drinks pale brown tea out of a stained pink cup, has cleaned feces from her idiot son for years, until maybe the last five years—as he used to hold it in, holding on and on, not going for weeks, she'd feed him mineral oil, and special herb teas, and constantly scrub his underwear in bleach, he'd hold on until a huge ball of leaden feces would build in his colon, blocking all passage, until finally a sluice of liquid would trickle out from around the block and stain his underwear, unexpectedly, anywhere, and it took years to fix this, because the colon had become permanently stretched—she hasn't gone out to dinner at a nice restaurant ever, has occasionally taken Ton, on New Year's Day, and treated him to a special *eight courses of beef,* a Vietnamese specialty. But she didn't eat that, she instead had a simple steaming bowl of *Pho,* a peasant dish of noodles, tendon and beef broth, a breakfast food. Carol, real name of *Huong Li Phuo,* got pregnant in Vietnam two weeks before they left in the black night on a boat, refugees, her husband sick, then as they fled, his encephalitis, *pushing him overboard, watching his dead body float like a pale jellyfish, going forward to a new place, crazy scared, pregnant.*

How about Carol stays with a Vietnamese restaurant owner, making rice noodles in their house, at their kitchen table, until Ton is born too early, two months too soon, water gushing from her like a small flood she couldn't stop, it stained the rug, and his cord came popping out between her legs, not a head, or a leg, but the cord in the taxi, the wife of the restaurant owner didn't recognize it (Carol's skirt up in the car, she kept pushing it down modestly, then after a while her modesty disappeared in the midst of shaking pain), a whitish blue twisted nob darting out of the bloody entrance of Carol, like an anemic snake, she says nothing, touches nothing, but knows from the horrified looks of the doctor, the expression *prolapsed cord,* that it isn't good, Carol is whisked away, Carol is sliced open in exactly three minutes.

Three minutes in which, as they cram the tiny triangle of plastic on her nose and mouth and say *breathe,* she lurches into some upside-down place where she can't move, she can feel the plastic throttle of the ventilator in her throat, hears voices, and then a pain so sharp it feels icy, it feels so hot it is like ice, she feels them slice her stomach open, the anesthesia hasn't kicked in yet, only three minutes yet Ton has suffered, oxygen cut off in the cord and Ton's Apgar scores are low, his tongue lolls from his mouth until six months old.

How about at night, Carol washes her face with Dove and smooths on a crushed pearl cream you can buy in Chinatown, wears a limp pink polyester gown over her small, mouse body, brushes the hair she has permed every three months, her only concession to beautification, and lies in her cool slim twin bed and plans her future, saving her money to take care of Ton, putting aside five hundred a month in a small box, to take care of Ton, to seal his future. Lying in the black room, she sometimes thinks of her husband, her hand tries to caress between her legs but that part of her is over and gone, she remembers nights where it was fun with her husband, but she remembers his bleeding and she turns away, then she sleeps.

Having fun. What *is* fun in her life? Well, briefly on Sunday mornings after church she has Bible study with the Vietnamese Ladies Coalition and they eat *cha gio* (spring rolls, Mrs. Thuyen makes them but they are dry), they talk about their children. That's fun, she would say. (No, it's not. Carol spends the time trying to make a brave front, *Ton is soooo good to me! Ah, so good.* Sadly, Carol lies and the women know it and she knows it.) Well, then, it's fun when she gets her hair permed by Miss April in the Rex Salon, many Vietnamese people there from her church, and it's fun to chat (How's Ton, Carol? *Oh, he, he amazing me these days. So smart! So smart!* Carol sees the people look up at each other, little smirks, with the corner of her eye. Carol sees). Then, it's also fun when she and Ton watch those game shows on TV, each with a tray in front, stir-fried noodles on paper plates (Ton doesn't talk, and Carol thinks, *these are people's sons, maybe one day Ton goes on this show, I'll be proud and wear a nice dress, sit behind him. He know all the answers. Then the Coalition sees*).

Carol just now tells herself she is protecting Ton from problems with this old Japanese man, but, as evidenced in the smile which seems to crack through her stiff face, Carol is having a bit of a good time, in the oddest way.

Ito returns with three mugs of coffee balanced in his clutched hands, he puts them down and whistles as he returns to the back to cook fried rice for breakfast, and Mariane and Carol sit and wait, and Mariane thinks, *what the hell,* goes to the bar and grabs the bottle of Courvoisier and pours it over her coffee, enjoying the fumes, and says *Hey, Carol, you up for some?* and wags the bottle in her face, and Carol says, *oh, no, no, no,* and laughs an embarrassed laugh, and when she does, Mariane notices with horror, she has *black teeth,* keriist! How the hell does one get black teeth, and she remembers reading in *National Geographic* about betel nut chewing in Thailand and she says, *wow, your teeth. Betel?* Huh, what, what? says Carol, thoroughly mortified, hand at her teeth, *oh, oh, yes, small nut,* and then in a moment of kinship somehow, Mariane says, *come on,* and passes the bottle again and Carol says, *ohhh-kay, little bit, little bit,* and she drinks it through her stained teeth with a whistling sound, the way she does hot tea, coffee and cognac, a weird combination for her, but OK, Mariane swigs it, then says, wait! She scampers over to the cooler and pulls out Reddi Whip, froths the tops of each cup and they both giggle.

So what do those, like, small nuts taste like? Are they good?

Huh? Carol looks up at her, with whipped cream on her top lip. Mariane notices the creases around her eyes, like bent leather.

I said, those nuts? You know, you chew? Chomp chomp?

Oh, yeah, good. You try?

You got it here?

Yeah, yeah.

She whisks around in her pocket, pulls out a green nut with ridges, wrapped up in a shiny leaf.

Chew this.

The whole thing?

Yeah. Chew.

Mariane takes a tiny bite and it's just bitter, she spits it out in the tiny sink and says, still spitting,

Ohh, I'm sorry. Yuck!

No problem. This very special in Vietnam. Lot of history. When we marry, we chew this—says Carol, holding it in her tiny palm—it's good for heart and they say a story about this thing, there were two, two *kids* who love, right? Love a lot but their family too different, not want marry, so they kill other one next to river—

They killed themselves?

Yeah, kill selves, and King goes to be sad, you know crying by river, and betel nut fall and he see the, the red water come out—

Juice?

This, and he see it like blood, so he say, this king, always when marry have to have this one, this nut, the man and woman eat it—

That's cool.

And then Ito comes out, with a plate of steaming food, and bowls for them, and chopsticks and he notes their frolicsome spirits.

Party, *ne*?

We are, we are! says Mariane, and truth be told, Mariane feels damn good, liquor seeping on the edges of her frayed hungover nerves, and the disappointment in her life, as her mind, when sober, tends to back up, to analyze, which is not what she wants at all, to review yesterday, and the day before, not remembering a lot, just shameful bits and pieces, and, sniffing around like a bloodhound, it starts to drag her back to real details, back to the baby, and, smack! she whisks that liquor back down the gullet, and that little pit of pain recedes.

Well, says Ito, music time, and he goes and puts on a dreamy CD of a bold, fluctuating Japanese singer's voice, cool and hitting all the ranges, with the vibrato of country singers in Japan, and he comes back, and says, with a bow:

Dance?

And both women laugh, and pick at their fried rice, and Mariane pours pure cognac in her cup, and Ito wants to hold her badly, just to hold her tight, he sees the drinking and it pains him, but he turns to Carol, with her small, lined face, the attentive rabbit eyes, and says, *come on!*

Oh, please, I can't.

Come, dancing! Pulls on her arm.

Oh, mister. No! But she's up and she feels very shy in his strong arms, he twirls her around slowly, her feet with corns nimbly tracing the steps, she smiles and sees the sushi bar, coming in and out of focus, the mirrors of the walls shine and glimmer, his hand against her back is infinitely comforting to her, a woman of such strength, who works so hard, the hand offers her a millisecond of freedom to relax—

OK, my turn, you two, says Mariane, standing there, and Ito releases Carol, who goes to get coffee for everyone, and she is curious to peer around the back of a Japanese kitchen, see what they have different from the kitchens she knows, she goes through the *noren,* and Mariane is enveloped in Ito's strong arms, he wraps them around her, dancing is a useful social convenience, allowing a presetting for intimate physicality, a rehearsal of the movement of arms and legs, of mutual synchronicity, and there is no problem here, he wraps up Mariane and feels great comfort to hold the frail back in his hands, and Mariane, in turn, is tired to the bone, about to reach the proverbial rock bottom, Mariane is getting drunk again, it's ten-thirty in the morning, she has no job, no man, no life, she dribbles sperm from a man as real to her as plasticine, like everything around her, a way to distract and waste time. Unbeknownst to her, Ito is deeply moved as the singer is crooning a particularly sad bit about love and losing love, thinking about Xiu-Xiu, about Tomoko, and overcome, Ito reaches down, as Mariane turns her head up instinctually, her lips turn to Ito at the right moment, he lays his upon her, her lips are warm, his are warm, he parts her mouth and he kisses her with fervor, as does she in return, they stop, he caresses her hair, she lays her hands delicately on his neck, caressing him, his mouth is soft and insistent, she darts her tongue, their eyes are closed in reverence, this kiss is the most pleasure they both have experienced in a long, long time.

★ ★ ★

Carol is at the *noren,* holding a steaming pot of coffee, and she stops, and watches, sees the golden forearms of Ito against Mariane's face as he grasps her cheeks sweetly and kisses her, sees Mariane's hands woven through his glossy black hair, and says, to herself, yes, this is good husband and wife, to love, it is good.

She thinks of Nguyen, his narrow face overcome with a smile, thinks of the day her father introduced them, and he wore an old suit of his grandfather's, thinks of his delicate hips, thready and narrow, dashing with insistent dips as her ankles had been tucked on his shoulders, and thinks of his eyes, puffed shut and swollen, his purple plum lips, and his senses gone already, *Nguyen, Nguyen,* but the other man, the man from their village, said, he is gone. She thinks of fish eating him. She turns to the wall and pushes these thoughts away, scratching at the paint, and in the corner of her eyes, she sees them still kissing, and the CD has stopped, and they still kiss.

She looks at the door, misses her son, and wants to leave, and Ito and Mariane seem unaware, the few sips of cognac has made her dizzy, she sneaks along the wall, and comes to the door, she opens it quietly, people outside walking back and forth, with business on their minds, she closes the door and wonders if the number six train is here, nearby, needs to go to work (at eleven), wonders if Ton has had breakfast, a flash of worry, pushes Nguyen away, pushes Ito and Mariane away, the sun, though it is cold, is shining brightly.

They notice her leave, peripherally, but they can't stop, Ito and Mariane, he doesn't want to lose this moment with her, and she also, and Carol needs to go back to her life, anyway, and they are getting a bit desperate now, Mariane finds she is attracted to Ito, he is strong and his arms feel solid around her, his mouth is kind, and she feels the falling, melting feeling of warmth through her body, and Ito feels out of breath, they lose balance for a second, and just knock against the bar briefly, the bottles shake, and Mariane stops, remembers Yoshi, a wave of ice chills her and she stops, she pulls back,

Yoshi. That Yoshi, I think he, he maybe *raped* me the other day.

What? What day?

Wednesday.

Rape? He pulls in and holds her head.

Yeah, he, he knocked me down there, pointing to the corner of the sushi bar, and like, grabbed my skirt up and just did it, but then I freaked so he, he, stopped, and then I left, next time I come to work, I, I feel really weird, he's kind of cold, and you asked me to dinner, was it to fire me?

No.

So, I screwed up and missed dinner, I fell asleep, and when I came in to work, you were all pissed and he was weird, he, he, acts weird and all nice, then he fucking *fires* me and gives me an envelope of money—

He told me, he finds you stealing—

Goddamn him—

But I thought, because I saw you drink at work—

Oh.

—that if we had dinner, I talk to you first—

Yeah, so he fires me, that's OK. Not the first time. Besides, I'm gonna blow this crappy town, I'm going to go down south, back to Raleigh, get my baby and rent, I don't know, some kind of bungalow or something and really get my, you know, act—

She takes a long chug on the coffee.

—together, get some kind of job, what have you—

Mariane, Mariane—

Yeah, hey, can you pass that cognac, you want some?

OK. Mariane,

Yeah, *what*?

How you going to take care of baby?

You know, love her, like any mother.
Sorry, *ne*? But. Too much drink.
I like a little drinkie once in a while, like yourself.
Mariane, this baby.
Yeah? What do you know about my baby?

Comes a time, sometimes, when you can carry a realization around in the pocket of your cerebrum, and carry it like a promise, a solution, and bring it out to finger and consider at times, and value the changes it can bring, and such is the case of Katsuyuki Ito, he had realized that Mariane's little baby, her plan, was a crock, that the baby was grown, and wished to relieve her of this dissolution, to save her from the heartbreak of discovery, to be, once again, the boss, the man in charge, the decision maker, and also, maybe, on some level, Mariane would be grateful to him, he would mean something to Mariane, say, he would have earned a measure of intimacy with her, there was this thought driving him.

No one had told him upright the truth, it had taken certain stages of realization, the startling dream of blood and the weight of Xiu-Xiu's dead body for the jolting realization that she was dead by his own son, and not the phantom he pursued, the *Miss Ling,* here in the States. Even though the resemblance was not close, he was pursuing the need for Xiu-Xiu, for the knowledge she had gar-nered in the years she had tended his body, that carried a form of intimacy there, more than the sex, but the fact, for five years, Xiu-Xiu had been close to his skin, she knew his sounds during lovemaking, his vulnerable moments, she knew the scent of his body and its particularity, the sound of his breathing, the texture of his skin, the flavor of his mouth, the feel of his hair—it was this knowl-edge, this closeness he pursued in Ling, perhaps thinking on some level, women were parcels that, if packaged similarly, would pro-duce the same effect, like dolls in the store that cry real tears, or

speak, and if one is damaged or lost, one can buy a similar model—
perhaps on some level, this is what Ito thought, in his rather self-
centered way, He could find a new Xiu-Xiu and feel a certain
wholeness in this large, harsh city, but Ling was not Xiu-Xiu, Ling
was on her own circuit, and Ito was a few nights to her in a terrible
and vivid life so far, she was not available to Ito on any level, to her
he was a hounding crazy man, a lunatic, she had the bouncers at
her club ready to pounce on him, and, in her book, he was dead.

So, Ito had been a vulnerable wound walking in the glare of
New York City, a man who had been trained for years in an art
wholly appreciated in his country, yet here he was a spectacle, a
dietary aide, he was a hungry man, on some level, and considering
this revelation to Mariane, it occurred to him that perhaps she
knows, that it's not a simple question of *knowledge* here, but a question of saving face, and personal dreams, that if Mariane did not
have this particular idea to work for, as is the case with all people,
she would dissolve fully in the drink she consumed, for that is a
symptom really, the problem is that Mariane wishes to die, and by
holding the faded snapshot of a baby in pink, however dated, she
could move forward in her thoughts, it was this realization that came
to him quickly, and in doing so, Ito saw sides of this woman he
had neglected to see in all women, he saw beyond her looks and
their quantification in terms of meeting his pleasurable needs, beyond her femininity in terms of boosting up the booty of his masculinity, he saw her simply as herself—Mariane, a woman, who
drinks too much, who leads an unexamined life, but who seeks still
some redemption.

I think, we should go get your baby.

My baby. I don't know if I'm ready and all, I mean, *money*—

That's no problem.

He kissed her again.

Come here.

And Ito unraveled some of the armor of samurai propriety that he had wrapped himself with through the years of being a sushi chef, which had essentially plastered his sentiments in an icy cave, and by doing so, had imperiled himself, and he now cracked this shell, and loosened himself. He had lost Yoshi's money—this was a fact—and replacing it would mean more than simply being docked a week's pay, it would mean a certain psychological loss of respect by Yoshi, already Yoshi thought he was inept in his choices of weekly menus, too specialized, too esoteric, he could catch the half-sentences between Yoshi and Koji, mocking the old man for dreaming American palates would approve of *O-toro* or appreciate *Devil's tongue* or *the liver of whale*—

Down this way.

Ito led her down the musty stairs to the basement, where they stored boxes of sake, sacks of rice and other large items, and they came to Yoshi's little study, with sheaves of papers and *Manga* comics, an antique pachinko machine he would play by himself, *Penthouse* magazines, some Japanese novels, and Ito knew just what he was looking for, he reached down behind the desk, and he found the orange tin box that the crisp seaweed for sushi had come in originally, placed it on the desk, loosened the edges and it sprung open, and inside, as Mariane gasped, lay bundle after bundle of bills, hundreds, fifties, tied in bunches with rubber bands—

Holy shit, Mariane said. She reached out and touched one with her index finger.

For years, Yoshi had been skimming money from the register (*Don't ring up, just take out change, then ring up every other one,* he told the waitresses) and placing it in the box, taking out what he needed to spend (his Jeep was paid for in cash, $28,687 dollars, in an envelope) or his trip and operation in Tokyo for the penile implants ($14,559, including a night in a love motel the night before) and then adding more, each day, wrapped in different thicknesses of rubber bands and different colors,

Take this, all—

Take Yoshi's *money?*

Yes. Take. Go from here, You and I.

But—

Yes, get baby. I want to—

He held her face and kissed her nose,

I want to help you. Get baby.

Mariane was quiet, she leaned against his shoulder. She was grateful. She was crying.

No drinking.

Hell, Ito, she mumbled. *I don't know if that's possible.*

This was said as a whisper.

Is possible. Very possible.

She held him really tight, *I'm afraid, I'm going, to die or something before I get her!*

No die. Come on. Going to get her and later, get Daisuke.

Daisuke?

My son. That I left.

Ito picked up that tin box and held Mariane's arm. He led her through the restaurant, turning off lights as he went. He straightened their coffee cups, turned off the music and they went outside, it was lunchtime and these two stragglers appeared wrinkled, dirty and tired in the sea of crisp business Manhattanites, he flagged a taxi and Mariane and Ito got in, he had an idea to go to *La Guardia Airport, please* and find a rental car company, get a nice car, maybe a van, pack Mariane in it, lay her down, drive down south, and clean her up, get the poison out of her, make her well, and then demand they see the child, when she could handle it, when Mariane was well.

So Mariane fell asleep against his arm and Ito is thinking about Daisuke, about fixing Mariane, he can give up this absurd thing with Ling, he is overcome with shame for his behavior with that woman, he thinks now what he has to do, about Daisuke, how he'll call his sister and have him sent, and Mariane will be better, how they'll have a home, with her baby (young girl), they will find a new town, he thinks he will leave this harsh city, the sun beating down now, it's twelve.

Ito breathes deeply and calmly and doesn't feel bad for Yoshi, he feels nothing for Yoshi, he has left that world behind, like abandoning a seat in a restaurant, it was yours, and suited your purposes, it fared you well, but you can leave it easily because it was not your place, it is for others just as easily, it held you temporarily, and now, sated, you move on.

chapter twenty

Carol leaves the restaurant, closes the door, walks down the
steps to the street, leaving Ito and Mariane, wants to got to work,
wants to see Ton later:

Carol feels, this a departure and doesn't feel good, anything
feeling like departure or leaving makes this woman Carol feel queasy
inside, shaky, her heart is rushing, *I don't want move or change from
here, this is good spot,* Carol sits on the curb, breathing gently.

Carol still has *post-traumatic stress syndrome,* not everyone has
to leave their wooden plank bed below corrugated steel roof, hens
on top, to dash to an anchored boat on the river—*leaving warm home
about three am morning, wife of dad friend waking me, come on, I and
husband sleeping dead as dogs on the road, come on, this is your opportu-
nity*—not everyone has to slink down to the river, holding their
husband's hand to the canoe—*maybe Nguyen needs medicine, he not
feeling so good, fever all night, last night, making bed all wet, this might
not be most best time, but can't help*—you can hear the paddle hit the
water, making that *thwok* sound—*but we can't cough or talk, we get on
the boat, I have sticky rice and red bean in a paper bag*—on August 3,
1983, to travel across the black South China Seas to get to some
safe spot, Malaysia or Indonesia, across the choppy seas in the pitch
of night—*you can hear the rustle of the people moving quietly, like snakes
in the bush, you can hear the water's sound, we get on*—laying down,
across the waters to international seas, the boatman pulls into reeds

and everyone wonders what he does, but can't speak, he waits, and waits, then he lights a piece of incense and puts it on the top—*I am smelling incense, I hold Nguyen's hand, he is delirious, I pray to all the saints boatman won't see, hear him, or turn us back, leave us in this canoe when the big boat comes*—and the big boat comes, and they have to get on carefully, Nguyen is nodding out, Nguyen has advanced-stage mosquito-carried encephalitis, if anyone catches whiff of this they will expel him, he is as good as dead, unless he can get medical attention now, but this boat will be sailing seven days, if there are no attacks from Thai pirates or storms, and she doesn't address all of this, there is always hope and miracles—*they cover up the boat muffler with a cloth so it is quiet, we sit but no space, we find one in engine room with his brother-in-law, bags of rice and bananas, we sleep a bit but towards morning of the next day*—there is always hope but destiny, she knows, is predetermined, she holds him and pours water in his mouth, a storm rocks the boat, splashing water at each wave, the water pump can't empty fast enough, and finally after four hours it is over, she is sleeping and feels the boat still shaking in her sleep, brother-in-law voice sounds funny and it wakes her, looks down and Nguyen is shaking, shaking, shaking, not the boat, the water is still as cloth, he's bleeding from nose, Nguyen is dying, now dead, she screams, he grabs her, they have to pull her aside, they check him and say no, says prayers, someone lights incense, they have to throw him overboard—*I see them throw him over, not sure if he is really dead, because there are miracles*—she has to sit down alone and close her eyes, the water-rocking feeling still, and she throws up again and again, someone offers her pickled pork, but she says no, she gets sick, she doesn't think of Nguyen at all, she only has two gold pieces, after paying seven for this trip, she drinks some water, a small drop, she sleeps—*in morning of ninth day, because storm set off course, we see dolphins swim in water, see land, myself and the people see the joy in us, all this time shit and piss in the same place, like birds*—they arrive to the shore of Malaysia, and came aground where they are welcomed, to the island of Letung, and Carol drags herself up the shore to the van they take to the camp, a long gray shape of cinder block, of men with tiny dried monkey faces the color of smoked pigs, standing still with rifles, pointed wire, with her brother-in-law, no husband now, which is terrible bad luck—*they give us bag rice, bag salt, bag sugar, little can Spam, small tea bag, one liter diesel for cook, five Singapore dollars, we wash in stream, we get five gallon water to use, they have two minimarket to buy thing, if you leave camp, police beat you, this is thing, while wait for leave you must take ESL class, must wait turn, I waiting and during this time, I find I have baby growing, during this time is miracle.*

So travel is an imperiled state for Carol, even going across town brings high anxious feelings, she sits on the curb and deals with her shakiness, she sees a phone across the street and she will go there and call Ton—

August 3, 1983, as Carol sat in a boat with her dead husband:

Katsuyuki Ito, in Hokkaido, Japan, on this particular Saturday, had vacationed in a hot water spa with his wife Tomoko (whose tiny pearl of cancerous fiber had just sprouted in her lower stomach) for a summer vacation, on this particular day, he and Tomoko (no Daisuke yet) had awoke on their tatami mat, eaten grilled baby flounder, made hurried love on the futon, gone to the hot waters and soaked, followed by a mud wrap, and had taken a mountain trek in the afternoon. In the evening, they went to the town's harbor to view the spectacular night-glowing squid, famous in this town. They held hands at the water's edge. After a bit, they returned to the inn and ate a dinner of those live glowing baby squid, presented in glasses, to be dipped in wasabi and soy sauce, and crunched between their teeth, enjoyed with sake. This was followed by a grilled sea bream and rice. That night, they slept soundly in each other's arms.

★ ★ ★

August 3, 1983, as Carol sat in a boat with her dead husband:

It had been two weeks since Bobby Baxter had packed his two duffel bags, one mahogany red with a gold Redskins insignia and the other a faded blue, *Raleigh Hills Health and Sport Club* on the side. As Mariane's head pounded, from a vertical angle, she watched the painstaking way he packed his socks, speaking a clump of words each time he placed some socks in a cavity in the bags, *I really have tried to understand,* prod, pack, *what, what you're going through here,* prod, prod *and Mariane, it ain't, it just ain't been easy, you know, shit, now where's my,* prod, pack, *I mean you got men calling here at all kinds of hours and I just didn't expect,* prod, pack, *I mean, I'm sorry but.*

So, on August 3, 1983, at some point she got up and made macaroni and cheese. At some point, she called her friend Nagaris, and agreed to meet at a bar, at some point Mariane, who didn't work that day, dressed herself in black leggings and a white T-shirt and combed her then-long-brown-haired spiky shag, applied some black liner, some red lipstick and went to a Polish diner on Third, where she had two beers and some cabbage soup, she went to a bar on Avenue A and met a guy she knew, she drank two kamikazes, they went to a burrito restaurant and she had chips, he had a beef burrito, they went to Lucky Bar, as Nguyen's body was heaved over the side, for it was eight at night for Mariane, but a misty eight in the morning outside of Vietnam in the indigo South China Seas, his body rocked a bit on a wave, his shirt caught a bubble of air and poufed up and then went under, at this time, she met Nagaris, they tossed a round of Yagermeisters, at this time she thought of Bobby, and was glad she was free.

Carol skitters across the street like a crab, grabs the phone. She calls Ton.

It rings, and then picks up.

Ton? Who this? Who this? says Carol, shocked to hear a *woman* answer. Huge adrenaline rush—social services lady?

This is *Ling.*

Who?

Ling.

Where my Ton? Carol's heart is jumping.

Your little boy, Mother, is right here, your little boy—

I want to speak my son! (She is defiant.) Now, my son!

There is the sound of *clunk,* then silence.

Mother!

Ton, always trouble! Always trouble!

Mother, come quick. Come quick. I am leaving, Mother. I am leaving—

Ton!

The phone is dead.

Ton! Ton!

Carol's head spins and she can't see, wetness from her eyes everywhere, she sees the blurred yellow of a taxi and runs to the street.

Help me! Help!

She bangs on the door, You must help me!

He opens the door for her and she falls in,

Oh, mister, unh, unh, unh (great sobs breaking from her tiny, pruny face), get me my home fast now (throwing money in the front).

OK, lady, calm down, lady—

Unh,unh,unh, home, *unh,unh,* please.

Just tell me where, lady. Just tell me where.

Unusually, because in New York they don't do this, he pulls to the side and turns, holds her hand,

Everything's OK. Just, tell me where we're going. OK, just, just relax.

She looks at him, calmly, and speaks.

I need go 5 Ludlow, *please.*

OK, there you go.

Something all wrong with everything. Oh, something wrong!

What happens then, is the woman passes out, Marty Carbotta (Tiny) tells his wife, *like this crazy lady, she screaming and crying all over.*

Pobrecita, what's her problem, baby? His wife is six months pregnant, she wears a tight white slip pulled across her stomach as she sits on his lap, her head resting on his shoulder, his wife is only eighteen, from the Dominican Republic,

I holds her hand and she passes out in my cabby, so I pull over and get a wet napkin, there, at a hot dog stand, she all moaning and shit, saying in Chinese or something, and she comes to—

Oh, shit, that chicken's burning, says his wife as she heaves herself up, *go ahead, I'm listening—*

I, I take her to that address and she get out all shaky, so I carries her, she crying and she ring the buzzer and then this freaky weird-looking guy come out, Oriental, and he looks all white, you know, and this woman, too, all *dressed,* you know, they say thanks and all that and put it in my hand, just lay it on me—

Two hundred *chicas,* mi amor.

You got it. Two beauties.

In his hand the two hundred dollars crackle.

When Carol's OK, she's in her bed, and she feels a wave of thanks to her gods because Ton is there looking happy to see her, and she vows in that millisecond to give one hundred dollars to the church tomorrow and burn a candle and pray to Nguyen for his soul to rest in the South China Seas, that he swim with dolphins, that the sun shine pleasantly for him and that *he leave her and Ton alone now,* that he'd caused enough trouble with his sadness and his longing to get into their lives, she loved him yes, but it was time he got on with his life on the other side of things and she knew, people asked for ghosts, they come to you at all weird times and places, and she knew Nguyen had come to them, maybe to help, but he was upsetting her with his damn chewed-up face and his smelly, fishy clothes.

And she knew, if his brain got diseased and blew up, like her brother-in-law insisted it did, he said it was the fever from the mosquitoes, he said he shakes because his brain is suffering, then she knows that brain is no good now, that he's not thinking right, that this dumb ghost of her husband couldn't see that he tormented her and made her crazy, it was hard enough to raise their son alone, without his presence wanting something.

When she tries to get up, she's shaking and that's Nguyen again, like he comes in her and says, *You see what I go through? You like that shaking? You think that feel good?*

Get out this place, Nguyen! Get out! she yelled in her angriest Vietnamese voice, get the hell out and don't come back, don't ever come back!

And someone spooned some broth in her mouth, and she saw Nguyen, in a chair in the corner, crying.

Oh, Nguyen.

She fell asleep and Ton and Ling sit on the sofa, Ton says:

She always talk like my dad is here, when she's upset. Like he's a ghost or something. He drowned when she came over here, or he was sick, something.

Poor lady.

Ling lit a cigarette.

He put his am around her.

This is what I'm thinking, we go to Graceland, and we get married there. What do you say?

I say, what about mother?

We can bring her or maybe she be OK. Oh, I can call her friend.

I don't know.

Oh, Ling! I need you!

Well.

She sat on the couch and the plastic that covered it crackled, I'm not sure.

It'll be good.

Yeah,—

Oh, yeah.

OK, I got to get some stuff.

Yeah, Ling? Yeah?

I'll be back.

She grabbed her coat, wrapping it tight. It was spring, but still cold. She hated spring for that reason, it always taunted. Ton kissed her hard, and grabbed her ass and he said, come back, soon, and she said, OK.

And she went down the stairs, and she found a taxi, she asked for a sleek address on Sixty-fifth, and the driver had no problem with it, he drove fast, edging through the stalled traffic like a wiggling goldfish, and she took out a mirror and reapplied lipstick, and she felt a real sad ball of pain somewhere, she knew she wasn't going to see Ton again, she knew what that meant, but it was the intensity of the old lady she couldn't bear, the feeling in that apartment, it was a different thing than her moments one-on-one with Ton and his sweet body, it was the suffocating atmosphere of belonging they had with one another, and the way it made her feel more like a side dish, she tried to ignore it, it was the plastic on the couch, the hot chili garlic sauce in the plastic squeeze container on the coffee table, it was his underwear, scrubbed by the mother in the bathroom hung up to dry, it was the two plastic noodle bowls in the rack drying, it was the gray shaggy carpet, it was the sliced-out place she saw herself fit in, saw herself as *daughter-in-law,* and knew what that role meant, she'd lose her special spot, she'd be in a family, and families weren't for her, she'd have to go to temple, she'd learn to cook, she'd have babies, she couldn't bear the smell of that old lady's room, and the way she had no clothes in her little closet, but most of all, what really drove her to change her mind, to throw away Ton was that she loathed that man in the chair, with the rotten face, the one looking at her and laughing, the one Ton refused to see, the ghost who would follow them and tease her and ruin her life, she could bear a lot of things in life, but not that.

And Ton, pretending he can't see him. No shame.

How many people in life have spent their time looking out a window, clouding it with their breath, waiting, looking? Wiping away the wet foggy spot or making little designs, or in Ton's case, writing a little heart with "Ton" plus "Ling" and putting a little arrow through it, and then rubbing it away quickly, then looking, watching the scurrying of people on the Lower East Side, seeing people go into the old man's fabric store across the street, following coats, black hair, but no Ling, no glossy, permed hair, seen from above, no taxis stopping, he waits and waits, his mother screaming or crying for him occasionally, he waits and waits, it gets bluish outside, dusky, he waits as it darkens further, it becomes night, and then he realizes Ling is gone, won't be coming back, but there's always hope (maybe she's lost?), maybe in the morning there will be a note?

He doesn't have her number, or address, he holds on to hope for a long time, a long, long time, until one day, he realizes, *it's over.*

chapter twenty-one

The Twelve Steps

1. *Lives had become unmanageable*

The radio is broken in the car. Mariane lies in the back covered by his coat, she says:

I'm bored, Ito, sing to me. Or tell me a story. Something.

Her hands are shaking. It is about eleven.

You want story? OK, OK. Let's see.

A good one.

Yes.

Uh, OK.

So, long time ago this emperor love his courtesan very much, more than others.

Courtesan?

Girlfriend.

Oh.

He love her very much, but everyone disapprove. Everyone say she is very not special, very common, but this no problem for him. This make a lot of people angry, because there are rules he disobey. But he doesn't care. Then she has child, and he love him too. But then she get sick, too sick.

Sick?

She is like sick. She smoke opium too much. She get very skinny, not eating. The child get no attention, she lose control.

He wants the child?

He wants her to get better.
There's a diner, can we stop, get some lunch? I'd love a beer.
No drinking.
What do you mean?
I mean, you stopping now.
Sure, I can stop.
For baby. No drinking.
Look, it's not like I can't.
Everything no good because you drinking.
That's crap, everything—
Everything! This is all drinking problem.
I will admit, things could be better, but—
Things are out of control—
But I can easily get control, if I want—

Mariane looks out the window, the dingy pallid landscape of New Jersey whirls by, and she thinks, should I ditch this old man? But she's grown fond of his presence and now sober, she is feeling bursts of great fretfulness, just seeing an airplane in the sky makes her worry it'll crash into a ball of fire and the speed of the car sends wave after wave of adrenaline through her body, she sees the huge rattling Mack trucks barreling close by and she shakes more, she is achy and greatly sad, she can feel herself groping around in her memory like it's an old laundry basket, looking for some item to pull up, she wants to think about what she is doing and why, but she is clutched by anxiety, she is scared of Ito now, maybe he'll kill her, a lack of trust, her chest is feeling tight, the word *pathetic* comes to her mind.

2. *A Higher Power*

It is three o'clock and Ito stops at a McDonald's and buys some Chicken McNuggets, a fish fillet, some milk shakes and they find a grassy lot, off to the side in a small town in Delaware, the sun is trickling through, and Mariane seems pale and distant, she keeps saying that a beer wouldn't be a problem because she's in control, that she's got problems traveling in cars, the small space and all, and the speed just shakes her up and so she could really use a few stiff ones, but Ito says we have to keep in mind our goal, firm and controlling and she feels like jelly and pain mixed in a bowl, hungover, headachy, shaky, dehydrated, nauseous (she doesn't stomach the Chicken McNuggets, she salivates and pukes in the green grass), Ito, don't be a fool, and he replies, everything is OK.

God in heaven, she says, the first time these words have sprung to her mouth in a long while, lying in the grass as Ito sleeps draped across the front seat, *deliver me from my life right now, from this terrible pain, this situation, stop my head pounding, stop this poisonous feeling, and let me be*—uwungh! she lies back, recovering from the horrible, puking action—let me be OKOKOKOKOK, sun is sparkling through the leaves, in truth there is God in all things around me, she thinks, she has prayed as a child for safety, for a real life, learning of God from school and from early Sunday TV shows about sinning and heaven and hell, and has gotten this convoluted sense of God as a lost father she never had who would one day enter and fix everything, like a holy handyman, take care of faulty plumbing and bad carpets and make good dinners and help her get ready for school, who would clean up her room, and help her with homework, get her mother together and keep her home so Mariane wouldn't have to stay at the baby-sitter's all day long, this God Daddy could come now and give her a drink, or better yet, fix her up, make her feel calm and happy, stop her fear of speed, fear of accidents and injury, make sure Ito is not going to harm her, the sun is beating on her face, she goes back to what they said, that God loves all, she holds on to this (to her, there is nothing left, this is foxhole religion, this is the last straw, the end of the line), this gives her a tiny flash of joy, because if that's true she might hope, will this baby love her, she thinks. Could this baby love me? Because in the grass with puke on her mouth, the Daddy God was fading and now she entertained the idea that she could save herself.

3. *To turn our will*

And it seemed she lay puking in the grass a hell of a long time, a long, long time, it seems Ito wiped her mouth with a Wet 'n Dri, in a fast little efficient way like he was some old Asian orderly in a hospital, a night shift type, the ones who come at three and wake you to rub your arm with alcohol and draw blood, *like why at this particular time?* Because it says in the chart, miss, ma'am, funny, she is back at the hospital again after the water broke, Carl holding her in his arms like a small child who wears a balloon under her dress, he says, *hey there, buddy,* to a man in scrubs, *hey buddy,* it's all so vivid right now because Carl was frantic and sweaty and he said, I need a doctor right here, *son,* and the orderly just strolled over.

Lying in a curtained (green) room, not real walls but fabric, hearing the guttural screams of a woman next room over, and they strapped up her belly with a heavy, cold metallic belt, and plunged a rod up her and on the screen came the milky machinations of some being, shifting like algae under a microscope, indefinite edges of matter and tissue, underwater sounds, Carl next to her holding her hand, with both hands.

Zoom in on: Carl, next to her, Carl, flawed, old, unfashion- able, smelly, herniated, balding, old Carl, *holding her hand with both hands,* and this concept of God comes creeping back, God as a kind, old man who rescues her from trouble, she says, to the wet mush in the grass that her head is pressed into, the churnings of her stom- ach, Oh, God, help me now, give me some help. And then, it's not so much God as a kind, old man but God as an abstraction of that moment, though she doesn't quite get it, but it's coming across in tiny flashes of feeling: God exemplified by Carl holding her hand with both his hands. Something gnaws at her, a memory of peace.

And this old guy, who is Carl, is talking to her in his kitchen and he's making her tea, on the day she came over there, stirring sugar into it, smiling as she talks, the old Carl has stopped to listen and he listens to every word, not interrupting, until he goes to check on his cancer-ridden wife upstairs. This is what is in her head, right now, Mariane.

4. *A fearless moral inventory*

Back in the car, driving though Maryland, she drinks some Coke, sipping it slowly, it's about five now, and she holds Ito's hand across the front seat, and she is looking at the hills sliding by (eyes glued on the horizon to relieve nausea) and Ito is talking about being a chef in Japan, describing his day (at this point), and below the pink stretched skin of her forehead (she stops to scratch exactly there) at the *reward cascade* section of her brain, the tragically undeveloped and damaged bundle of neurotransmitters on the blink, fouling up and drying up the supply of dopamine and endorphins and we get a Mariane again with bolts of adrenaline, shooting nerves, scared of the cars, the road, the dark approaching, scared of boys, men, children, scared of cancer in her body, of needles, of smells, of holding animals, of eating slime, of eating germs, of Ito, of murderers, of babies, of holding them, of accidentally pushing them or flinging them out windows,

Oh God, Ito, and she falls to his lap with such pain.

I am not capable, she says, of much.

He stops the car.

He holds her.

Night is coming on.

5. *Admitted the exact nature of our wrongs*

And he stopped at a Hampton Inn but it was booked—*booked?* she asks, what the hell for?—and so he finds the next best thing, a faded Econo Lodge in Fairfax, Virginia, off the highway of 66, he

went in while she waited in the car, into the burgundy demi-lobby
with a burning pot of coffee sludge (this is the smell of crematori-
ums in the U.S., he was told, because they add a cup of coffee grinds
to mask the scent), he walks in slowly, in his Hawaiian shirt and
jeans, his baseball hat, he slowly looks around at the beige plasticine
couch, the tiny chandelier like a fancy woman's ring, glittering with
shards of diamond dust, an Easter lily wrapped in blue crushed
decorative foil, he sees a standing ashtray, and a TV in the corner,
dishing the evening news of earthquakes, hurricanes, missing children, murdered adults, he watches for a moment, he pulls out his
cigarettes carefully from his chest pocket, packs it down, sticks it in
his mouth, shields it and lights it, coughs, then—

Can I help you, sir?

Enter Barjani Pajandab.

Yes, please, uh. One room please, for two. For my wife and
myself. No animal.

Of course, *no pets,* until when (*clickety-clack* on computer)
would you require the room, sir?

Until, tomorrow, please.

Double or two singles? (I am serving you, yes, but I am a student of cultural anthropology at Georgetown, I'll have you know,
I am not of *subzero* intelligence.)

Double.

OK, please fill this out (for you and your hooker), I will need
a credit card (as if it is any good). Very good, sir. I-T-O, may I
presume this is a Japanese name?

Uh, Yes. *Japan.*

Ah. Interesting. You see, I am a student of cultural anthropology at Georgetown University—and my thesis is, coincidentally,
on *the Japanese soul and Anime,* are you familiar with *Anime,* ani-
mated film merged with *manga* comic books and the popular video
game culture, such as Nintendo, sir? Ahem, sir?

Anime? Anime? Yes, yes.

Can you tell me why, in a few words if possible, sir, your *Anime* is so melodramatic, romantic and fevered, yet the model of ideal Japanese conduct is reserved and quiet, unobtrusive and unindividualistic? Why the dichotomy, sir? Can you explain?

Uh, said Ito. Uh.

And why, in a largely male-dominated society, the emphasis on female characters, albeit scantily clad? Do you defend the idea of a unified Japanese longing for that which is feminine, romantic, subterranean?

Is, is this the key?

Yes, 421. And, in terms of *Anima* as a play on words of *Anime,* the female aspect of a male personality, according to Jungian—

Thank you.

He whirled to the door. He was embarrassed, he did not understand what the man said, he caught some words, *Anime, romantic, Japanese,* but the rest was a babbling creek, he felt ashamed he might have insulted the man, or been insulted, he staggered out the door, he heard more words, like many times before in this country, he would have to distance himself, he would remove himself from the source.

Sorry, he said, as he closed the door.

6. *Were entirely ready*

Sitting in the transparent moonlight as white and pale as smoke, the moon peering out of bluish clouds, thoroughly sick and anxious, unfathomable anxiety and shaking all over, Mariane hated everything and everybody, mostly herself, hated having to feel a throbbing headache damaging her skull and mostly to know, with even more pain, she has been doing this to herself every day for years and she thinks clearly that it is Poppy's fault and the baby's fault and Carl's fault, and Bobby Baxter's fault, she would not have drunk if it hadn't been for him, and that sends her back to dry dull afternoons in Carl's house, where he lived with her, where she brought her baby, a four-walled space with geraniums, and something not shown before, Carl a loving man, he brought flowers some afternoons or picked a few roses from the side porch, or made soup sometimes with white beans and salt pork, he was generically kind, and this is the most maligned trait one can have, kindness is bulldozed most of the time, preferred by sexy or seductive or smart, kindness came from the man gently, he would make coffee for her in the morning and bring it to her, not because he was a lecherous old man but because he was simply *kind,* it seemed a decent thing to do for one's wife, Carl had felt true despair in his situation with Janie and Mariane, he was sweet but not sensible, it did not occur to him that it was unseemly because, when Mariane approached him at the diner, refusing her entry into his life would have been tantamount to throwing his life out the back door, as Janie died the cells in his body did a slow death, and to hold a young girl in his arms, in his veiny arms, he was saying *yes yes yes* to life once more, so kindness becomes gratefulness and to Mariane it all means a quiet place of calm and order and that is where the great chasm starts, or reappears.

Wanting to die seems to be the recurrent thought. Having tried that slowly, now wants to do it fast. Wants to feel her veins ripped apart. Cars zipping by on the freeway and her mind can feel the impact, feel the heavy weight of the cars as they zoom over her, crushing and mashing her, and imagines them not killing her, just smashing and damaging her more, the pain greater and greater.

7. *To remove our shortcomings*
Ito believes there is a demon in a bottle that looks for a vulnerable heart, and if it sees one, it leaps up when you drink and grabs the heart and hangs on, ripping with its teeth. He believes that a bad one, a trickster grabbed on to her and held tight and he can unloosen its grip, he knows the forest holds all sorts of evil trick-

ster gods that ply the susceptible types and he knows he and Mariane have been attacked.

The bottle god just needs prayer and sacrifice and commitment, and it will be gone.

His own heart was eaten up by the fish god, when he was young and scaled fish, when he thought stories as he swept the floors, when he exposed too many secrets and the fish gods grew jealous and they ruined love for him, made it seem like a clear liquid that pours through his heart, and can't be grasped, this is a theory he has thought about all day and night, that now he has a defect, he is willing but his heart is full of holes and nothing can stay.

But sir—

It is the Indian clerk, once more as Ito tries to leave.

You need to sign, sir.

Oh, yes, of course.

That's OK, listen, not meaning to beat a dead horse, but I'm rather agitated with this thing, you see, I am finishing the thesis on Tuesday and—

Thesis?

You know, the *Anime* I discussed and one more thing, please—

I have to—

Just, just—

The man had come around the front of Ito, his eyes were dark and intense, he spoke in blasts of coffee breath in Ito's face.

Is it the heavy load of, of conforming all the time, the load of academic pressure, the rejection of mundanity in life that makes Japanese such fans of escapist *Anime,* is it the connection to epic, to a desire for the profound?

Ito stopped and looked at him.

It was quiet.

Yes, he said. Yes, that is it.

The man nodded and chuckled, I thought so! Great! Thank you, sir!

You are welcome.

The man spoke gibberish and now he was silent.

Ito pushed through the door.

More thievish gods were at work, stealing hunks of his brain that modified his reasoning, his understanding. He was becoming a child. Ito thought of the Shinto of his youth, his mother and father washing his hands before the temple, that large metal chalice burning incense in the wind surrounded by people waving the perfumed smoke towards them, the young Ito choking on the heady fumes, the tiny shelf in their kitchen with a miniature temple and mirrors, he thought of aligning himself once again with the way of *Kami,* the gods, and how he was off this trajectory, that gave Ito some ideas, he had lost his way from the *Kami,* he would amend this soon, he had allowed bad energy in his life because he had forgotten his Shinto.

In the parking lot, crawling on her hands and knees towards the road, Ito saw Mariane.

8. *To all the people we have harmed*

There was glass on the road and it was cutting her hands as she crawled but she didn't care, in fact it felt good, one particular piece had lodged under her palm and every time she pulled it up and put it back down on the ground, it stabbed further and she felt delight in that pain, it was far better than the suctioning of remorse that was centered in her mind or the acidic guilt. Instead she focused on the glittering black asphalt in the moonlight, and the rushing whirl of cars, the wet, slick sound of their tires flying by, the subtle bump of their carriages as they hurtled over potholes and she plodded forth, crawling, because she didn't want them to see her, she wanted to be crushed instantly under their tires, and, though improbable, but this was a fantasy, she wanted them to drive on and think they hit a can or a McDonald's package, she wanted to be plastered thinly to the floor like a grease mark, to make all her volume squeezed down into flatness, she wanted to feel the hard impact of the car, she—

Couldn't help it but she was forgiving her mother but she was angry because she made her old and ditched her before she had her baby and that was mean of her, she was angry for her preferring nights out to being with her, she was mad because of the nights, endless nights, when she was seven, eight, alone with a TV.

And that pulled her mind to Carl, and she missed him, she wished she could be with him, so he could get her now, but she had fucked him up and that was her fault, and Bobby Baxter whom she lied to, and the endless others in bars as she giggled and made love, the lies her actions and words held, most of all, her baby, she thought of her baby,

9. *Direct amends to such people*

He ran out towards her, whispering *Mariane* and he grabbed her shoulders and she said, *no, no*—

He grabbed her shoulders and pulled her back, no, Mariane, listen.

She looked up at him, and her hands were bloody.

This is not the way.

I want some kind of *relief*, please, some fucking relief.

Come to the room, I make bath.

No, Ito. I'm through.

It will be OK.

I want to go.

Come on, now. Please.

Leave me.

Shh, shh. Up now.

He hoisted her on his shoulder and walked her to the door of the room. She was as light as a branch, he thought. He put her on the bed, and she was crying, contorted but without tears. He wrapped a towel around her bleeding hand, then he went to the bathroom and turned on the water, then put down a white pad on the floor, he went to the bed and she was sleeping, he started to remove her clothes.

First, her socks, they were simple and navy blue and he un-rolled them and placed them on a chair, then he unzipped her jeans and slid them off and he noted her slim, boyish hips and pale waxy legs, almost emaciated, and she wore a striped blue and white string bikini underwear, tiny curls of pubic hair curling around the edges, he reached around and took off her shirt, she wore no bra and had rather flat brown-nippled breasts, and a distended stomach, he found himself yearning to kiss her breasts, but she was sleeping and he felt it would be an invasion, soon she is naked, emanating a sour odor of unwashedness, but she adjusts to her side and the angles of her hips popping through and the delicate lines of her ribs showing through the transparent white skin seem almost otherworldly, he thinks he has never seen anything as beautiful, and this may be partially due to the fact that he cannot touch, if he is honorable, in any way other than that of a kind benevolence, she is ill, very ill, and possessed, and to take advantage of this would surely be some great offense, so he feels pure thoughts, he reaches under her shoulders, lifts her and brings her to the water, where she opens her eyes as she sinks into the warmth, and he pulls back in anticipation of her anger, but instead she looks up at him with great eyes of sweetness, and she smiles, Mariane lies in the water and it swirls around her, and she feels OK as Ito holds her hands and washes her with a crumpled washcloth, the bubbles and suds feel warm in waves and she maybe feels happy.

I am sorry, she says.

10. *And continued personal inventory*

He sits on the toilet and smokes a cigarette as she sinks in the water and they say not a word. Ito thinks about Genji and how he courted so many women, and that maybe each one represented a part of himself, he thinks about himself like this and tries to understand the role each of his loves may have afforded him, and Mariane suddenly says,

Ito, you said you had a son. Before you went out that time to get beer, you said you had a son.

I do.

So, why isn't he with you?

He paused and sucked his cigarette. One image was in his head, the tiny white hand of Xiu-Xiu dangling out of the futon as he and Daisuke, on that dark night, got rid of her body.

Mariane, before, in Japan, my wife dies. She has cancer. She dies. It is considered by family best if he is in family situation, I think they—

They?

Tomoko, my wife's family, they consider too unhealthy for Daisuke alone, by himself, so they say this and I, think, OK.

The tips of her brown nipples peep through the bubbles.

So I just do, I say, OK.

And how old is he?

He is, now, fourteen.

Oh.

And, I make mistake, I realize.

Why?

Because he is my son, my responsibility. I will go get him, we go get him.

We?

You and me, we get our children.

OK.

You getting better.

I'm getting better.

I take care, it's OK.

★   ★   ★

11. *Sought through prayers and meditation*

He came over and he washed her hair and he rinsed her, the water covering her shoulders and hair, smoothing it all like glass, and then she stood, feeling shy and awkward, suds caught in her pubic hair, and he wrapped a towel around her and led her to the room and as he turned to look for her clothes, she dropped the towel, she stood in front of him naked, sober, her eyes were sore, her palms were sore, her body was sore from yesterday's fiasco with the businessman at the hotel, she was shivering, she stood and looked at him and she said, *Ito,* and he dropped her clothes, he went to her and said, *oh, oh,* and put his hands on her breasts, his palms like warm dry blankets, and he moved them slowly and brought his wet mouth to her chest bones in the center, he kissed her there, and she grabbed his head, and stroked his hair, and said, Ito, my dear, and he picked her up and draped her across the bed, he kissed her slowly from her belly to her arms, she enfolded him in her arms, and their mouths met, their tongues met, he wanted to wait but she was urgent and soon he was inside Mariane, she had urged him inside, she was warm and receptive, and he was holding her face, he—

Knock, knock.

Ito pulled himself up, but remained locked in the velvetiness of Mariane.

What—what is it?

Mr. Ito, can I ask one more thing?

Later! Later!

Please!

Busy!

Oh, oh, OK. OK.

And then they laughed, he laughed so hard he slipped out of her, but then he wrenched himself up and they began in earnest, and for several hours, he visited her body, he took residence there, she opened herself to him, she thought not of anything but him, not even the baby or the drinks, he knew her in every sense, she understood this man called Ito, they engaged in the act of love, and in some ways it became an act of forgiveness, too.

12. *Having had a spiritual awakening.*

It was late, she woke up and it was dark, she was attacked by a weight of terrible, wracking pain across her chest, she drew up and breathed heavily, sat up and went to the bathroom for water and Ito was out, draped across the bed, she put her clothes on and stood in the room and couldn't breathe, she clutched at her heart which was filled with dread, embedded with a sharp, sad pain, not unlike the glass earlier in her palm and she couldn't even cry out, she stumbled to the door, and she opened it, and Ito was still out— *my baby*—he was sleeping—*there is no baby!*—she needed air—*it's been too long*—she was filled with the panic of a bad dream, she saw the cars and the driveway, and the asphalt, the outside of the motel, and the pseudo-colonial entrance of the lobby—*goddamn, I left my baby for too long*—images of a child, left, for years, in a crib filled her mind with the savagest thoughts, she stumbled to the lobby, she saw the cars flitting, speeding—*how does a baby grow without a mother?*—she wants to get down, and go to the cars again, but she then sees the sign—*babies become kids become adults*—the sign says, next to the lobby, it says *Fire Hearth Lounge,* and she can see through the yellow windows people around a bar, she sees movement, she swallows and darts for the door, she brushes her hair back, and doesn't hesitate—*baby*—she enters to the rush of voices and smoke and music from a jukebox, stumbles in and heads straight to the bar, sits down, but she has no money, she says quickly to the man to her left, *hey, hey, hey,* losing all subtlety, going for broke,

He turns, it is the clerk.

I need, can you buy me a drink?

Oh, well, uh, certainly. What will you have?

Vodka. And soda. Double.

OK, heh, bartender, one vodka, uh, Stoly and soda, please. Thanks.

It is down her throat in seconds and how do you describe the relief at being with her friends, all the bottles looking down at her smiling, the molten river of assuagement that the sips afford, the numbing, she feels so happy, so giddy—

God, this is great.

She grabs his arm,

God, I like you. Are you like, Indian?

Well, Punjabi, to be exact.

Ooh. Poon-*jobbie!*

You like this?

Sure. It's sexy.

And she smiles and she has another, it's getting late, the bar is closing and he says he has an apartment off the lobby, would she like to visit, and she says sure, and now she is good and drunk, they leave the bar and walk outside through the parking lot, by the motel rooms, she sees the cars whirling by in the night and she merely acknowledges the blur of lights as lovely, the shiny paint of the cars zipping by glossy in the moonlight, she is laughing, and she sees Ito in the doorway of their room.

Mariane.

Hey, Ito!

Mariane. Come here.

He has a towel wrapped around his waist.

Can't! I'm having fun! Whee!

Oh, listen, is this your husband? I think maybe, says Barjani, this is awkward.

Hell, no, he's not my husband! Right, Ito? You're not my husband!

Mariane, please.

Listen, I think it's best I, uh, move on here, I'm sorry, miss,
but—

Wha-? Hey, we're partying, I thought! Wait!

Mariane.

The clerk moves away, and she watches him.

Damn you, Ito!

Mariane. The *child*.

Damn you!

Mariane, please, stop. The children!

Whose children?

Ours!

Fuck you, she kicks a can, fuck you and I'm out of here.

Mariane.

She picks up a stick and runs along the doors of the hotel,
scraping each one, poking the doorbells, lights come on, she hears
voices, she is running, yelling through the court yard and Ito stands
there, listening,

He stands there and he gets cold.

He closes the door, and he sits on the bed, his eyes closed.

Child! Her voice is high and squeaky and he can hear the bark
of a man telling her to pipe down,

Child!

She is still scraping the doors, but her voice is farther away.

Want!

To!

Be!

A!

Child!

Again!

Want!

To!

Be!
A!
Child!
Again!
Child!
Again!
Want!
To!
Be!
A!
Child!
Again!

He doesn't hear her anymore. She has run down an alley with her stick, and she doesn't want to turn around. It is threeish and she likes this hour, she runs through an alley, she goes running, and running, and running and she sees cats.

He sits on the bed with his eyes closed. He stays like that for a long, long time.

Twenty-one Things About Moi
by Daisy Fry

1. *My name is Daisy Fry, though friends call me Day.*
2. *Pompom girls rule over cheerleaders.*
3. *Except Cheryl Parkinson and Samantha Perigrine.*
4. *My mom died when I was a baby.*
5. *But I know she sees me. Is that weird?*
6. *I think she's like some really pretty angel.*
7. *I can eat ten chocolate chip pancakes when my dad makes them. Am I gross or what?*
8. *I've been known to hurl after.*
9. *I wonder what my mom was like.*
10. *Dad says she was the sweetest lady in the world.*
11. *Prettiest, too.*
12. *I hate my life. I drank a glass of vodka once, on a dare.*
13. *He said my mom was a "fox." He's kind of dweeby, in a Dad way.*
14. *I would way prefer living in California or something.*
15. *I'm in Raleigh High right now, but I hate it.*
16. *I think of my life as pre-Joey and after-Joey.*
17. *My favorite animal is a kitten.*
18. *After-Joey, I wonder what's the point?*
19. *It wouldn't be so bad if his locker was farther away.*
20. *I tend to be more myself on the Internet than in life.*
21. *I think my dad is a hero.*